Eugene Landon Hobgood

Country Roads

The Internal Life of a Mannish Rascal

Editions Dedicaces

COUNTRY ROADS.
THE INTERNAL LIFE OF A MANNISH RASCAL

Published by:
    Editions Dedicaces LLC
    12759 NE Whitaker Way, Suite D833
    Portland, Oregon, 97230
    www.dedicaces.us

Library of Congress Cataloging-in-Publication Data
    Landon Hobgood, Eugene
        Country Roads. The Internal Life of a Mannish Rascal /
        by Eugene Landon Hobgood.
        p. cm.
        ISBN-13: 978-1-77076-413-2 (alk. paper)
        ISBN-10: 1-77076-413-5 (alk. paper)

Eugene Landon Hobgood

Country Roads

The Internal Life of a Mannish Rascal

This book is written in recognition of all the secrets and untold tales flowing in the undertow of every rural county of the United States since its founding and still...

Chapter One
Reflections

That old buggy seat was still joined to the shade tree. For as long as Randolph could remember, at least two of the five slats had been missing. Now, only two were left. He adjusted his backside between the remaining strips. His balance and weight felt different than last year when he was ten. It wasn't cause there was one less slat, it was cause he was bigger and stronger. The oak bark felt zigzaggy against his back like it always had.

The front yard looked the same too. Right there between him and the corner of the front porch, where it turned past the bay window and headed toward the rain barrel, was the place where something happened he was never gonna forget. Every time he passed the spot or looked at it he was back to being six years old.

Jack was his favorite dog, bigger, whiter and and fluffier than Jabbo, his brother. Jabbo had almost no hair, he looked a lot like a Bulldog. The mother Trixie was fluffy like Jack although she was smaller than him and Jabbo. From the time Jack was a puppy, he came to Randolph right natural. Didn't make no difference who was there, Jack would always nudge up to Randolph.

Everybody had just come up from church. Randolph was all decked out in his 'Little Lord Fauntleroy' Easter suit. Elmore had his Brownie and wanted to take a picture of his nephew-dressed all sharp and everything. That was fine with Randolph-Jack had come halfway down to the church to meet him and naturally would be in the picture with him.

Randolph was used to having his way. Some grown folks would tell him he was spoiled. They didn't call him a brat like he'd heard them call some other boys. They would just kinda grin and say. "Boy you're so spoiled!" Then they'd laugh and tickle his stomach.

So, it surprised and confused him when Elmore said the dog couldn't be in the picture. Jack was already standing there posing beside Randolph-his tongue hanging out in a big old grin. Randolph had told Elmore twice he wanted his dog Jack in the picture. Both times Elmore said no. The second time he said no like there was no way he would change his mind.

Elmore had been away in Crestville at Booker T. College. Before Elmore went off to school, Randolph remembered that of everybody, he was the nicest to him. Something or other must've come over him up there in town.

In his best baby voice Randolph said, "Please, Elmore!" Elmore said, "NO!" It didn't take another minute to know he was gettin' on his uncle's nerve. That was ok, he knew just what to do.

He commenced to cry. It was easy for Randolph to cry. This time, it was even easier cause he was hurt by how mean Elmore was acting.

Randolph started out with a simper so he could build up to a good cry without working too hard. After he got wound up and could hear his own pitiful voice whining, it shocked him to see his cryin' didn't mean nothing to Elmore.

Letticia, Mozzelle and Arlene had kept out of it. But the boy's tears made them ask Elmore to let Jack be in the picture.

"There's nothing wrong with it."

"Why don'tchou go on and take the picture? Jack's already standin' there anyway."

"Come on Elmore."

The Devil musta been in Elmore or something. He wouldn't give in.

Behind his crying and carrying on, Randolph found himself asking The Lord to help him. He promised that if He helped him this time, he wouldn't do it no more.

How it came to him to do that, he had no idea. He had never even admitted to himself that he knew it was wrong to be crying to get his way.

Elmore, who had been frowning like King Saul or somebody, relaxed his face and in an easy voice said, "Ok. The dog can be in the picture." Jack had not moved the whole time. All Elmore had to do was click the camera.

The zigzag feeling from the bark had gone, Randolph was deep into the time when Cedar Grove was home.

"He's your cousin." Mozzelle said when Jesse got there yesterday. Randolph and Jesse played together all afternoon. Last night, Mozzelle, mama and them made like it was Randolph's idea to let Jesse sleep in his bed with him. He didn't care, it was good to have a cousin-whatever that was. The more time he spent with Jesse, the more of a chance he had to find out if a cousin was different than anybody else.

At age two, Randolph could tell what grown folks thought was good or bad, what was pretty or not, what tasted good or not. By now he knew what he thought about stuff too. Sometimes he felt the same way they did. Sometimes he didn't.

Jesse was a year older than him. He was from Washington and was yella and he was his cousin. Randolph could tell right off what Mozzelle and them thought about the big city Washington, and what they thought about Jesse's yella skin. They talked about how much they enjoyed going up to Washington. Mozzelle said Jesse had pretty yella skin. Everybody seemed to pay more attention to that than anything else about Jesse. Randolph was gonna have to find out how he felt about all that stuff.

He and Jesse got along right nice, all night and through breakfast. For about a half hour now, they had taken turns riding Randolph's red tricycle up and down the back yard between the oak and bay window at the top, and the chicken coop at the bottom. Mozzelle came out to the back porch to get a dipper of water. "You havin' a good time Jesse?" "Yes mam." For much of his two years and one month, Randolph had been the apple of everybody's eye. "You havin' a good time Jesse?" sounded like Randolph was in the chicken coop or down at the spring or somewhere else. That was what he felt and it hurt. Mozzelle went back into the dining room. Randolph was about to take his turn on the tricycle. "Let me go again?" "Alright." It would not have occured to Randolph to not let Jesse go again even though there was something hot runnin' around inside himself. He was mad about Mozzelle talking to Jesse like he was there by himself. But every time he had been mad at somebody before, they were too big for him to do anything but pout or cry. He didn't have any practice at being mad at somebody his own size. Besides, it was Mozzelle he was mad at.

7

Jesse was back from gis extra turn. Randolph reached for the trike, Jesse pushed his hand away. "I'm going again." "No you ain't." "Aunt Mo!" Jesse called so loud Randolph almost jumped out of his skin. At the very moment Jesse saw Mozzelle open the screen door, he let out a whine. "Randy won't let me ride the tricycle!"

"Boy! You better behave yourself. Go ahead Jesse. You ride as much as you want to. And Randolph, you'd better not stop him. You hear me?"

Randolph watched Mozzelle's back until she disappeared inside. The hot thing that had been running around in his body, settled behind his eyes and burned right there. He had to summon tears to douse it enough that he could stand it. Soon as relief came, he lit out up the yard where Jesse had got to. He lifted his fist high as he could reach and brought it down on Jesse. He didn't know where or how to hit, he just struck out. The blow landed on Jesse's shoulder and didn't hurt him much. But it scared the living daylights out of him.

"OWWWW!" Randolph knew he was gonna get a whipping. That didn't matter much to him cause he was so satisfied to know that out of nowhere he had, for the first time in his life, made somebody pay for making him feel bad.

* * *

"Trixie died last Winter." Mozzelle scooted him into the kitchen for some fresh ham and creamed potatoes. He wolfed down the red-tang and round-beige flavors along with cracklin bread and buttermilk. Still embracing his reintroduction to country fare, he had asked about the dogs. "Oh yeah? What'd she die from?" The repast of a moment ago tempered the sadness Randolph might have otherwise felt. "Old age I reckon." Mean as she could be sometimes, Mozzelle had a soft heart. "We lost Trixie. But she had had another litter of pups since you were here. We gave all of 'em away 'cept one. Her name is Flossie-a right pretty thing."

Jabbo had died a long time ago. Jack and Flossie were the only two left. Randolph went out to the back yard to whistle for them. They came running-wagging and grinning. Jack still looked about the same. Like Mozzelle said, Flossy was right pretty. She was a little bit smaller than Jack, fluffy like him but wasn't solid white like him. She was black and white. Flossie kept nudging Jack aside to be close to Randolph. Trixie and Jabbo might be gone, but Randolph still had two favorites. When he sat on the buggy seat by the tree, they both stood right there next to him.

* * *

Back, down past the chicken coop and woodpile by the outhouse, is where the pigpen used to be.

Just before Thanksgiving was hog killing time. Liticia told Randy that it came around every year. This was the first he remembered any talk about it though. It sure was the first time he had ever smelled that stink in the air-a deep-gray kind of stink.

Liticia knew the boy was gonna get around to asking about Piggywiggy. It was better not to be the one to bring it up, she let him get to it in his own time. Randolph had asked how the hogs were killed? "Shotgun." Who was killing them? "Gregory and two men from the sawmill." What do they do after they kill the hogs. "They cut them up and we eat the meat." All of us? "All of us." Me too?

Liticia felt bad for the boy. She well remembered back when she had to start hardening herself to the realities of life. She leaned forward to place her hands on the shoulders of her four year old grandson. "Yep. You too Randy." He didn't pause. "They kill Piggywiggy?" Liticia kept her hands on his shoulders. She looked into his eyes. "Son, they kill all the hogs. Piggywiggy is a hog." Randolph reached up to remove his grandmother's hands. Liticia chose not to say anything further. She let him walk away.

Randy had been in her care since he was four or five months old. She knew him like a book. She watched as he walked from the kitchen through the dining room into the hall. As she knew he would, he walked around the staircase to the space underneath, where they stored patch squares and rags.

For over two years now, he would go into that dark closet and lie down on the soft pile to think. At first, Liticia had considered that a queer thing for a child to do. She soon realized she shouldn't be surprised. Like Reverend Winston once said. "That boy came into this world already 40 years old."

Randy entered his innersanctum still as quiet as he was when he left the kitchen. He sat on the cloud of linen to let his mind retrace the last few minutes. When he felt confident he was hearing for the second time what he had heard in the first place, he lay back on the soft pile and cried.

The old sow gave birth to four little pigs. From the day they opened their eyes, one of them would look at Randolph. After a while he would come over to the edge of the pen. Randolph would reach through and pet him. He wanted to climb over the log-barrier to play with his pet that he had named Piggywiggy. Gregory didn't allow him to do that. He said you couldn't trust the grown hogs.

As well as Liticia knew her little man, she had no idea that, from time to time, he would sneak out to the pigpen and climb over the barrier. Not only did he play with Piggywiggy, he would pet the big hogs too.

Randolph continued to cry while these memories slid across his mind. He was sorry they had killed Piggywiggy and his whole family. In a way though, he was crying more because he had been reminded of what he first realized when he was one year old; the more he learned, the less he knew. When would he know everything? He cried himself to sleep and did not eat pork for a week.

* * *

South of the tree, across the narrow driveway, the yard sloped down several feet to the hollow on the right and the beginning of the churchyard straight ahead. On the first Sunday of September, the churchyard would be filled with new and old polished cars; "Big meeting time." At the end of the churchyard was the Baptist church, it looked like almost every picture Randolph had ever seen of a country church-a church in the dell-a white clapboard structure with a square bell tower topped with a wooden Cross.

When he remembered to do it, he would stand beside the church and look back toward the house. From there, you could see

the roof of the house where a rooster weathervane sat at the peak.
Every so often, he caught the rooster spinning one way or the
other. That only happened when the wind changed directions. it
was a lucky day when the rooster turned to look behind himself.

Across the road from the church, was an empty house
where the Camerons used to live.

The Cameron sisters were his girlfriends, except for
Sundays when boys their age were around. Those eleven and
twelve year old boys had the two girls giggling and telling
Randolph to go away and stop following them.

Miz Cameron seemed to always be in the kitchen baking
biscuits or cooking stringbeans with field peas or making some
kind of pie or cake.

Soon as he was on the porch, a mixture of aromas came
through the house from the kitchen to fill his memory. He couldn't
pick one to settle on-the yellow and green smell of succotash, the
baked-brown sweet potato pudding pie or whatever those other
smells were. He just took all of them in-like gathering flowers. The
wall next to the front door sparked a memory of doing a headstand
against it that mixed in with the medley of aromas. He got on his
knees and attempted a headstand. It was more difficult than he
remembered, he gave up.

There was no lock. At his touch, the door swung open and
a gust blew puffs of dust across the floor. Randolph's footsteps in
the empty house created an echo that erased his sense-memories.
He wanted to turn around and leave but refused to.

All the rooms evoked recollections of happy experiences.
None of them matched the moments that came back of the three of
them down by the spring where he touched one sister then the
other.

* * *

Across the yard to his left-up past the house-were the
orchard and garden, side by side. Across the road from them was
the Methodist church. The Roebucks were Baptists, the Cedar

Grove Baptist church was founded by a member of the Roebuck clan. However, the Methodist and Baptist churches were attended by everybody in the community. To facilitate attendance, services were held on alternate Sundays. Randolph knew that his family was Baptist but didn't understand what difference that made. Both churches looked just alike. Anyway, Reverend Dew the Methodist minister was his favorite preacher. Mama and them said he was a fire and brimstone preacher. Since he liked Reverend Dew, Randolph preferred Sunday school at that church.

Cesar Logan was a young Deacon and Sunday school teacher at the Methodist church. One Sunday when Randolph was four, Cesar asked him to read from the lesson. Earlier in the week Cesar had dropped in on the Roebucks. They were playing records on the Victrola. Cesar asked the boy which was his favorite. Randolph picked through the record stack until he came to one with a yellow label. He handed it to Cesar.

For a month or so, fifteen year old Arlene had been teaching Randolph to read. He only knew a limited number of small words. It had not yet occured to him to attempt to read the label for, "Well Done" by the Harminizing Four. What he did know was that there were only two records in the stack with yellow labels. One time, when he selected the wrong one; he studied the two yellow labels to make certain he would choose the right one next time.

At the very moment he selected his favorite today, Mozzelle said to Cesar, "Randy can read, you know." Because he was actually learning to read, Randolph didn't feel like Mozzelle was telling a tale. He let it go.

Here they were in Sunday school in front of several children and three grown folks. Cesar handed a picture book to Randolph, pointing to the paragraph he was to read. "Lord have mercy!" Ran through Randy's inchoate mind. Yet, to say, "I don't know how to read," did not seem to be a choice he could make. The book was a New york, American Tract Society publication. Like most of the books Colored churches and schools used, it was a hundred-odd years old.

A PRETTY PICTURE BOOK; author unknown. Page two, from which Randolph was expected to read, depicted in sepia, a white woman and her three little girls to whom she was reading.

> *"Those little girls are listening to*
> *their mother, who is sitting in*
> *the chair, and reading to them. I dare*
> *say they are very happy to hear her,*
> *and I am sure she is much pleased to*
> *see them so attentive. I hope you*
> *will give as good attention, if your*
> *mother should read to you."*

The first four words flowed without a stumble. The word, 'listening' stumped Randy. Cesar pronounced it. To his own astonishment, Randolph then read all the way to, 'attentive' on the fourth line before faltering again. After Cesar pronounced that word for him, he completed the paragraph. His only mistake was pronouncing, 'attention' as 'attentive.' Cesar allowed him to finish, then he corrected the boy's error and added, "Randolph, if I hadn't heard it with my own ears I wouldn't have believed it." Cesar beamed and searched for words. "Young man you are special. The Lord has truly blessed you. Give him a hand everybody!" All the children were proud of their own. The adults showed a deeper and more enthusiastic appreciation. Cesar looked in Randolph's eyes. "Boy! You're gonna be a preacher. That's all there is to it. You're gonna be a preacher. Yessir!"

Randolph tried to look as if he had done this before-read a paragraph from a book other than the First Grade Reader. Everybody kept congratulating him for several minutes. For all practical purposes, Sunday school was over.

Randolph hoped he would be able to hold himself together until he got back to the house. He longed to crawl into the soft-darkness of the linen closet where he would try to figure out, "What in the world..."

Chapter Two
Home Again

When Randolph got back down here in June, Leticia seemed fit as a fiddle. By the beginning of August, she was in her bed more than she was up and around. Even before grandma was bedridden, she took to calling him Junie. What bothered Randolph about her calling him Junie, wherever that name came from, was that back when he was a crybaby and the apple of everybody's eye, grandma (he called her mama then) had called him Randy. She was the first one to call him that. He took that nickname the way she intended it, as a term of endearment. "Junie?"

That she was losing touch with the moment-to-moment of her life, was beyond his comprehension. The suddenness of her decline made him think she was deserting him again just like she did when she took him to Washington and left him there when he was six years old.

At about the same time as grandma started to slip away, it occured to Randy to write to his real mama in his real home to ask her if she would please send his bike down here. He had only two playmates. One was Archie who was four years older than him like his big sister Lucille. Archie didn't live far away. If you took a shortcut through the woods by the Methodist church, it won't no more'n a quarter mile. The only other Colored boy in Cedar Grove was Reverend Easterbrook's grandson Holly. Holly was two years younger than Randolph. He lived near 'bout two miles away.

* * *

If Randolph ate too much watermelon or drank too much lemonade after dark, he would go behind the chicken coop to take a pee. That way he was only in the dark for a short time and distance from the house. He could take a quick pee and dash back inside. Even before dark or in broad daylight, it wasn't fun going to that little shack the old folks called "The closet."

When he lived here before or during Summer visits it became clear to him he was never going to get used to anything about an outdoor toilet. His favorite thing about the new house he, mama and Lucille moved into in Washington, was the indoor plumbing. Outhouses just did not seem like they were meant to be. He thought it was kinda strange that smack dab in the middle of the smell of morning glories, persimmons and all kinds of nice stuff, was a stinking little hut. When he had to doo-doo, he held off as long as he could.

It was Randy's chore to take Liticia's slop jar-grown folks called it a chamber pot-out to the closet once or twice a day. That made it kind of easy to resent grandma for seeming to stop being crazy about him and spending night and day in bed in the dark. If he turned the light on when he came into her room, she would order him to turn it off. She didn't talk to him no more than she had to neither. It was really hard to keep liking her. Now, on top of everything else, he had to carry her stinking shit out to the toilet every day.

Randolph loved his grandma; at least that was what he told himself. The few times he had asked an older person to explain what love was, they had not told him anything he could grab hold of. So, if they could say they loved somebody without being able to say what that was, he could too.

* * *

The sun was high enough that the mist a foot above the ground was dissolving into thin air. The stall floors were covered with manure-stained yellow straw. Two mules, one big like a horse-she was Jane and, Sadie, a donkey-sized one. "You got to keep your eye on Sadie, she spooks easy. She'll kick you. If you go behind her, make sure you let her know you're comin' back there." Randolph wondered why Archie was telling him what to do when he crossed behind the mule. Won't no way he was gonna go behind Sadie or Jane or any other mule. He stood outside the stall's half door and chipsed for Jane who stuck her head out. Archie let him bridle her. "You done that good. You know how to put the harness on 'er?" Archie took Randolph's silence to mean that he knew how to harness a mule. "Alright. Go over yonder an' git it off the hook." Randolph walked Jane out of the stall and maneuvered her around so that her head faced the door. He held onto the bridle strap while he took the halter down. Archie got a kick out of how his little buddy went to so much trouble to keep from being kicked by Jane. Randolph didn't care, he put the halter on right, but he criss-crossed two chains under the belly. Archie straightened them. "Don't feel bad. You ain't never done it before."

They walked the mules around to the shed side of the barn where they backed them up on either side of a wagon tongue. Randolph had forgotten that they would have to hitch up Sadie and Jane. He felt his breath quicken. There was no way to hitch the tracers to the doubletree without getting behind the mules. He slid his hand along Jane's side so she knew that he was going back there. He stroked her haunch before he knelt behind her to hook the chains to her side of the wagon. Jane lashed her tail kinda easy; she wasn't bothered by him being back here.

When he and Archie were on the wagon, it crossed Randolph's mind, 'Folks say animals can tell when you're scared. They get spooked.' Jane didn't seem to know he was scared no more'n his buddies in D.C. knew that he was scared when they went swimming in the half frozen Potomac.

The sun threw shadows behind the stacks of hay. They looked like wigwams in shoot'em-ups. He even imagined an Indian maiden coming out of one of them. "You ever loaded hay before, Randy?" Archie's question caught him short, he couldn't come up with a bluff. Archie continued as if Randolph had answered. "Well. It ain't all that hard. Just be sure you don't put more on your pitchfork than you can handle. Archie dug his fork in first-veins popped on the backs of his hands and the fifteen year old's biceps bulged in his denim sleeves. The lifted hay hung on the fork like a weeping willow. Randolph dug his pitchfork deep into a pile-too deep. He pulled the tines back a few inches and still couldn't do nothing with it. A few tries later, he only pushed the fork in a little bit, he was able to toss a heap onto the wagon.

The sun was all the way up by the time the boys had a full load. Archie let Randolph drive. He undulated and slapped the reins against the mules' backs. "Git up there!"

Archie leaned back until his head touched the hay piled from the tail-end of the wagon bed up to the seat. Randy saw him out of the corner of his eye. Archie was grinning like a cheshire cat.

It didn't seem to take any longer to toss the hay up into the loft, back the wagon into the shed and unhitch the mules than it had taken just to load the wagon.

Verniece and Archie were tall like their daddy. Archie looked like Mr. Irvin, Verniece didn't. She didn't look like her mother either, Miz Annette was short. All ten of her younguns were tall like Mr. Irvin. Verniece and Archie were the only two still living at home. All the others were married and livin' up the road a piece.

One of the pleasures of working over here was being around Verniece. Sometimes she worked in the fields along with him and Archie. When the sun was high and she was sweating, her cotton frock hung on her body so you could see her shape. "My Lord!" Randolph would think. He wouldn't imagine anything carnal or even picture her naked. He would just get that feeling... the same one he got the first time he saw a woman in pants. He was six and had just come out into the front yard. There was a woman who had come down home for Revival Week. She was standing with her back to him talking to somebody. He couldn't remember who she was talking to. He did remember later learning that her pants were called slacks, and the tan material hugging her behind was gabardine. All he knew in the moment was how the shape of her butt sent something through him, something 'nother like one of those hymns about half way through a revival meeting. "My Lord!" "Want some more peas and corn, Randy?" When she asked, Miz Annette was already spooning the mixture onto his plate. "Yes, thank you."

Randolph was a precocious boy, but only experience would have let him know that Miz Annette saw how he was staring across the table at her youngest daughter like she was something good to eat. Nor would she let on that she noticed. Still, she thought it was 'so cute.'

Mr. Irvin and Archie were too busy shoveling in their vittles to pay attention to anything else. Verniece was fully aware that little Randy fancied her. At age seventeen, she thought it quaint that the eleven year old showed an interest that seemed beyond his years. She only allowed herself brief consideration that there was something grown about his gaze... she gave him the kind of non-committal smile girls her age have practiced to perfection.

18

"We ain't done." Archie was grinning again. Was he reading his little buddy's mind. "The mules got to be watered." Randolph angled Jane over next to the wagon tongue so that he could get a leg up. Archie didn't ask if he knew how to ride so he didn't say nothin'.

It wasn't difficult to stay on. The only thing was, Jane's backbone was like sittin' on a log. He had to dig his knees into her sides to protect his balls.

The watering hole was a fair ways down a slope of bumps and gulleys. That part of the land was so uneven and dry that all the previous trips down there hadn't made a path. You had to steer your mount so that she didn't stumble too much.

At a patch of woods halfway to the watering hole, "Look here Randy, I'm gonna go in the bushes an' take me a quick smoke. Why don't you get down and hold these mules til I get back. I won't be long." Randolph didn't know if he was surprising Archie, but the words that came out of his mouth sure did surprise himself. "While you take a smoke, I'll take Jane and Sadie down to the watering hole. Gimme sadie's rein." He wasn't all that sure he wanted to take the mules to the watering hole by himself. At the same time, he was...sure. He let it run through his mind and didn't see nothing about it that was scary. He waited anyway for Archie to discourage him. "Ok Randy. I'll be right here when you get back."

Randolph's mind was like a blackboard, early in the morning. It just sat there waiting for something to be written on it. He took Sadie's rein from Archie, nudged Jane forward with Sadie in tow. His mind was still blank. With no help from him, Jane headed straight for the watering hole. They had almost reached it when the first thought to enter his mind was the realization that Jane knew where they were going. The big mule walked to a ridge that sloped down a foot to the water. She stopped but did not put her head down to drink. Sadie came forward and started drinkin' right off. She made a familiar noise-the same sound Randolph made when he sucked soup from a bowl or pot liquor from the edge of a plate of greens. Oh how the noise of liquid drawn through the teeth and around the tongue made him wish that he could take a drink. The little mule continued to tickle his fancy with the music of her slurp. Jane stood there like she was posing for a picture. Maybe it was because he couldn't take a drink

19

himself; maybe it was because he thought he had to show this mule that he was in charge. Whatever the reason, Randolph decided to make Jane drink. He tried to push her neck down. Because of the relative strength of his arm to that of her neck, jane was not alert to his intentions. He thought she was being stubborn, ignoring him. "Damnit! Drink!" He struck the tuft of mane lining the back of her neck. The mule felt that. She gave her head a loose toss. Sadie was done drinking. She stood erect. The height of her head came up to Randolph's thigh as he sat on Jane. "See! Sadie's finished and you haven't even started." He pounded the back of Jane's neck. "Drink, damn you. Drink!" While Randolph was lost in his tantrum, the mule dropped her head down to the water. Like somebody had pushed him down a slide, Randolph plunged into the watering hole. His feet landed on the miry bottom and slid out from under him. He bounced on his butt, but it didn't hurt; his mind flashed back to a near drowning two years earlier. It took him several moments to realize that the water only reached his chest while he sat in it. The fear of drowning melted away leaving a space to be filled with embarrassment and blame. "Jane what the hell is the matter with you." He tried to stand up twice, slipped back onto his ass each time.

Something Archie had told him about a local farmer, popped into his mind. According to Archie, the farmer, Jack Richard, had got mad at his mule and punched him in the jaw.

> *"I swear, Randy, that ol' mule's knees buckled."*
> *"You tellin' a tale!"*
> *"Naw I ain't."*

Randolph had only half believed Archie at the time. Yet, in his memory, Archie's words were right as rain. "Are you crazy mule!" He jumped up and, with all his might, slammed his fist against Jane's foot-long-two-inch thick jawbone. "Ohh-shittt!" Randolph had not felt so much pain since his three front teeth were knocked out. He coddled his right knuckles in his left palm and prayed-sobbed and was tempted to try once more to buckle Jane's knees. The awareness that such a thought had crossed his mind made him feel like a fool and his knuckles throbbed even more.

He stood thigh deep in the water blowing breath onto his knuckles until little by little the pain eased. Sadie had been startled back by the noise and splash. She and Jane who had by now joined her, nibbled on grass in a patch several yards away. When Randolph scrambled out of the watering hole he felt the soggy weight of his clothes. He tightened his belt a notch to keep his dungarees from sliding down. He had the wherewithal to strip excess water from his shirttail and pants by pressuring his hands against his belly and sliding them all the way down. The action did not make him feel less wet, but he was proud that he had thought to do it. He collected the mules and tied their bridle reins to a dogwood branch. His nerves settled enough that he allowed himself to enjoy the cool wet clothes clinging to his skin in the scorching heat. Next, he had to get back up the hill. Archie must be wondering where in the world he got to. He looked around for a way to get a leg up. He saw a stump near the tree he had lashed the mules to. He led them to either side of it. "Ok." He managed to step onto the stump and keep control of the mules while keeping balance until he could jump onto Jane.

The way he imagined he looked congered the vision of himself as an old prospector riding away from a gold mine with a little pack mule in tow.

The afternoon sun leeched much of the the moisture from his clothes.

It had been in August when he and Lucille got caught in a hale storm that time. This Carolina heat had dried their clothes lickety split.

Archie was waiting by the woods at the top of the hill. He wore a wide grin that hid how he was scared to death. He hadn't dared go down to the watering hole. The thought that something terrible had happened kept him waiting and hoping. He knew he would be blamed if something happened to little Randy. "Boy, you sure a sight for sore eyes. Where you been?" He was too relieved to notice Randolph's still half wet pants.

On the way to the barn, Randolph told Archie about falling into the watering hole, almost breaking his hand and cursing at Jane. Between guffaws at each detail, Archie said, "Boy, you a mess." Randolph had to laugh at himself. On one level he got a glimpse of the truth that what had just happened wasn't nothing when he thought of some of the stuff he'd been through.

Mama's letter got here three days ago. Randolph knew that a letter usually took at least four days. She might've sent it a week ago. Waiting for the bike to get here was gonna be like waiting for Christmas. He wished Mozzelle and them had a phone so he could call Washington and ask mama to send Suzie Q. by Special Delivery.

* * *

A big stack of fire-wood was chopped, the front yard was mowed-he did the side yard two days ago. There was no clabber to churn or stringbeans to snap. Mozzelle had studied for several minutes before she accepted that there were no more chores for him to do. To his surprise, she didn't make up something to keep him busy. It would be hours before he would have to go down to the bottom and bring the cow back from grazing, he didn't know what to do with himself. He wandered over to the trash pit at the top of the hollow. Once, when he was little, he found a toy truck under some bottles and cans. Nothing in the pit caught his eye today. But near the edge of the hollow, toward the church, he saw a cedar branch hanging low. Right at the end was a smaller branch. One part of it made a perfect Y, it was like the Lord had meant for Randolph to see it and think of a slingshot. He broke the small branch off and took it over to the woodpile. After he chopped it down to the 'Y' he used a scythe edgw to whittle the bark off. Now, all he had to do was find a piece of inner-tube, an old shoe tongue and some twine. He found an old pair of brogans Gregory had thrown in the pit a while back; only the rubber and twine were left. There was twine in the sideboard drawer. Where could he find an inner-tube? Gregory didn't have a car right now-no old tubes around.

...When Randolph got back from Archie's house, Mozzelle didn't even know he had slipped off almost an hour ago. He cut two even strips of rubber, tied them onto the tops of the smoothed Y and tied the shoe tongue to the other ends. "Hot dog!" This was the first slingshot he had made all by himself. "Hot dog!"

At first, Randolph shot stones at bottles or cans in the junk pit. Then he got the notion to go into the woods, go bird hunting. He stuck the handle of his slingshot into the pencil slot on his overall bib so that the rubber strips and tongue hung down like a watch fob and chain. "Hot dog!"

22

Bird hunting stayed at the heart of his thoughts.Usually when he got in bed, he went right to sleep so as not to lie there in the dark any longer than he had to. This was one of those nights he couldn't just fall off, make his escape.

An image of the slingshot hanging down across his overall bib, floated in his recollection. After satisfying himself that it looked, "Cool as a fool in a swimming pool," he thought, 'can't go huntin' without huntin' dogs.' "HERE JACK! HERE FLOSSIE!" Neither of the dogs came into sight. He whistled and called again. This time they came out from under the house wagging their tails and grinning. "Hey ya'll. Been up under there out of the sun, have ya'?"

Flossie got to him first. She rubbed against his leg. Jack moved in and nudged her aside. Randolph imagined for a moment that his dogs knew how good they were making him feel. "Come on y'all, let's go bird huntin'." The dogs followed him around the trash pit, down through the brush. After a distance about as long as a block in D.C., they came out by the spring and baptizing pool. A few birds flew over the open space. Randy ignored them. He was looking for one that was sitting on a limb where he could take good aim. The hunter and his dogs went down below the spring-deep into the hollow, past the blackberry patch into the real woods.

After seven or eight shots at birds-close and not so close, he had not hit a single one. Most of the intended prey didn't even fly off, he missed them by so much. A heap more times, Randolph went down in there to sack him a bird. Each trip, he missed his target by as wide a margin as the first time.

What kept Randolph awake tonight was, "Why?" He needed to figure out why in the world he never could shoot him a bird? When he shot at cans or bottles, he hit them at least sometimes. How come he didn't ever hit a bird? His memory camera scanned across the hunting trips. The floating light fixed on an image he had conjured the very first day. He had imagined himself shooting a bird then seeing it lying in the weeds with a bleeding broken neck. It looked like a chicken that had been killed for supper. It looked like a dead pullet a hawk had left because somebody came up on him before he could eat it. The sight had disgusted Randolph just like the thought of dead piggywiggy at hog killing time.

All the fistfights he had back home in D.C. came swirling into review. He remembered clearly he could not get going until the other boy threw the first punch. It was alright to beat the hell out of him after that. He had never understood why he was like that. He didn't try all that hard to figure it out. Still, he wondered why he was like that. The same thing with the way he hated bullies so much. "Shit!" Why'd he think about how much he hated bullies? Just remembering the way they looked down and barked at smaller boys made him mad. (Feeling his eyes squint in anger gave him enough satisfaction that he was able to move on.) He lay there chewing on his cud until finally in a blast of light... Randolph didn't want to kill no birds! Deep down, he knew it would tear him up if he did. Folks would sometimes say, "So and so wouldn't hurt a fly." Randolph never paid much attention to the saying. Now he knew what they were talking about. It bothered him when he had to kill a fly. He would always try to wave it off until it stayed around long enough to get on his nerve. Then he would try to kill it.

Randolph continued to go bird huntin'. He always made sure he missed-he kept that a secret between himself and himself. But he had to go out there in the woods and make like he was gonna shoot him a bird. Inside, it made him feel like a grown man.

The moment settled on him. He felt pretty good to have lay here in the dark all this time without being scared. The thought didn't last long, sleep overcame him before fear could.

* * *

"Fuck you!" Lincoln acted like somebody had spit in his face. Randy's new school chum hung his head and turned to walk away.

"What the hell is wrong with you?"

Lincoln had done exactly what boys back in Washington did. He teased Randolph by singing, "All I want for Christmas is my two front teeth." He could not have known that Randolph hid the gap in his mouth from himself; as far as he was concerned, he had all his teeth. If he didn't keep his snaggle-tooth appearance out of his mind, there was no way he could smile or even talk without feeling self conscious. Nor could Lincoln have known how much it bothered Randolph that the song talked about 'two' front teeth, when in fact, he was missing 'three' front teeth.

Lincoln turned back to face him. "How come you cuss so much?" Had he asked his friend from D.C. how come he was smart in class, it would not have thrown Randolph one whit more; he was as proud of his ability to cuss real good as he was of his aptitude for speaking properly or talkin' like country folk. "Don'tchou cuss?" "Not like you do. You cuss a whole lot." That observation stumped Randolph. Lincoln turned again to walk away. This time, Randolph did not stop him. He watched the guy he had secretly nicknamed Beanpole walk around the end of the three room schoolhouse. He kept his eye on the the end of the long-white-one story building as if an explanation for how much Lincoln's reaction confused him was going to fill the space left when he turned the corner.

* * *

The school bus was full and loud. Randolph sat all the way in the back. He tried to figure out-not why Lincoln thought he cussed too much, but why that notion seemed to make sense.

Three sisters who lived in Ash Grove were getting off the bus. It wasn't until then that Randolph remembered he had not cussed much at all before school started. Archie didn't cuss that much. He smoked and chewed tobacco, he even sneaked drinks from the bottle of Schenley's his daddy kept under the bed. Except for saying, "Shit" sometimes, he didn't cuss that much. Nobody in Grandma's house cussed that Randolph could tell. There was no liquor in the house. Most of the records were church music. There was not even a shotgun in the house. He could not think of another house that didn't have a shotgun somewhere in it. This stood out for Randolph cause back in D.C., mama had a shotgun in her closet and a .38 special in a shoe box under her bed.

He knew good and well why he cussed around other boys. As far as he was concerned, that was one of the things boys did. Anyway, he enjoyed cussin'. He enjoyed every kind of language he'd ever heard including the few Spanish words and phrases he learned in the fourth grade. But nothing he thought or felt let him know why he didn't curse from the day he got down here in June until he started school.

There was a place underneath his thoughts; way down below the things he pretended not to know or feel because he did not know what to do with them. The place was so far down, it was beneath the dark that was his secret closet. That place was like the end of the tunnels in his dreams where sunlight came out of nowhere-everything was clear. But what he saw way down there came and went like a lightening bug-one lightening bug. It wasn't like the bunch of lightening bugs he saw every night. It was like it would be if there was just one of them. He would see it and know what it was.

All Randolph could say about it though, was that it was a little bitty light. Every time he saw something way down there it was like that. He knew exactly what it was, but the blink never came a second time. It was a brief impression. This time, it had more to do with what was not than what was.

Here, in the country, he was not scared all the time like he was in Washington. He was afraid of the dark-and Lord knows it got real dark down here. But back home in Washington with all those street lamps, it was like it was dark all the time. Cursing seemed to ward off the scariness in that kind of dark. Cursing was a lot like a diptheria shot. It kept you from getting sick. Randolph Wilford did not think or feel this. It was something that blinked and went away. Yet, it planted a seed while it was there. Out of the corner of his eye, he saw ARJAY'S general store. He'd better get ready for his stop.

He got off the school bus knowing that he had not talked or joked with the other kids like he usually did. He was not bothered by that, the look on Lincoln's face was still with him. "Damn!"

He was at the 'T' where ARJAY'S road crossed the end of the Cedar Grove road. How long had he been there? All he knew was, he didn't hear the school bus any longer. It must of got past the mill already. 'Ok, Randolph. Git to steppin'.'

Archie quit school when he turned sixteen last month. These days Randolph has to walk the mile or so by himself. Although It is November, there's still light from the setting sun-not dark like when he leaves home at five thirty in morning.

About a quarter of the mile walk home, he passed cousin Hilda's house. She was on the porch. "Hello Randolph." She called out. "You haven't been to see me in a while!" He answered that he would come to see her soon. Cousin Hilda was real nice. He liked being in her company.

By the time he crossed the creek, at the bottom of the hill, Randolph had decided to stop cursing. At least he would stop cursing at Lincoln. Last week he called him a dumb motherfucker. Tomorrow he would tell him he was sorry.

* * *

"Junie. Is that you?" He knew it was no use to correct her. Grandma had moved to somewhere else. Randolph did not have a name for it, he wished he did. It was sorta like who she was had gone away and left a stranger here in her place. And she didn't tell nobody she was leaving, neither. "Yes maam." He had not yet accepted that Leticia was never gonna come back. On the rare occasions when she said as little as she just had, he took it as a sign his grandma was 'bout to return. "How you feelin' grandma?" He might as well have been talking to the man in the moon. She had called him from wherever she was, then hung up. He laughed. 'And she ain't even got a telephone.' There was no further sign that she knew he was in the room. Like he did every morning, Randolph picked up the chamber pot and held his breath until he was out in the air. He emptied the pot into the outhouse pit then came back to the rain barrel where the side porch turned to the back porch. He took a bucket of water from the barrel, used half of it to clean the chamber pot. The other half, he poured into a wash basin for his bird bath.

The first two months of school, Randolph would wash up before he did his slop jar chore. He wanted to put that off long as he could. As the mornings got colder, he found it harder to stand washing up with cold water. But he was caught between a rock and a hard place. In order to have hot or even warm water to bathe with, he would have to start a fire in the kitchen stove. It would take the stove a good half hour to get hot. The cold water took another half hour to be warm enough to make it all worth while. That meant he would need to get up at least an hour earlier. He already got up at four to milk the cow before taking her out to

27

pasture. "Shit! Cold water ain't all that bad." He figured it was better to empty granma's mess after he took Bessie to the bottom to graze. That way, washing up with fresh, cold water was almost a pleasure.

The school bus used to come by the house. That fulfilled Randolph's dream from the first time he lived down here when he was little. It would pick him up, drive to the 'T' where it turned right and headed to Ash Grove. Now, instead of coming down Cedar Grove road, the bus went to Ash Grove first. Then, it had to go way down pass the mill and drive up into the mountains. There were six kids who lived up there. They were four sisters and two brothers. the boys were Second and Third Graders. The sisters ranged from Randolph's age to Archie's. The ride was long. But there were only those two stops.

By the time Randy got all the way to the T, light would be breaking. But when he left the house it would be dark as night. Across from the Baptist church was the house where the Camerons used to live. A little further down was aunt May's house. But they were both empty-dark.

The dogs were still sleeping when Randolph left, it was pitch dark and so quiet he could hear his breath. Because his yard and the churchyard were in the open, he didn't begin to get scared until he got out onto the road and passed the two houses. Below aunt May's house, there was nothing but woods on both sides of the road. No crops, no fields, just woods. The woods were always quiet during the day except for birds singing. No birds sang in the dark. But there were other noises that Randolph never heard in the daylight. Creaking, cracking and something that sounded for all the world like whispering.

Today, and every morning, he told himself, "I'm a child of God, it doesn't make sense for me to be scared." His attempts to be calm and sensible did not prevent him from feeling a slight shiver run over the surface of his skin. 'Felt like something 'nother in the woods breathed strong and loud enough to let him know it was 'bout to leap out of there. At the base of Randolph's mind was a notion to run. But every other instinct told him that the haints in the bushes would be mad at him for thinking he could get away from them. Their long-shaggy-tree-limb arms would grab him and shake him until his own arms and legs flew off. These thoughts accompanied him around a turn that sloped down below aunt

May's. The closer he got to the creek bridge at the bottom of the slope, the tighter and tenser he got. He was half way down the slope flinching with any and every squeak or crunch that came across the drainage ditch from the woods. The way his heart bounced around in his chest made him wonder how long it was gonna take before he had a heart attack or took a cramp and locked in place so the haints would just stroll out and tear him to pieces. No matter, when he got all the way down to the creek bridge, he could still see-still hear-he was whole.

A little bridge separated the end of down from the beginning of up. After he got across it, woods were only on one side, going up to where there was a corn field on the right and a sweet potato patch on the left.

Getting across the little bridge meant a lot. Approaching it, he could hear the sweet-trickle of the shallow flow over creek-rocks. When he took his first step onto the bridge-and he had learned to walk on tiptoe all the way to the other side-whatever critters there were underneath, scattered and splashed to beat the band. None of them ever came up the banks to the bridge. But Randolph knew, one of these mornings, some little critter with blazing red eyes was gonna come up the bank at the beginning or it would wait until he thought he had made it all the way across, then it would dash up the far bank to scare the life out of him.

Some mornings when he tiptoed across the little wooden span, he would tense up so much that he would stumble. All the creek creatures in the world would skitter and make little creature sqeaks that made him sure that this was the day one or two of them would run up onto the bridge.

Today he made it across without tripping or stumbling. He heard just a few skitters-making tiny splash-noises that didn't bother him too much. Once again, Randolph had made it across the bridge. Breathing came back and blew off the twinges that bit at the ends of his nerves.

The road sloped up on a curve to the right. He passed the spot where he and his sister Lucille once took a short cut through the woods to ARJAYS.

Daylight was breaking. He could make out the rolling clay ridge above the drainage ditch to his left by the time he reached the crest of the hill where he could see a sliver of the rising sun above sweet potato vines. Ahead of him the road sloped gradually up to

Mr. Mason's house and, a little bit further, Cousin Hilda's. He loved her house. The fondness was multiplied by memories of being up in Glady's room, and of the treats cousin Hilda baked for him and for him and Lucille when she was down here.

The wide front porch ran along the walls of the parlor, hallway and Cousin Hilda's bedroom. Behind those rooms, the house narrowed to the den and dining room. Further in still, was the little kitchen and ln the back, the pantry. The house was shaped like a Christmas tree laid on its side.

And from here at the top of the creek hill, the sliver of light reflected off the windows and made everthing else up there, a gray silhouette.

Ten minutes later, Randolph was beyond cousin Hilda's and was at the T waiting for the school bus with his back against the bank. He retraced his feelings.

He was halfway to the church before his eyes were used to the dark and he could see his hands. He wasn't good and scared yet. He was alert to look back at the house roof to catch the weathervane, it was not spinning; there was no wind, the rooster's silhouette faced due East.

Randy's body was still half full of home, the outdoors took a while to push its way into him. When he went onto the road in front of the church and was almost down to aunt May's, home eased out of him. The dark outdoors came in and took charge of his feelings and thoughts. He reached the turn toward the creek trying to hold on to good sense. The haints didn't allow him to. Their noises twisted his imagination into a space filled with cobwebs and shadows from Wolfman and Frankenstein movies.

Halfway between the turn and the creek, he became a sapling bending to the chill of invisible things that tried to huff and puff him into little bits. He forced himself to keep in one piece. But something in the bushes moved, he flinched and quivered. From then until he got to the creek bridge, pinching cobwebs floated in him causing tiny hot itches. Beads of sweat popped out on his forehead.

Halfway across the bridge, the fright and perspiration commenced to dry up.

"Thank you Lord." Randolph relaxed against the bank and like he did every morning, wondered how long he could keep this up.

* * *

"I am forty three years old; a lot has accumulated in my mind over the years. Yet, I had enough space to memorize these verses." She walked from her desk at the front of the classroom. Halfway to the back, she made a semi circle around the potbelly stove that was not yet fired up for Winter, then she walked to her desk near the blackboard. "You children are eleven and twelve years old. You have not been on this Earth long enough to have crammed that much inio your little heads. So, you should not have any trouble learning and remembering them." Elizabeth Merriweather had been teaching children for over twenty years. She-Randolph had not failed to notice-was a plump, brownskin woman with cow eyes behind round, wire rim glasses. It was one of his favorite looks. Mrs. Merriweather offered Randolph double pleasure, the chance to learn verses from the Bible and, he would be able to show off for her by reciting them. Of course he would have to be the first in the class to memorize the verses in order to win the contest.

The children were to commit to memory the first chapter of Genesis and the first two verses of the second chapter. To further challenge them, Elizabeth Merriweather added the Ten Commandments.

Randolph looked around the room. Among the dozen other members of his class, there were only maybe two who could learn the verses as quickly as he could. Lincoln sure wasn't one of them. His eyes stopped at Debra Gill. She was smart, with her cute self. She might be able to learn the verses before him. He skipped over several faces until he got to Henry Hill. He was the only other person he had to worry about. Randolph corrected himself. He didn't really have to worry that either one of them would beat him out. He knew that if he studied hard he would win the contest.

The lunch bell rang. He and Lincoln looked at one another. They were good buddies now. Every chance they got, they hung around together. Neither of them got up until after the rest of the children filed out of the room. That way, they could wink back and forth while they watched the girls' legs. When the show was over, the two chanted, "MAN-OH-MAN!" and headed for the play-ground.

Randolph and Lincoln usually went out the door on the Schoolhouse Road side of the building. Randolph didn't know if Lincoln was just following him or if, like him, he enjoyed seeing the two school buses parked under the trees. Since back when he was four and being taught to read by Arlene, he had loved the big yellow one. Now that they had switched the routes around, he had come to love the little bus that went to Ash Grove and to the mountains. It was like riding in a small room with everybody sitting close to one another.

The two buddies walked around the end of the long, three room building. Most of the seventy odd students were already out there making a racket. Lincoln tugged Randolph's sleeve. Debbie Gill and her friends were skipping rope. Debbie was up and was jumping double-dutch to beat the band. Her skirt bounced up and sometimes it bounced high enough that the boys saw her sky blue panties. "Let's go over yonder." Randolph didn't have a particular place in mind. Nor did he know if he was jealous of Lincoln looking at one of his secret girlfriends or, if he felt guilty about looking up a girls dress when she didn't know it. He, in fact, might very well have wanted to walk away before he got too excited. All he knew was he wanted to move on.

The playground was bordered on one side by four out houses-spaced five feet apart. Across from them was the baseball field. Big boys who had quit school or graduated, were on the field taking grounders and shagging fly balls. Randolph and Lincoln went to watch them. The buddies shared a stick of Doublemint gum while they watched the ballplayers do their stuff.

At the end of the day, Mrs. Merriweather passed out carbon copies of the verses. Randolph's copy was burning a hole in its folder. But once he was on the little school bus, he forgot all about it. He sat next to the youngest of the Ash Grove sisters. Her name was Margaret. She was just a year older than him.

The sisters looked alike in a way; all three had heads of thick ringlets falling on their foreheads. Deep set, slanted eyes brightened their smooth black skin-not the cool blueblack that sometimes tickled Randolph's delight, but toasty, deep-dark brown like gingerbread crust. They were all bowlegged. The older two, Mary, fifteen and Magdalene, thirteen were kinda skinny. Margaret was built up from the ground. Her bow legs had thin soft looking hair on them. To Randolph, that hair was something or 'nother like glory.

He searched his mind for a way to start a conversation. While he roamed around in his head, he remembered smiling at one of the girls skipping rope during recess. The girl smiled back until she saw he was snaggletoothed. She frowned and turned away. It was difficult enough for him to talk to Margaret without remembering the doubledutch girl's reaction to his gap. The memory plus his withdrawn nature, weighed too much to manage. He said not a word.

The dentist had decided not to fit him for dentures because he could expect his teeth to grow back in by the time he was ten. For the first year or so, Randolph had checked his gums every morning for signs of new growth.

At eleven, he has given up. Since he went to the dentist that time he has never thought again about dentures. Everybody he knows who has dentures is old like grandma and them. He couldn't fix his mind on the notion of a child wearing false teeth.

His attention shifted to the other kids in the bus. It felt strange to see that just about all of them were laughing and talking to one another except him and Margaret. He mustered gumption. "It's hot on this bus isn't it?" Margaret fixed a gaze on him that said he must be talking to somebody else (at least that was what he convinced himself she was thinking.) After that, Randolph couldn't think of a way to make himself comfortable. He couldn't change seats, he couldn't do the one thing that was easy, get mad. Moments later he settled on a promise to himself he would start all over on anuther day. Meanwhile, it was a long-hot-stiff-half hour until the sisters got off in Ash Grove. Randolph was tied in knots; he hid in sight the rest of the way to the T.

* * *

33

The heifer's bristly tail flung around and struck him across the cheek. "I'm sorry Bessie." Randolph didn't need to wonder why the cow was uneasy. He stopped milking her to change from the 'four finger sqeeze' to the 'two finger strip.' These were names he made up for the milking styles Mo had taught him. She had explained that if his fingernails were too long they hurt the cow's teets. Bessie would always let you know by swinging her tail at you or kicking the milk bucket over. Sometimes she turned her neck and mooed like she was saying, "Hey! What the hell you doing!"

At first, Randolph stuck his pinky in his mouth. He was intending to chew off the ends of his fingernails. "Shit!" Again, he had forgotten thet his front teeth were missing.

The minute Bessie felt the gentle downward slide on her teets, she stood easy and chewed her cud. Randolph loved the cow almost as much as he did Jack and Flossy. Her slow, soft way made him feel peaceful. And the way she looked at you with those big brown eyes was real gentle-with those Betty Boop eyelashes. Sometimes she made him mad, though.

Mozzelle had just beat Randolph the third straight game in a row. He was thinking how he was never gonna play checkers again when the sound of Bessie lowing, came in from the night. Arlene turned her attention from The Record Mart, on the radio. Mo looked at him. He couldn't pretend he didn't here the cow.

"Boy! How many times do I have to tell you to lock that cow shed good?"

"I locked it good." He could have saved his breath.

"You're gonna have to go down to the bottom and get her before she wanders off somewhere." This had happened once before. Randolph was sure he had turned the propeller-like lock across the door. He was letting a vain hope slide into his mind when Gregory took his pipe out of his sorry mouth. "Git to gittin' boy." Gregory did not tell him what to do often enough for him to be used to it. So, when he did, Randolph was tempted to tell him to mind his own business. Before Mozelle could give him her squinty-eyed glare, Randolph got up to get the flashlight.

He went to the cow shed to get her collar and chain. Sure enough, the door was wide open. Randolph still shined the flash-light inside as if by some miracle Bessie would be standing in

34

there. "Don't be so damned stupid." After chidng himself, he felt less like a fool. But that only freed up his mind to focus on the darkness. The flashlight-glow gave him some release although he had to turn it off every few minutes. He knew that if he kept the light on the whole while, he looked for Bessie, there was a good chance the batteries would burn out. The thought of the light dying while he was down in the bottom in total darkness sent chills through him.

He could take a shortcut from the cow shed to the spring if there was a path over here-not just tall grass. He wasn't sure whether or not snakes came out at night. No need to take a chance. He walked back to the yard to take the path down the hill to the spring. Like the other time the cow got loose at night, he passed the spring and baptising pool marveling at how this spot that he was crazy about in the daytime, was just another scary dark place at night.

At the bottom of the hollow, close to the blackberry patch, he turned the flashlight on-no need to get caught up in those briars. The whole time he had been out here in the dark, Randolph had managed to think about everything he could to keep from being scared to death. In the blackberry patch he kept the light aimed at the ground because when he was little he and Mozzelle had been picking berries and seen a snake down here. Despite being tense with fear, the memory made him laugh out loud. Mozzelle and he had seen the snake at the same time. He saw that it was a black, pilot snake, not poibonous. Mozzelle nearly yanked his arm out of its socket when she grabbed his wrist to pull him behind her. When they ran past the pool and spring, Randolph yelled through panting breath. "It's just a pilot snake!" Because she was pulling him behind her, Mozzelle's voice was barely more than a gush of breath. "Hush boy!"

They reached the top of the hill-the edge of the yard, Randolph saw that Mo had lost one of her loafers.

Here, four years later-in the dark of night-was a rotten brown loafer, still right where Mozzelle ran out of it.

Occupied by the thought of Mo losing her shoe that time, Randolph reached the field beyond the blackberry bushes. "Huh!" A bulk blacker than the dark sround it, was right in front of him. He lifted the flashlight. "Bessie!" While he was searching for the *cow, Randolph had imagined that when he found her he was gonna grab her by the horns and shake her. Then he would curse at her for making him come out here in the dark. But the memory of the day he and Mozzelle saw the snake had erased his anger. "What am I gonna do with you? When I put you in your shed every night I give you extra hay...you break out anyway. What's the matter with you heifer?" He put the collar around her neck and stroked her shoulder. It came to him that this big old cow made him feel safe. He didn't expect that if some haint came after him Bessie was going to protect him. It was just that she was big and was an animal. The thought put him enough at ease that he decided to avoid the briars and keep the cow from getting all scratched up. He led her around to the sandy bottom down behind her shed.*

Randolph came back to now. His reflection had kept rhythm with his two fingered milking. The pail was three quarters full and only thin streams were coming out of the teets. "I'd better stop before I milk you dry."

After depositing the pail of milk in the kitchen, Randy skipped back down the steps-feelin' good. He had already chopped a nice pile of wood and some kindling for tomorrow morning. Milking Bessie was the last chore for the day. Instead of walking ahead and leading her to the shed, he held Bessie's chain slack and walked beside her urging her forward with a hand on her neck. Along the path, Bessie looked at Randy a couple of times. He understood, like he did with the dogs, something was going on between them. He did not pretend to know what it was. He just knew something was going on.

"Well alright now!" Gregory had replaced the propellar-lock on the shed with a wooden bolt lock. It was good and secure. Randolph was grateful to Gregory. He gave the cow a bunch of hay. "Good night Bessie girl."

Chapter Three
The Good Book

Much as Randolph was enjoying Mo's chicken and dumplings, he was anxious to go up to his room to study Genesis. So far, memorizing up through Chapter 1:13, was easy as pie. *"And the evening and the morning were the third day."* That, the tender pieces of chicken and dumplings-oozing gravy, had him rocking to and fro.

"Be still boy." Mozzelle was tickled to death. She knew good and well that it was her fine cooking that had Randy so excited. She did not know that he was feeling double pleasure. He made sure to be still enough to keep her from messing up his flight.

Gregory was quiet as usual-sittin' there looking like a skinny white man. Arlene-with her big round belly-couldn't help giggling. She thought it was funny that Randolph was slurping and chomping in time with his back and forth movement.

* * *

"'And God said, let there be lights in the firmament of the heaven to divide the day from the night; and let them be for signs, and for seasons, and for days, and years.'"

When Randolph read the word 'sign' he pictured the neon sign on the 7th & T Cocktail Lounge he used to see near the Howard Theater in D.C. Intuition led him away from that image; it was confusing. He went about commiting verse 14 to memory. Then, he went back to the beginning to recite the old through the new. As usual, he stumbled a few times-not because he had not retained well, it was still hard to believe that he had. Confidence and satisfaction melded when was able to go from the beginning through verse 14 with no bad mistakes.

Randolph's introduction to memorization was "Twas The Night Before Christmas," when he was six. It surprised and exhilarated him when he was able to recite the poem. On the other hand, when at age nine, he read "Moby Dick," a world broader than his imagination touched him in the deep places he came to frequent and explore with increasing satisfaction, ever since.

* * *

"I thought'chou knew Arlene was pregnant."

Randolph did not respond to Mozelle. He made a move that took her king. Mozelle still won most checker games they played. But, it was satisfying to know that as time went by he got better and better. As for Arlene, he had thought she was just fat. Yeah, Mo had told him she was pregnant. For some reason though it had not resgistered. Besides, although everybody knew that babies came from inside a woman, this was the first time he could remember anybody in the family having one. Back in Washington some girl or other would have a baby. It always seemed to be somebody he didn't know.

Arlene had a little girl. The child, Naomi, was several weeks old before she was real-really real-to him.

"Grandma. Here's Naomi." Randolph was now toting the baby about. He had come to be possessive of her. "You've met her haven't you?" He extended Naomi so that Leticia didn't have to lift her head from the pillow. To his surprise, she smiled as though she did indeed recognize the child. "You do remember her don'cha?" The smile faded and Leticia retreated to the place where she lived these days. After the moment of encouragement Randolph accepted grandma was too far gone for him to continue hoping that she was gonna ever come back. "Naomi. That's your great grandmother." His words were more compensation to himself than anything else.

Randolph had the baby in his care, by default. Arlene and her boyfriend Willie spent a lot of time in town. Gregory hung around with the white men over by Arjay's. It seemed that when Mozelle wasn't cooking or cleaning she was at church meetings. He was glad Naomi was just as much his baby as anybody else's. He fed her, changed her and sang ditties to her. During the first weeks since Naomi was born, he studied Genesis downstairs in the living room. He memorized it well; along with the Ten Commandments.

38

One month to the day after Mrs. Merriweather passed out the copies, the recitation competition was held. As Randolph had guessed, only the three, himself, Debbie Gill and Henry Hill had bothered to work on the project. Each one stood to recite. Henry went first, he made just a few mistakes. Randolph was sure Henry would win. He went second. He made more mistakes than Henry had. His fate was sealed. Cute Debbie made even fewer errors than Henry. Now Randolph was sure Debbie would win.

Mrs. Merriweather explained that there were three criteria she would use to judge the participants; memorization, comprehension and presentation.

After recess, she announced her decision. "Debra Gill showed superior memorization. On the other hand, Henry Hill showed a high degree of comprehension. Randolph Wilford," she continued, "Presented the recitation with great skill that indicated complete comprehension. And although he made a few more mista-kes than either Debbie or Henry, his overall delivery, as indicated by the children's applause, gave the listener a more complete understanding of the material. Randolph Wilford is the winner."

To his delight, the 1st Prize turned out to be, The Four Gospels. Each one was in its own little, hard cover book. "Hot dog!

When he had become familiar with Mathew, Mark Luke and John, Randolph read aloud from them to Naomi. At six weeks old, she laughed a lot when he made faces at her. He thought up noises to make. Sometimes they were attempts to mimmick animals, sometimes he just made up sounds. Naomi seemed to enjoy his company and he surely enjoyed playing daddy.

* * *

Grandma, in her dark room, was slipping further away. Randolph had never seen anyone in her condition. The last time he saw daddy alive, he was up and around. You could see that he was way off somewhere, but daddy was up and around.

Randolph tried a number of times to believe that something had taken hold of grandma and wouldn't let her go. In the end, his good sense wouldn't let him deny that she had just given up.

Sometimes he wondered what made her do that. "Well, they say, 'The Lord works in mysterious ways.' He mustered a grownup voice. "I reckon..." He leaned over Naomi's crib. "Guh-guh-guh." She kicked her little brown legs so that her white booties were a blur and her laughter tickled Randolph out of his thoughts about grandma and stuff he could not understand.

For a while, he amused and jiggled Naomi. Then he read to her from the Book Of Mathew;

"1) A record of the genealogy of Jesus Christ the son of David, the son of Abraham:

2) Abraham was the father of Isaac, Isaac the father of Jacob, Jacob the father of Judah and his brothers..." Randolph read in earnest. Naomi lay still in her crib as if she comprehended. Engrossed in the language and lineage, Randolph took what he read as he had, *"In Fourteen Hundred Ninety Two, Columbus sailed the ocean blue..."* The Gospels were historical document-tation of olden times. Back when he memorized the first book of Genesis, his belief was that it was a factual account of the begin-ning of earhly time. Further, he concluded, by learning biblical stories, he was preparing himself to live, as the old folks said, "In Grace." His reason for reading the Gospels to little Naomi was to do the same for her. That she seemed to be attentive was not surprising to him. As the old folks also said, "It is written." He continued to read from The Gospel According To Mathew until he realized that the baby had fallen asleep. He closed the book and placed it on his lap.

Quiet embraced Randolph and he too fell asleep.

Chapter Four
Up Up and Away

Bessie was fed and put out to pasture. The kindling was piled beside the kitchen stove. When he took his bird bath with the water from the rain barrel, Randolph did not feel it. It was December, yet the icy water felt just fine. He hurriedly washed his ears, neck, under arms and feet before going back up to his room to put on his shirt, cap, coat and shoes.

In the yard, he buttoned his macanaw and turned the collar up. At the same time, he checked the back door to make sure Mo wasn't looking out at him. It was important that nobody learn his secret. The coast was clear, Randolph took a deep breath then leapt straight up into the air like Rocket Man. As usual, he rose high enough that he wouldn't clip the tops of the tallest trees in his path.

One of the best parts of flying was leveling off. During take off he only saw the sky. That was good at night. But here, just before dawn, there were no stars to see. When he leveled off though, Randy could see the woods and fields and houses-everything down below.

He looked back at the roof to see if the weathervane was spinning. As it had been ever since Randolph got back down here, the iron cock was stone still.

The flyer headed straight for the T. He was sick and tired of being scared to death every morning. From now on he would fly to meet the bus.

When he passed over the woods between aunt May's and the creek, a light appeared through the trees. It wasn't a lamp or a candle. It was just a light, a glow. Randolph felt a shiver run through him; a haint, just as big as day, sat stoking a camp fire. It had to be a haint, sure wasn't an animal. There were not any deer, bears or any other big game around here. Anything this big had to be a haint. Randolph swooped down a little to get a closer look. Yes indeed, it was what he thought it was. It was the size of a gorilla or a bear. But instead of fur, the thing had other stuff all over its body. It looked a lot like THE HEAP in comic books. Except the haint Randolph saw down there had tree limbs for arms and legs. And his body was made of wild grass and weeds. "Oh shit!" The haint was looking up at Randolph flying over. He jumped up and down and roared like a lion. The roar hurt Randolph's ears. "I'd better get back up to where I was." Before he could swoop up, the haint grabbed the fire glow and hurled it up at Randolph. It missed, but it put out so much heat when it went by, Randolph broke into a sweat.

He swooped up and up some more before leveling off again.

When he passsed over cousin Hilda's house it was a blurr.

At the T, he had to skid to a stop; his speed almost took him past his stop. Randy laughed 'til he near 'bout cried.

"Boy you'd better get up from there!" Mozelle yelled from her and Gregory's bedroom next to his. "You don't want to miss the school bus."

"Alright" Randolph swung his feet to the floor before he was awake enough to realize he was gonna have to do everything all over again. This time though, he would have to do it in real life. Worst of all, he would have to take that long scary walk down cross the creek. Would this be the day he would finally drop dead from fear?

By the time he fed Bessie and put her out to pasture, his finger tips were numb. The bird bath water felt colder than ever.

Up in his room, Randolph squeezed and rubbed his hands together for several minutes before he got feeling in them.

* * *

At the T, Randolph reflected back on this morning's walk. It hadn't been all that bad. When he was going down the real dark part near the creek, his memory of flying over and seeing the haint scared him a little bit. At the same time, his mind was not able to separate dream from reality clearly enough to get him wrapped up in one or the other.

"Naw. It wasn't all that bad." The little bus was in sight. It was passing Arjay's. "Doggone it. I'm gonna talk to her this morning!" While he pictured the soft hair on Margaret's brown, bow legs, the bus pulled to a stop and the open door waited for him to get on board.

The driver Pete fit the bus. He was a little guy. Pete was nineteen but not much taller than Randolph. He had a dark brown handsome face-Pete was a nice guy, easy going-the kind of older boy you could kid around with.

Margaret was sitting next to the window halfway toward the back. Randolph spotted her as he walked by Pete. He forced himself to smile, gapped mouth and all. Margaret smiled back. That didn't surprise Randolph. He had learned that when he could muster confidence, things seemed to go alright. The seat next to Margaret was waiting for him to walk right up and sit himself right down.

"How ya doin'?" "I'm fine. How're you?" Everything had felt right natural up until now. How should he answer? Should he say, 'I'm fine too.' Naw, that wasn't hep. 'Everything's copacetic.' Was too much. By the time he settled on, "I'm ok," enough time had passed that he felt awkward like he had been loping along and tripped over his own feet. Margaret was waiting for him to pick himself up. Still, Randolph decided, she knew he wasn't reet petite and gone like he made out he was. Further, Margaret would make fun of him for trying to be cute.

He shifted around in the seat and said nothing, but hoped against hope, she would give him a look that said, "It's alright Randy. Start all over."

Margaret stayed quiet just like he did. From the way she shifted every few minutes, she had the same sweat-pin-pricks across her forehead that he had and was afraid to scratch.

Soon, Margaret turned to talk with her sisters, one behind her, one across the aisle. Randolph wanted-once or twice, to say something to one of them. He held back.

It wasn't so much that he was scared as it was that Randolph was punishing himself for not getting it right the first time. Except to laugh with the girls from time to time, as if he was a part of their conversation, Randy didn't make another peep.

On the way up the winding mountain road, it crossed his mind that the mountain kids were the only people he had seen up here. He was about to make sure to remember to ask them about that when, like cutting in line at the movies, another thought slipped in between. He had never seen where they lived. They were always standing by the road when the bus got there. Margaret and her sisters waited by the road too. But you could see their house at the end of their driveway. There was no driveway up here.

His thoughts were interrupted again. Margaret's voice went across his shoulder to make fun of a darkskinned boy at school. She called the boy, "Sambo."

"You stupid hussy!" The words almost came out of Randolph's mouth. He clamped his lips just in time. Margaret's slur made him glad he had not made her like him. He wouldn't be that bowlegged heifer's boyfriend or any other kind of friend if his life depended on it.

When they stopped to pick up the mountain kids, Randolph took notice for the first time that all six of them were lightskinned. Soon as they were on board, he made it his business to talk to them. He wanted to show Margaret that these yella kids, who could talk about somebody's dark skin if they wanted to, were not dumb enough to do it. Still and all, brown-skinned Margaret had the nerve to call... he stopped the thought.

Randolph was satisfied that he had made his point, even if it was only to himself. From then to the schoolhouse, he and the mountain kids laughed and talked. Margaret's two older sisters even joined in. He could tell by how quiet Margaret became, she knew something was going on. He felt kinda sorry for her. But he held on to his anger until recess.

* * *

On this humid September evening, Randolph was well attuned to the magic of 'angels singing and joy bells ringing in Glory.' He was certain the sensations dancing through and around him were The Holy Spirit summoned by the Reverend and the elders-the tried and true.

Reverend Esterbrook had already bounced his little brown self about the pulpit proclaiming the perfection of The Lord God Almighty and the wonders of His ways.

The preacher promised a burden free life for those who would become saved, get on the road to salvation.

JEE-SUS KEEP ME NEAR THE CROSS
THERE A PRECIOUS FOUN-TAIN
FREE TO ALL A HEALING STREAM
FLOWS FROM CALVARY'S MOUN-TAIN

Now, down at the alter, John Esterbrook wiped sweat from his face with a big white hankercheif that was already soaking wet. The preacher's confident grin and the shining gold cross at the rear of the pulpit, made Randolph comfortable in his belief that this holy space was full of the Power of The Almighty. He joined the congregation in surrender.

NEAR THE CROSS, NEAR THE CROSS
BE MY GLO-REE EV-ER
TIL MY RESTLESS SOUL SHALL FIND
REST BE-YOND THE RIV-ER

Most of the grownups sang, "raptured soul." Randolph had always heard and sung it as, "restless soul."

At the beginnig of the service, ninety minutes ago, he busied himself, looking up at the pine beams supporting the high apex, back down to the dark men in black pin stripe suits, the women in mostly black frocks and fluttering cardboard fans.

Since, all but the honey-butter-soul-sweet Glory of The Savoir has dissolved into nothing. The Lord God Almighty is in Command!

Every voice as one continued in a soft, plaintive croon.

NEAR THE CROSS A TREMBLING SOUL
LOVE AND MERCY FOUND ME
THERE THE BRIGHT AND MORNING STAR
SHED ITS BEAMS AROUND ME

"The doors of the church are open." The preacher's voice was barely louder than the hushed singing. "Won'tcha come to Jesus? His arms are waiting to enfold you."

Randolph wanted so much to get up and join church. He knew better though. He and Mozzelle had talked about it and agreed he should wait until he was older.

One of Archie's older brothers, who was home for Revival Week, broke down and had to be helped to the alter. Until then, Randolph had thought he was full of the spirit. He had not been. Now, he was; his chest pounded-tears poured down his face. He no longer had to guess, Randolph Wilford was filled with the Holy Spirit. He embraced every bit of that which consumed him.

NEAR THE CROSS
NEAR THE CROSS
BE MY GLORY EV-ER

The sight of her big brother entering the doors of Salvation, inspired Verniece to rise and turn her cares over to The Lord.

TILL MY RESTLESS SOUL SHALL FIND
REST BEYOND THE RIV-ER

The siblings knelt at the alter. Reverend Esterbrook placed a hand on each of their heads. "Gracious Lord, see these young people and receive them into the fold. Lord, let them feel the Glory of your precious love. Let them partake of that sweet joy which has filled those who have come before them. He paused, and with his eyes closed, Reverend Esterbrook smiled broad brightness that made Randolph think that he knew and felt all that the preacher did. Again, piety spilled from his own eyes.

NEAR THE CROSS
 NEAR THE CROSS
BE MY GLORY EV-ER
TILL MY RESTLESS SOUL SHALL FIND
REST BEYOND THE RIV-ER

* * *

It wasn't easy to figure out what was going on. Mozzelle was one person, then she was somebody else but still Mozzelle. The first Mo was chasing Randolph with a switch the size of a black snake. The second Mo kept him hid behind her to protect him from haints. The first one would find Randolph hiding back there, and grab at him. Mozzelle number two would slap her hand away.

He woke up with the surface of his mind still confused. On the level that keeps track of what goes on, Randolph saw what was happening. He rolled over and let his secret part remember.

10:00:AM
"Randy. I want'chou to mow the grass."

"Aw Mo! Do I have to?" He had just finished shelling butterbeans.

"Boy! You better get yourself out there'n do what I told you." She wiped her hands on her apron while giving him a familiar squint-eyed glare.

"The grass" meant every part of the yard from up against the garden, down across the part between the front porch and the road. Then, the patch on the church side of the driveway, just above the hollow.

After the couple of hours it took to mow those parts, he would have to do the side yard and the back, down to the chicken coop and chopping block.

Randy did this chore once before. It took him over four hours. Mozelle didn't care how long it took or how much his hands and arms hurt after pushing that damn lawnmower up, down and across all that yard. All she knew was that it had to be done. Randolph kinda understood that. But he was not able to connect his understanding with the need for him to be the one to do it. He pulled the mower out from behind the chicken coop and drug it around the the chips and the chopping block.

By the time he pulled the mower to the starting point up by the garden, he was tired enough that he had to rest. The thought that he hadn't even started yet, stuck in his craw. "Shit!"

This part of the lawn sloped down; he mowed down hill and back up until he had done the area from the house corner to the road.

The yard in front of the house was flat. It wouldn't't've been all that bad except that it was so wide his hands got sore.

The last time the family went to town, Randolph bought two hankerchiefs-one blue, one red. The two paisley bandannas were like the ones real farmers used.

Today he had stuffed the red one in the hip pocket of his overalls.

At the big oak, he paused to pull the habkercheif out and wipe it across his brow. 'Lord! that felt good. He squirted spit from the tip of his tongue through his gap. "Aaa-boy! Shake a leg!" An old farmer, now long dead, used to say that. Randolph paused as if to pay homage to the dearly departed. He put the big red hankerchief back in his pocket. Enough energy now flowed through him he was able to mow the whole far side of the driveway before he whipped out his sweat rag again. This time he peered into the trash pit at the top of the hollow, s' been a long time since he went in there to see what he could find. "Yessir!"

The nearly two hours it took to finish the side and backyard down to the chicken coop seemed like half that time.

2:00:PM

Randolph returned the lawnmower to its place behind the coop and waited for several minutes to see if Mo had noticed that the mowing noise had stopped. Nothing. That meant she was too busy with her own chores to study him. He knew better than to ask her if he could go over to Archie's or to Holly's to play. Mozelle (number two) would say, "No!" She would look around until she found something else for him to do. Randolph Couldn't remember the last time she said, "Yeah, you can go play." He bided his time until he was sure Mozelle didn't miss the sound of the mower.

Randolph's bike, Susie Q, was in the driveway-next to the big oak. With the side of his brogans, he eased up the kick down stand, stepped on the pedal and pushed off with the other foot. Then he swung his leg over the seat like the Durango Kid mounting his big white steed.

Randolph came out onto the road grinning. When Mozelle found out he was gone, her voice would ring across the woods between the Methodist church and Archie's house. "RANNNDOLPH! SAAAY! RANNNDOLPH!" He would wait until she called several times before hopping onto Susie Q. to come home.

Every time he slipped off, he enjoyed himself for as long and as much as he could because 'Sure as Carter made little liver pills,' Mozelle was gonna wear him out when he got back. Still, he had to admire her for being able to be heard loud and clear all that way.

48

Mr. Irvin was sitting on his front porch licking down a Bull Durham he'd just rolled. He told Randy that Archie had taken the pickup into town to get a block of ice. That didn't make Randolph no never mind. He was gonna hang around anyway. "Yessir." A smile went across Archie's daddy's lean face. He lit his smoke and well remembered, not long ago, Randy had been playing here in the front yard when Mo's voice came from cross yonder.

"Boy, don't I hear Mozelle callin' you?"
"No sir."
Mr. Ervin had told young Randolph that he'd better go home 'fore Mozelle got mad enough to give him a whipping. He didn't know, won't no way the boy was not going to get a whipping. 'Course Mr. Ervin also didn't know that Randolph had slipped off.

"Can I play 'til Archie comes home?"
"Sure can."
Randolph went around the house to the grape arbor. He knew a coat hanger hook and a '16 inch' wagon rim were back there. Nothing was more fun than using the u-hook to run the the iron rim around. He would push it along listening to the ringing sound it made-the faster he ran, the louder it rang.

3:40:PM
"RANNNDOLPH! SAAY! RANNNDOLPH!" How the hell could she yell so loud. It was more'n a quarter mile, as the crow flies.
Randolph had been having the time of his life running up and down a path between Archie's house and the barn. Mozzelle's voice reached him as he was about to head back toward the barn from the house end of the path. He could have gone ahead and pretended not to hear her calling him. But if Randolph Wilford was anything, he was proud. He knew good and well Mr. Ervin had heard exactly what he heard and was sitting out there on the front porch waiting to see what young Randy was gonna do. Instead of turning back toward the barn, he pushed the singing rim around to the back of the house and parked it by the grape arbor.
Randolph was ever concious of himself. He knew without thinking about it that by not leaving the hanger and rim in the side yard, he took enough time that his aunt would have to call a few

extra times before he got back home. He took his time getting to the front yard to pick up Susie Q.

When he pedaled away, Mr. Ervin's voice came after him. It would have made him mad if it hadn't been so funny. "Well-suh! Young Randy's hearing done got a heap better'n it used to be!"

He laughed as long and hard as he could. He was sparing himself from spending the whole way, thinking about the whipping Mozzelle was surely gonna give him.

She was standing exactly where and like Randolph knew she would be-on the side porch between the bay window at the corner and the rain barrel. "Boy! I'm gonna make you mind me, if I have to kill you." He came as close as he could without actually blurting it out. 'How the hell you gonna teach me by killing me?'

"Take yourself out to the holler'n get me a hickory."

Neither now nor on the several occasions he had broken off a switch to be whipped with had Randolph realized he was breaking off a branch from a hickory tree. He only knew about pines, cedars and dogwoods. Far as he knew, hickory was just another word for switch. The hickory he pulled off a low branch was green enough to last through a good whipping. He had learned the hard way not to bring a sorry switch that would snap before Mozzelle was satisfied. He'd have to go get another one.

She waited, there on the side porch, hands on hips. "Give me that hickory and get'chourself up on this porch." Like, every time, he hesitated before stepping up to take his medicine. When one of his Brogans finally did land on the edge of the porch, he had a quick moment to notice that Mozzelle looked like she was about to dig into a slice of blackberry pie. He held onto that look, from the first whack across his back until she got tired.

Maybe it was eight times she brought the whistling green hickory down across his back. He lost count... Yeah, the first blow hurt like hell. And every one after that hurt just as much. What had Randolph Wilford's attention though, was that it seemed crazy to take such a whipping. It was hard to believe he let somebody do that to him.

6:30 PM

The mixture of field peas, corn and string beans with chicken and dumplings chased down with buttermilk, had Randolph wagging his knees under the table just like Mo always did. He had not forgiven her for the beating but he could not bring himself to hate through the 'gracious me' flavors dancing around in his mouth.

8:30 PM

Tonight was another of the few times Randolph ever beat Mozzelle at checkers. By the time he went to bed, he had beat her three games to two. On the way upstairs it came to him that he had completely forgiven his mean-ass aunt.

With his feet over the edge of the bed, he wiped the sleep from his eyes, smiling like a cheshire cat. It felt right nice knowing he had solved the problem. "Yeah. Mo is two people. He chewed on it a bit to be sure. "Yessir! She is both the good witch and the bad one."

* * *

No two ways about it, this was as good a day for baptising as you could hope for; Mozzelle said as much. Randolph couldn't see how anybody could dissagree. It rained up until about a half hour before Rev. Easterbrook was finally able to lead the congergation down to the pool. The sun streamed down in shafts the way it did in Sunday school books. The grass between the pool and the blackberry patch glistened beads left over from the storm. Randolph, as he did every year, had cleaned the sludge from the spring and pool down to their red brick bottoms. The pride in his eyes sparkled near 'bout like dew-like droplets on the wet grass.

Last year, and the year before that, if it hadn't been for the spanking new look of the pool's bottom, would;ve seemed like a waste of time, nobody joined church those years. Today, 'halleluja' Verniece and her brother from up the road, were about to be baptised into The Spirit.

The pastor and a big deacon stepped in the knee-deep water to receive the lambs into the flock. They and the Mills siblings were dressed in white robes that Randy, without knowing they

51

symbolized purity, knew so anyway because he was put in mind of new fallen snow.

Vernieces brother was first to be laid prone until his body and face were immersed. "I now baptise you in the name of The Father, The Son and The Holy Ghost." Although Verniece's brother wasn't underwater long enough to get his mouth full he came up coughing. Randy half hoped-half prayed that Verniece wouldn't act the fool like that. He was not dissapointed; she went under and stood up without a sound. Her robe, however, clung to her hips-titties and thighs causing him to nearly go into caniptions. He did not allow himself to show it, but he could not help, dispite being in the presence of The Father Son and Holy Spirit, near 'bout going crazy at the sight of her voluptuous curves. He fought it with all his might, to no avail. Sure, he had told The Lord how he felt about sex. That did not help him one whit at this time in this place. his guilt was palpable to a degree he felt certain those around the pool could tell he was aroused. There was not a sign anyone was studying him. The truth was, he knew they were not. There was within him a need to inflict himself with the pain of self loathing when he did not meet what he perceived as high moral standards. He was in pain from this moment until he went to sleep that night. The following morning, Randolph remembered every aspect of the baptising ceremony except his lust.

* * *

Back in Washington when he was nine, Randolph's big sister Lucille took him up to the linen closet and showed him their Christmas gifts. Until that moment, he had thought that Santa Claus was real. The memory of Lucille convincing him that she was telling the truth about there being no Santa Claus was not a pain like the memory of getting his three front teeth knocked out. It was a lasting-different kind of pain. A month or so after Lucille shocked his life, a Sunday School teacher gave him a copy of Moby Dick. Although that book changed him, it was clear to him that the story about the big white whale was make believe. Maybe before Lucille broke his heart by telling him there was no Santa Claus, he had thought that Jack and Jill, Little Black Sambo and Snow White were real like Saint Nick was. "Yeah." Now he knew Ishmael and them were make believe because Santa Claus was.

And the people in fairy tales and in school readers could not be real if the jolly old elf was not. By now, the word 'tale' was in his vocabulary and he knew what it meant.

Bible stories were different, though. Everybody Randolph knew had a special look in their eyes and spoke in a real serious voice when they talked about the Bible. They didn't act that way except when they talked about 'The Lord' or 'The Lord.' He hadn't yet figured out the difference between "The Lord God" and "The Lord Jesus." But folks commenced to act serious when they talked about any and everything in the Bible. The many sermons he had heard, the way everybody treated preachers made Randolph know when he read the Gospels in the four little books Mrs. Merriweather gave him, he was reading the truth-God's truth. Like some of the church hymns said, he got comfort from them. The Scriptures taught him that so long as he believed on "Him" he did not have to worry about a thing.

* * *

At first, Mozzelle giggled when Randolph chided her for using the mild epithet, "Darn." Then she realized her nephew was ernest and devout. Thereafter she watched her mouth when he was around. One day Randolph explained to her that he had figured out that 'lie' was a bad word. He knew, he made it clear, it was not cussing to say it but it just wasn't keeping the golden rule to say that word. She nodded yes. After all, she did not want to discourage him from being a christian in whatever way he thought was right.

* * *

The two boys walked up and down between the toilets and the ball field. They were talking about Scripture-Randolph was talking about Scripture, Lincoln was content to listen.

Of all that Randolph had memorized, the thing that most appealed to him was the Seventh Commandment. The miracles performed by Jesus in the Gospels awed him, but Jesus was The Messiah. Randolph knew better than to try and identify with or even understand Him. All he could do was love and worship The Son of Man.

"Thou shalt not commit adultery."

They were walking back toward the schoolhouse when Lincoln looked around the end of the building. He stopped and pointed to the two buses parked under the trees. "I'm gonna drive one of them buses 'fore too long."

Randolph had been speaking from somewhere in Bible days. Lincoln's boast brought him all the way back. In the middle of his mind when he returned to here was the awareness that he could not drive. The first thought he had that he believed might equal Lincoln's skill was the Seventh Commandment. This was prompted by the reason that commandment struck him in the first place.

Every time Randolph did something that Mozzelle thought was disrespectful, like sassing her or expressing an opinion about an adult, Mozzelle would say, "Boy. You ain't grown. Don't be actin' so mannish!"

So that Lincoln wouldn't know that he was bluffing, Randolph looked his buddy dead in the eye. "You committin' adultery." "Say what?" "You heard me. You're tryin' to act grown."

Lincoln looked down and studied him long enough to be sure he was saying what it sounded like he was saying. "That ain't what commit adultery means. It means to do it to somebody you ain't married to." Both boys knew that it was a rare day when Lincoln could correct Randolph. Randolph usually got A's while his lanky friend got C's and D's when he didn't get F's.

Lincoln's wide grin near 'bout shouted out loud that he knew he had bested Randolph who had thought long and hard about the word adultery. He had not looked it up, but he had cogitated on it enough to be sure he knew what it meant.

Lincoln had the kind of dark eyes-in a pool of milk-that forced Randolph to come clean when he looked into them. "Ok. I'll take your word for it."

Lincoln's full, reddish lips smiled benignly. He had no notion to laud it over his buddy. He was content to best him fair and square.

* * *

54

For whatever reason, when grand daddy and them built this house, they put the attic above the dining room. It had a low ceiling like other attics Randolph had been in. But this ceiling was level with the floors of the bedrooms across from it. Looking back on his earliest memories, it always felt kinda funny when he reached the top of the stairs and turned right. A little bit ahead, to the right again was the space he would learn was called the attic. On the left, were the three steps leading up to the two bedrooms.

The attic not only had a low ceiling, it was dark and dusty like other attics. Even now, in his teens, Randolph would sometimes find himself in there digging through trunks and decaying pasteboard boxes looking for a magic lantern. Now and then he found an old vase that he would blow the dust off to see a miracle. He always came to his senses when he commenced to cough. That way, Randolph Wilford managed to keep himself this side of right good sense.

It was in the attic that he found what became his favorite book, next to the Gospels, Moby Dick and The Night before Christmas; the story of a sailor named Dorie Miller. Dorie was a worker in the galley of a ship called the USS West Virginia. It was on that ship in Pearl Harbor when the Japanese attacked, that Dorie took over a machine gun when the regular machine gunner was killed. He saved the ship's Captain and other members of the crew by shooting down several Japanese planes. There was a picture of Dorie Miller in the book, he was a Colored man. He was dark complected like Randolph. In Randolph's mind, Dorie Miller looked a lot like him.

On the same day, he found another book in one of the trunks, an old dictionary.

Randolph got home from the T faster than he ever had before. He rushed through the living room. At the foot of the stairs he yelled "Hey!" to Mozelle in the kitchen. He didn't hear her response as he leapt two steps at a time up to the landing. In his room he did not take the time to wipe his sweat or catch his breath. He went straight to the shelf where he kept his ten or twelve books. He sat on the side of his bed.

The first definition of adultery was, copulation between two people who were not married to one another. He continued to the other definitions. Randolph read each definition at least three times before accepting that there was no way he could twist any one of them into meaning, a youngun trying to act grown.

He moved from his concern about being so wrong to a new worry. A christian couldn't do it to nobody unless he was married to her. Without hesitation or doubt, he climbed off the bed and knelt beside it. "Lord. I'm gonna keep all your commandments except the Seventh one. Lord, I can't help it, I want to do it to a girl so bad... I can't tell you how much..." He tried for a moment to think of words to further express to The Lord how he felt. Then a lyric from a hymn came to him. "Lord, I want to be a christian, in my heart."

* * *

Old Rob Roy was the only route mailman Randy had ever known. The blue-eyed, blue veined man put him in mind of Santa Claus-a skinny Santa Claus. Rob Roy was also the only adult Randolph called by his first name-not exactly by his first name; he addressed him as Robroy like it was a single name.

There was no doubt that the bony man's eyes twinkled just like old St. Nick's in The Night Before Christmas. He had an easy, gentle way about him like the jolly old elf.

Randolph's clearest memory of the mailman was back when he was four and Arlene had begun to teach him to read. At fifteen, she still had her First Grade Reader. They would bring it up to the mailbox where he would sit on a moss patch and practice while Arlene waited out by the mailboxes. When Randolph heard the chug of Rob Roy's Model A Ford, he would run out to the road.

The old man was a lot like cousin Ames. Ames was a jolly, round, chocolate colored man. His laugh and "Belly like a bowl full of jelly," were like Santa Claus's. Cousin Ames died while Randolph was in D.C.

Given that Lucille had distroyed his belief in the real St. Nick, and Ames had done gone on home, Rob Roy was the only Santa left.

The Ford coupe had been new when Randolph was younger. Now it had lost it's shine. The chug sounded the same, though. "The little old driver so lively and quick." pulled up to the line of mailboxes.

56

"Ain't we lucky to have such a lovely day?" He waited for Randolph to acknowledge his greeting before getting out from behind the wheel. Randolph gave him a show off greeting. "Yessir! The Lord done spread sunshine all over the county."

Rob Roy got out and came around. On his way to the rumble seat, his crinkled grin seemed near 'bout brilliant as that sunlight. "Sounds like you're gonna be a poet someday. Yessir. Whatta ya think?"

"I reckon." He watched the old man go to the open trunk he had added slats to. The slats were worn and faded although they still made the rumble seat look like the bed of a little pickup truck. Rob Roy had one piece of mail for the Roebuck household; it was a letter for Randolph. Usually when he got a letter, the walk home took forever. He did not feel comfortable opening his mail ubtil he had carried it to the house. It was not a decision Randolph had made, It was simply what felt right. Today, the trip down the road to home was secondary to the mailman's words. "Sounds like you're gonna be a poet someday..."

Ever since his Sunday school teacher gave him a copy of Moby Dick when he was nine years old, Randolph had thought that he would like to write a book. This ambition was even stronger than the notion that he would like to be in the movies that entered his mind when he saw his first flick. That desire was no stronger than the expectation that he would be a fireman or policeman. 'Poet' was not what he had stored in his mental attic for later consideration. No matter, it was close enough to reawaken the writer urge he kept in one of his mental trunks. Maybe he would be a poet as well as a novel writer.

* * *

Monday July 26, 1948

Dear son,

How are you? Fine I hope. I am well. Lucille is too. She will soon enter the twelfth grade. She is quite a young lady now. She is seventeen. It has been raining a lot here. But we are making do.

Randolph, I am enclosing two dollars for you to buy new sneakers. I am also enclosing ten dollars for you to get a new outfit for Homecoming.

Give my love to mama, Mozzelle and the others. Tell them I will see them (and you too) the first week of September.

Love,

Mother

* * *

Holley lived about a half mile beyond Arjay's. He and Randolph were paying for their sodas before leaving Arjay's store. "Let's go nigger." Holly winked at Arjay and another white man. The two men laughed in a way that meant they thought Holley was cute. Randolph grinned as if he agreed.

They mounted their bikes that had been leaning against the shed posts in front of the store. "Hey Holley. Let's go into the woods and drink our sodas.

"Ok."

The woods were half way between Arjay's and Reverend Esterbrook's house.

Randolph found a clearing. The boys parked their bikes. Holley was ready to drink his bottle of pop. "Put that bottle down!"

"Huh?"

"You heard what the hell I said." He glared at Holley. He had meant to slap him up side the head. But Holley stood a half head shorter than Randolph and had just turned eleven.

A moment ago Randy imagined this would be the first time he ever hit somebody who didn't swing on him first. He thought about all the bullies back in Washington whom he hated and got

58

into fights with because they picked on boys smaller than them.

"Shit."

"Whatchou cursing about, nigger?"

Randolph had slapped Holley across the mouth before he knew it. The word nigger flashed him back to Arjay's. Before he could appologize, Holley took a swing at him. He smiled before his hand flew out to slap his little buddy harder than the first time. Holley didn't make another attempt to fight back. He took a step back and whimpered. "Why're you hitting me?" "Listen you little punk. If you ever call me that in front of white folks again, I'll beat the shit out of you." He was now comfortable with his anger. "You hear me motherfucker!" Spittle flew out of his mouth. Randolph wiped the corners of his mouth with the tail of his loose hanging white shirt. The lesson had been taught and learned. It was safe for him to feel sorry for his friend.

In all appearances, the two boys riding their bikes the rest of the way to Holly's house were at peace with one another and themselves. Randolph though, could not get beyond his violation of the Golden Rule. On most of the shelves of his awareness, he was sure he had done what he had to. On the level where his symmetry-his perfect nature held sway, he was unsettled. He didn't have to hit Holly. There must be something else he could have done to keep his anger from spilling over.

As if he were inside his buddy's head, Holly said, "I'm glad you got me back for saying that word in front of Arjay and his runnin' buddy. I swear you hit like a mule. But I know now not to do that again."

Randolph turned to him and smiled. He would have said something. He was too deep inside himself to speak.

The Esterbrook house had a wide porch like cousin Hilda's. The house wasn't gray like her's. It was bright white.

Reverend Esterbrook saw the boys pedalling up from the road. He had just pulled an empty wagon in front of a shed across the driveway from the side of the house. "You fellows are just in time to help me clean out this shed." Randolph loved the smoothe-proper way the preacher spoke. He wanted to talk that way although it didn't feel right when he did. Sometimes girls talked proper. But the only boys he ever heard do it were sissies. When he got grown, he would speak like Reverend Esterbrook.

"That is, if you would like to help?"

Randolph was so excited at the notion he didn't notice that Holly squirmed. They parked their bikes next to the shed.

"I've been putting this off for quite a while." He adressed himself to Randolph, giving him a double thrill. It made him feel special to have the pastor speak directly to him. He also felt grown like he always did when an adult talked to him straight on. "Now I can stop feeling guilty about my slothfulness." The preacher hoisted an old plow handle onto the wagon. This was a signal to begin. Randolph tossed up half of a buggy wheel while packing "slothfulness' to look up later.

Holly had no choice but to join in. He tossed up a rim.

The whole while, a big brown mule, hitched to the wagon, stood like a statue except when he lashed his tail.

The floor of the shed had been covered with the junk of seasons. After a little more than an hour, most of it was loaded onto the wagon.

It was Randolph who put the final piece, part of a halter, on top of the pile. Reverend Esterbrook winked at him. "Good work, both of you."

Randolph and Holly watched the diminutive pastor climb up to the wagon seat. "Giddup!" The mule did not seem to hear the command. Reverend Esterbrook snapped the reins. "Giddup Jody!" The mule's reaction was-or maybe Randolph imagined it was-to turn and look at the driver as if he must not have right good sense. Maybe the preacher saw what Randolph saw. "Goddamn you mule!" Randolph felt a quiver go through him. A man of God could not have said what Reverend Esterbrook just did. For a split second he pretended that the man of God had not actually said, "Goddamn you mule!" The self deception leapt out of his mind when Randolph accepted what he heard exactly as he heard it. Without further thought, he got mad. 'He just took the name of The Lord in vain. What kind of preacher is he.'

The mule decided he'd better get to stepping. Randolph waited until the wagon was out of hearing range. "Well. I gotta go little buddy." He and Holly shook hands in as manly a fashion as they could muster.

* * *

The shortest way home was the road past the graveyards. It crossed a creek bridge beyond the Esterbrook house. It was the same creek as the one below aunt May's house on the Cedar Grove road. Randolph liked this bridge better. The hills to it were straight down and up. He would come this way every time he went over to Holly's, if it were not for the cemetaries. Since he only came on this road in the day time, Randolph was only half scared when he pass the graveyards.

At the to the top of the downgrade, he pedaled hard as he could-all the way down across the creek bridge and up the hill. The graveyards were at the top of the hill where he would turn onto 'cemetary road' and head for Cedar Grove road beyond the mailboxes. When he crossed the bridge he pumped even harder so that he would not slow down until he got almost all the way up the hill. At the very top, Randolph used his fatigue to distract himself until he made the turn onto the cemetery road. To his left was the white folk's burying ground; straight ahead, across the road, was the Colored one. About three steps down from his good sense he knew that even if there was such a thing as ghosts, nobody he knew of had ever been hurt by one. Yet, there was some need he had, to scare himself half to death. He turned right toward the mailboxes a half mile away. The chill and thrill he created reached its peak when the graveyards were behind him and he was on a little slope going away from them. He got to full speed before he rounded out his drama by looking over his shoulder. "Oh Lord!" Something white and fluffy was about to grab hold of him. He turned his body more so that he could fight it off. The front wheel turned with his body and he felt himself fly over the handle bars. He had the presence of mind to stretch out his arms to keep from landing on his face. The feeling of hurting himself was familiar. Randolph had fallen when he jumped off a freight train; he once fell off his and his buddies' go cart. And nothing was like the time he got his front teeth knocked out... Knowing how it felt to get hurt and scratch himself up real bad did not make falling now any easier. It made it worse.

While he sailed over the handlebars, sense memory of all those times that he had messed up and hurt himself, settled in. The memory of each pain made him anticipate how unbearable it was gonna be this time.

Randolph landed on the pebbles and dust of the road and slid straight ahead on his palms until the bike scooted off to the side. Then the hardscrabble road scraped skin off his palms, forearms and knees.

He did not hear himself screaming until he came to a stop. "Goddamnit! Goddamnit! Goddamnit! His curses were not loud enough to drown out what leapt into Randolph Wilford's mind. No matter that he was in more pain than it seemed he could bear, it did not hurt any more than his awareness that something must be wrong with him; this didn't have to happen-he didn't have to do this to himself-he should've known that what he saw over his shoulder was his own damn white shirt-haints don't hurt nobody... "Goddamnit!" Maybe he expected that unscrambling the mess would make him hurt less. In fact, he only cleared a path for the pain to cling to his skin like hot bacon fat.

While he squirmed and screamed and cried at the top of his voice, another of his selves reminded him that he was in the middle of the road.

Randolph jumped up and grabbed his bike-it wasn't broken. The injured cowpoke mounted his steed Susie Q. and rode toward home.

He examined the stinging scratches and bruises and forced himself to know that they would soon heal. Another Randolph still, arose and told him he had better fix his crazy head before he wound up killing his fool self.

* * *

Unlike the first time Randolph missed the school bus and had to walk home, today he chose not to leave before the Cardinals and Bluejays finished a ballgame. His driver Pete played second base for the Blue Jays. A substitute driver took over for him. It felt kinda natural for Randolph to miss the bus since Pete had to play ball. He knew good and well his thinking was warped. To make everything copacetic, he was able to twist ridiculousness into reason.

The Bluejays won the game, making the price of Randolph's folly worth it. He shook Pete's hand before heading home. For the first quarter mile, he bouyed himslf by recalling, over and over, highlights of the game. A big pitcher-Randolph didn't know his name-threw a three hitter. Even better, Pete hit a base clearing triple. While the images ran and re-ran across his screen of reflection, he took a back road so that he didn't have to walk to the main Midway road to reach Cedar Grove road. A real darkskin old guy-tall and skinny like Lincoln-sided up along side Randolph on the narrow road. The man came out of nowhere. It didn't bother Randolph cause there was something about the old fellow that made him feel at ease.

The man started talking just like nothing. Before long he was telling Randolph about a job he used to have in the County Hospital before he retired. "Lemme tell you something. Dont'chou ever take up smokin'. Now, your lungs when they're healthy're nice and pink. You know what they look like if you take up smoking?"

"Naw sir."

"One time I was mopping the laboratory after a autopsy-you know what a autopsy is?" Randolph said that he had read about autopsies in books. "Good for you. Well, they had done a autopsy on this fella and I saw his lungs. They was black as coal. That's what done him in. An' it was from smokin'." The old man stopped short. "Hold on! Lemme git a good look at you." Randolph gave him a curious look. A bright smile lit up the man's black face. "You Connie Wilford's boy!"

"Yes sir!"

"Well, bless my soul! When I come up on you, I knew there was somethin' 'bout you... Boy, your daddy was somethin'. I mean he was really somethin'!" The man took another long look at Randolph as if he was determining if the boy was anything like his daddy. "Yes indeed. You know what your daddy done one time. We was eatin' Bar-B-Q an' havin' a little nip-ya know..." Randolph nodded.

"Well, another fella and your daddy got into it about somethin' or other. That ol' boy-an' he was a pretty big fella-took a swing at Connie. Connie commenced to whippin' on that boy til we had to pull him off'n him." The old man, who had walked ramrod straight until now, doubled over laughing. Randolph knew that whatever it was that he had to wait to hear was gonna be good. He made himself be patient until the old man finished being tickled. "I'm sorry son. My name is Horner." Horner chuckled a couple more times before he got himself together. "Well-suh. That ol' boy went home and come back with a shotgun."

Randolph started. Horner saw the boy flinch. He gave him a reassuring smile. "Well, let me tell ya son. Your daddy took that shotgun from 'im and give him another whippin'."

They shared a long laugh-Horner about his memory and near magical encounter with Connie Wilford's boy, Randolph about his father having been an ass-whipping son of a gun and, his conclusion that he Randolph, was a chip off the old block.

"What's your name son?" "Randolph." "Well sir, Randolph Wilford, I can't tell you what a great pleasure it is to meetchou. Yessiree!"

"Me too, Mr. Horner."

"This here's where I stay." It was a little white house with green shutters. "Now that you know where I live, you ought to come by and see us."

"Yessir. I will." Randolph knew he would never come by and see the man. He wasn't too sure he was seeing him now. He watched Horner almost skip along a brick walkway to his front steps.

Horner's house was next to a dump at the dead end of a lane. Up a rise, behind the heap of junk, Randolph saw the Cedar Grove road.

When he decided to take a short cut, he hadn't been sure he knew what the devil he was doing. He climbed over the dump feeling an uncertain pleasure that was layered on top of the pleasure given to him by the old man who came out of nowhere. He reached the road enveloped by a clear sense of having returned from a fairy place. He sank into its warm cuddle.

The shortcut had trimmed at least ten minutes off the trip.

From the beginning of where this dirt road came off the blacktop, to home, took the better part of an hour. From here, he would be at the house before it got dark enough to be scared.

The tobacco, corn and honeysuckle on both sides made Randolph feel like he was walking through a green valley in a Betty Davis movie he had seen. Strutting down the first slope of the hills and dales, he sang along with a Bing Crosby record running through his head.

THE OLD MASTER PAINTER
FROM THE FAR AWAY HILLS
PAINTED THE VIOLETS
AND THE DAFFODILS

The jaunty ballad was interrupted.

Slithering out of the drainage ditch to his right was a curiously shaped and colored snake. Randolph had seen a lot of black snakes. He had seen a fair number of brown moccasins and different colored garden snakes. The snake that came out of the ditch was almost square shaped. It had brown and yellow patches all over it. It was a pretty good length too-five feet or more. Randolph stopped to watch the curious looking thing cross the road leaving a serpentine trail in the dust.

After getting over how strange the snake looked, Randolph thought of finding a stick to kill it-he had killed his share of black or brown snakes-garden snakes were too pretty for him to think of killing...

He put killing notions aside. The mood he was in had him nearly floating along the way. He sorta felt that it would mess something up if he killed one of God's creatures. He had forgotten his song. The snake had left something of itself behind.

Randolph took an excursion into a place that lay beneath light, the place where answers were found. He thought about the times when he had killed snakes near his house or near somebody's house where he was visiting. He had made sure not to kill birds or rabbits. He did not even feel good when he killed a fly. Why in the world did he kill snakes when, the truth was, he didn't enjoy it all that much. He eased down a little deeper and saw what might be what he was looking for wrapped in a ball of mental twine. He tugged at a loose end until a cloudy image of the garden of Eden came through. He saw...yeah! He saw Adam and Eve and a serpent...

The reverie dropped off; it was not interrupted as the song had been. This time he volunteered to rise to the surface and leave the vision alone. Had he stayed down there, he would have had to try to figure out what was going on in the garden. That would have required him to form an opinion about it. The opinion would have led him to other conclusions which led to further conclusions. He did not go conciously through these permutations, he simply knew that it was not safe to look too closely at the garden.

A familiar house on the road from Midway was Chester Burns' house that sat on a hill. Grandma used to work for those white folks. Back when he was four or five, she brought him up here with her. The twelve room place had what they said were gables. Like every big house Randolph had ever seen-before or since, it was white. Looking at it now, he remembered that they had an indoor toilet. They had running water! Nobody else around here had running water. No matter how deeply he probed, Randolph could not find anything that he could even pretend was a clue.

He spent a few minutes wallowing in his memories of the days when little Randy was grandma's pet. She ranked above everybody in his world-including the preachers. He pulled himself away from the long gone to admire a house he had never been in. A little ways down the road from Chester Burns' house on the hill, was a long driveway to a rambling house that looked like a western ranch in a movie-maybe the one in 'Duel In The Sun.' He chose to let it slip away, his mind needed to rest.

Randolph glide-stepped down the hill. At the very bottom, in the dale before the final hill, was the house of another Chester, Chester Kennedy was also white. He wasn't rich though, like Chester Burns...he wasn't kin to him neither. Chester Kennedy had several grown younguns like Archie's daddy did. The difference was, his younguns hadn't left the county. They all still lived around here.

Mr. Ervin was done with his tobacco crop for the season. He sent Archie and Randolph to work half a day helping the Kennedys string the last of theirs. On the way down there, Archie told Randolph that his papa had borrowed some sweet potato slips from old man Kennedy. The two farmers had agreed that the repayment would be to have Archie work with him for half a day. Since Mr. Ervin was paying Randolph for the full day anyway, he sent him along with Archie.

There was a narrow road running in front of the Kennedy house that went pass the tobacco barn. Randolph looked down that road when he went by. His mind went back to the morning he and Archie were within earshot of the tobacco barn.

They heard one of Chester Kennedy's daughters telling her siblings that she was gonna get herself a job in town. Clear as a bell, one of her sisters asked, "Well, who's gon' tend to your younguns?"

"Why, I'll git one of these nig..." Seeing that sixteen year old Archie and thirteen year old Randolph were close enough to hear her, she cut the word off.

Half way up the hill to the mailboxes, Randolph saw why the memory struck him. He had wondered why he got so mad at Holly that day for calling him nigger in front of Arjay and the other white man. Hell! white folks didn't even call them niggers to their faces. And there Holly was, using that damn word in front of white men. He let it come back to him good and strong and got mad all over again.

By the time he passed the mailboxes on cemetery road, it also came back to him that he had made his little buddy pay. So, like the old folks say, "Let bygones be bygones."

* * *

Naomi was old enough now to run through the house. She was talking a little; she could say Arly for Arlene and the other nicknames, Mo, Randy and Greg. And Just as Arlene called her mother's mother mama, and Randolph had called her that as well, Naomi called her mama.

Litticia had long since stopped responding to her great granddaughter when she went into the room to say "Hey, mama." But most mornings, after Randolph came back from taking the chamber pot out, Naomi walked into Liticia's room and gave her that cheery greeting.

Today, Randy went into the room to get the slop jar. It was empty. Grandma's cover was half on the floor. One leg was out of her nightgown, hanging off the bed.

Elmore was home on vacation. He came into the room as if Randolph had called for help to push mama's leg back in bed. Randolph had not said a word. He was nervous about gripping grandma's naked leg. Elmore handled it with a steady hand like it

67

wasn't nothing much. After he and Elmore got grandma back in bed, Randy looked at how still she was. He knew, but kept it from himself, she was near 'bout gone on away from here.

He went to put Bessie out to pasture, chop kindling and crawl into the roost to fetch eggs. He made a fire in the kitchen stove, then went to the big oak and turned Susie Q. around. He then went onto the front porch and sat in grandma's old rocker to wait.

It took a while before Randolph knew that he knew the old woman whom he once adored so, wasn't long for this world. He stayed in the rocker waiting for the moment. When it came, he would jump on his bike and go tell the neighbors the bad news.

Somewhere in the back of his mind it came to him that in mama's bedroom he and his uncle had shared a silent understanding they were losing the woman for whom her son Elmore and later her grandson Randolph had once been treasured darlings.

Randolph began to regret that he had come to resent her for no longer favoring him. He had not been callous, he just had not witnessed someone's gradual decline into the grave. Daddy died in the hospital. Randolph only saw him in the casket. And he did not know daddy well like he did grandma.

* * *

The screams through the screen door reminded Randolph that his uncle was "funny." Elmore's voice that sounded like it belonged to somebody halfway between a man and a woman, made Randolph want to laugh. But the words that rang across the porch into the yard dared him to be tickled.

"MAMA'S DEAD! MAMA'S DEAD! MAMA'S DEAD!"

Inspired by a lone cowpoke-perhaps the Durango Kid, Randolph calmly approached his bike to go about sounding the alarm. At every house-first, Mr. Ervin's, next the families who lived back behind the Methodist church-he rode into the yard and, without stopping, yelled,

"GRANDMA'S DEAD! GRANDMA'S DEAD! GRANDMA'S DEAD!"

He rode by his house to go across the creek to tell cousin Hilda and Mr. Mason. There was another house on the hill. That house was where Mr. Melvin and his wife Miz Aretha lived. Mr. Melvin had done something that caused Randolph to resent him. That old man had once been his play grandfather. Randolph didn't stop by there anymore.

Cousin Hilda's was the first house he actually entered to give the sad news. Mr. Mason was there on dinner break from the field. As usual, Randolph marveled at how his sweet cousin looked like a lightskinned version of mama and Mo. She told Randolph that she would pray for Liticia's soul. Then she asked him if he would'nt sit to have a bite to eat. "No ma'am. I got to get back to the house'n tell Mo and them that I have told everybody."

He rode home to give his report to Mo and them. He was feeling right proud of himself when he walked into the dining room. Elmore was telling Gregory, "Mama died with her eyes open. I closed them before covering her with her sheet." He sounded kinda proper when he said that.

Mo told Randolph that the Health Department wagon had just left with mama's body. "Gregory drove Elmore up to Chester Burns' to make the call."

"I told everybody around that mama was dead."

"Good boy." Mozelle's eyes were red. Even if he had not looked into them, Randolph could've told by her voice that she'd been crying. Nobody said anything else. It felt like something thick was hanging in the dining room air. Without thinking about it, Randolph got up and left to go upstairs to his room. First thing, he walked over to the shelf he kept his books on-his library. His notion was to take down the Bible or the Dory Miller Story. Once he reached the bookshelf, he stood there. Normally he would have lay on his bed; his inner sanctum that replaced the linen closet. But he was in a blank space. It took a moment of standing there before it came to him to lie down and chew on his cud. It felt right.

When he came through the living room he took notice of the doilies on the arms and back of the settee for the first time in years. Grandma had crocheted them when Randolph was eight. It was about the same time it was in the paper that...what's his name, was gonna be electrocuted for raping a white girl.

It had seemed like magic that mama.. .granddma, could put all those little circles together from just a long white string.

Randolph shifted his weight on the bed and began to miss the first person who made him feel what he later learned was called love.

When he was four and Arlene was teaching him to read, mama was teaching him how to braid hair, how to thread a needle and baste a hem on a blanket or a curtain. Mama was the one who explained to him that Jesus was a man even if he looked like a girl to Randolph. Her explanation became less clear when she added that nobody really knew what The Lord looked like.

By the time he was old enough to ask her to explain the difference between Lord Jesus and Lord God, Liticia had taken to her bed.

When he was little, she taught him the difference between grits and hominy; that hog maws and chitterlings were not the same thing.

One time he called her a damn lie after he had overheard a man in the yard say that to another man. After she slapped him in the mouth, mama apologized and told him that the word he used was bad-it was called cursing.

Randolph's eyes were closed during these reflections. He opened them long enough to stare at the wall and wonder how long it takes somebody to get to Heaven when they die. He figured on that one until he was tired. He fell asleep.

* * *

Here was a Carnation milk smell he remembered from daddy's funeral. This time though he knew it was the flowers smelling like that. Randolph was gonna make sure he did not sleep through most of mama's funeral like he did when daddy died. Here in the Cedar Grove Baptist church the August sun poured-in patched colors through the stained glass windows onto the pews.

Daddy'e funeral was in a church that sat way down like it was in a cellar. The windows were up high so that colored sunlight hung in streaks, crisscrossing above everything.

70

Folks filed into this church breaking up the streams of light. They were filling the the benches but it was so quiet Randolph imagined he had cottonballs in his ear. The air was heavy like the dining room was the other day. He couldn't leave this time-he did not want to.

Verniece was playing a sad song on the old pump organ. He didn't know she could do that. He liked her even more now.

Mozelle, Gregory, mama-his real mama, Elmore, Arlene, Nadine and Randolph were on the front pew. Grandma-mama used to call it the "Moaners' bench." The casket was right in front of them. He did his best not to stare at it.

Wreaths and racks of flowers were butressed against the foot and head of the shiny brown coffin. Randolph did not like their smell. He had only noticed it in hospital rooms and at daddy's funeral. Flowers in the garden didn't smell nothin' like this. It was as if The Lord breathed stale evaporated milk on them when they were for sick or dead folks. In his reserve mind, Randolph wondered why they always put flowers around sick or dead people anyway.

Until now, Reverend Esterbrook had been preaching about how good Liticia Roebuck had been; how much she was loved by her neighbors in Cedar Grove. Randolph knew those things. He loved his grandmother too. And everybody called her Miz Liticia-even men and women her age gave her that respect. Old men and women did not call each other Miz or Mister, but they called mama Miz Liticia.

Randolph watched the little dark man whose good looking face and narrow shoulders were all he could see above the pulpit. He had forgiven the preacher for taking the Lord's name in vain. Because of that, he was able to again enjoy his smooth-clipped-nasal speach that bespoke of book learning. Randolph did not think specifically of education. He thought rather of well-to-do folks like the Burnses over on the hill toward Midway.

"Brothers and sisters. We have not lost a church Elder. And you Roebucks have not lost a loved one so much as The One on High has gained a new Angel...." "Amen!" It was Elmore's alto voice. He did not stop there. "Lord knows mama's an angel!" His voice broke. Myra embraced her little brother. Randolph was reminded of how strong his mother was. In not a bad way, he remembered how it had felt when she used to whip him before he told her not to whip him no more. "Can't you just see Miss Liticia, up there among all the other Angels, swarming around The Throne of The Heavenly Father?" Reverend Esterbrook took his hankerchief from his hip pocket.

On his level of expectation-deep in his well of hidden memory, Randolph knew it was time for some serious sermonizing. Every preacher he'd ever seen, gave the same signal. "Ha! Sister Leticia has finished her work down here. She has moved... MOVED!..."

"She done moved preacher!"

"The dear lady did evrything she could do for us here on earth. Now she has MOVED!"

"MOVED!"

Neither Randolph nor the rest of the mourners knew whose voice was echoing Reverend Esterbrook. They all just knew that he was speaking for each and every one of them. Reverend Esterbrook continued to extol the virtues of the departed. He took care to, ever so often, remind the throng of the wings of love that bore her home-of the Son of Man Who guided her path to the King of Heaven.

Randolph, in part because this section of the sermon was the same as in every church meeting, in part because he could not avoid looking at Leticia's casket, almost drifted off... 'Who is that!' Standing between the casket and the pulpit was a peanut butter girl in a pink satin dress with white ribbons in her black Shirley Temple curls. She stood right proud-like, with her head tilted toward the persimmon tones Verniece pumped out of the organ. The girl-with her Tokyo Rose eyes-looked like the name Yvonne and like fourteen. Her voice flowed into the purple, gold, green, red and blue streaming through the windows.

> I COME TO THE GARDEN A-LONE
> WHILE THE DEW IS STILL ON THE RO-SES

'Oh Lord! Mama was crazy about this song!'

> AND THE VOICE I HEAR FALLING ON MY EAR
> THE SON OF GOD DIS-CLOS-ES

There mama was, in the yard right in front of her bedroom. She's humming-watering that big old rose bush.

72

ANNND HE WALKS WITH ME AND HE TALKS WITH ME
AND HE TELLS ME I AM HIS OWNNN
AND THE JOY WE SHARE AS WE TAR-RY THERRRE
NONE OTH-ER HAS EV-ER KNOWNNN

The girl's voice and the song tasted like a hot buttered honey bisquit and milk from the icebox. *"Want some more Randy?"*

Teardrops slid down around his nose. He wiped at his upper lip. Until this moment, Randolph's thoughts had flitted about like a bluetail fly. Now, everything he didn't understand or didn't want to, poured out of the song-out of the rays of Heaven.

ANNND HE WALKS WITH ME AND HE TALKS WITH ME
AND HE TELLS ME I AM HIS OWNNN
AND THE JOY WE SHARE AS WE TAR-RY THERE
NONE OTH-ER HAS EV-ER KNOWNNN

The coffin-mama's coffin-was right there-shiny and brown. She was in there. He blinked at it and all those flowers and tried not to be scared. But he was scared and hurting in a new place. Now Myra-mama turned from her brother to her son to give him comfort. She hadn't hugged him like this since he didn't know when-maybe never like this...her words were soft, her voice was softer. "It's alright son. It's alright" But it wasn't alright. Still, mingled with his tears-snot she wiped from his nose and the hopeless-helpless way he felt, mama-real mama was here and he knew she would be forever. Grandma was gone forever-mama was here forever. It hurt so bad to know he wasn't ever gonna understand any of it but he was gonna have to live with it anyway. That hurt as much as anything else...Oh Lord...Mama wiped his tears and snot with her dainty hankerchief until it was wet and sticky..."It's alright son, It's alright."

* * *

As with a number of things, Randolph was of two minds about rainy days. When he woke up this morning it was pouring. The cow did not have to be put out to pasture but, fire wood needed to be chopped. On clear days, Mozelle would be sure to find something for him to do in the garden or in the yard. But rain or shine, Randolph had to crawl up into the coop to gather eggs.

Grandma was gone so he would never have to empty her slop jar again. He immediately wished he could smell that stench if...

It is now near 'bout three o'clock and the rain has not let up. He is up in his room, his acknowleged and confirmed refuge replacing the linen closet. The bedroom is not dark and soft like being on top of the big pile of rags. On the other hand, if he did not want to pray or just chew on his cud he could read, here in the bedroom. Today Randolph had some thinking to do. Myra had only stayed for three days when grandma died. She had to get back to Washington. They only gave her five days off to bury her mother. Anyway grandma had been his mama when he was small. When he went back to Washington to start school, it took a while for him to think of Myra as mama. Even after he did, she came home from work every day and went straight up to her room where she stayed except to come down and pick up a plate of food.

Mozzelle, when she wasn't being mean as a rattlesnake, was like a playmate. Most nights, she played checkers or pitty pat with him. He shifted his mood. He was sitting on the bed, looking out the window at the rain falling as far as the eye could see. He lay back and grinned; tickled that he had figured something out. In this moment he came to see that Mozzelle was kinda his new mama. She was a different kind of mother. But so was mama different than grandma-mama had been. Ok, that was cleared up.

There was something else to think about that was not going to be so easy to clear up. 'Eugene Chen.'

Not long before daddy died, he was home on furlough from the hospital. He walked by when Randolph and Lucille were playing Chinese checkers. He looked down at the name Chiang Kai Shek on the board.

"Eugene Chen is the name you should know."

Randolph and Lucille looked at one another, surprised as much that daddy had said anything as they were at what he said. Daddy had been gassed in World War One. He usually walked around the house like he was in another world.

The furlough lasted two weeks. After that first and only time spent with Conley Wilford, Randolph never saw him again.

The name, Eugene Chen was more clear in his memory than Conley's face.

The only one Randolph could think of who might know about Eugene Chen was cousin Ames. Cousin Ames told Randolph and Lucille about Akhenaten and Nefertiti. Sometimes he would call them his little Egyptian king and queen. Like grandma, Ames had gone on home. So soon after granfma's death, Randy didn't feel sorry about Ames being dead. There was still deep disappoint-ment that he would never be able to ask him if he knew anything about Eugene Chen.

Chapter Five
Jacob's Ladder

Every Autumn, cousin Hilda held a corn shuck. She invited all the local Colored folks. The ostensible reason for the gathering was to bring in the last of the corn crops for the year. The truth was, she and Mr. Mason had already reaped the harvest. Hilda's real motive was to get everybody together to celebrate that harvest-bringing in the sheaves-sharing the joy.

Archie and Verniece were there with their mama and papa. They, Arlene, Randy and little Naomi rode over in the back of Mr. Ervin's pickup truck. Mo sat in the cab with Mr. and Mrs. Mills.

As usual, Gregory was not there. Randolph did not reckon he'd seen Gregory at a gathering of colored folks but a few times in his life; he was surprised to see him at Leticia's funeral. For whatever reason, Gregory stayed stuck up around white folks. Maybe cause he looked about half white he figured that was where he belonged.

Cesar and his wife were there and as usual, so was Mr. Mason. When Randolph allowed himself to think about it, he was kinda envious of Mr. Mason. It seemed he was around cousin Hilda a lot. He must be doin' it to her. The reason Randolph didn't think about it a lot was because then he'd have to admit to himself that when he looked at cousin Hilda with her peach skin and smiling light brown eyes, he wanted to be with her. It seemed like a sin to feel that way about her. He wasn't sure why.

Hilda was tall and broad shouldered like mama and Mozzelle. Sometimes Randy wondered why she was not dark like her cousins. There was no special reason why he never asked her. She was the kind of adult you could ask things. He just never thought about it when he was alone with her.

From the way the name cornshuck sounded, you didn't expect there'd be anything more to eat than corn. Cousin Hilda fed them a whole meal. Along with roasted corn on the cobb, they had string beans and field peas with bisquits. And they had peach cobbler for dessert. Every time he tasted her cobbler, Randolph remembered the time he and Lucille got caught in a hailstorm on the way from Arjay's.

They ran to Cousin Hilda's. She had just baked a peach cobbler. Randy had already tasted some really scrumptious stuff-banana pudding, Myra's spareribs with sauerkraut and dumplings. One time, Arlene made an orange cake. All that stuff was good. Nothing! NOTHING! had ever tasted as good as that cobbler that day, fresh out of the oven. Especially since he and Lucille had just been pelted by hailstones.

Everybody was in a little group midway across the long porch. It was quiet for a spell; they were all stuffed. After a little bit, Mr. Ervin turned to Hilda who was coming out the front door after doing something inside. "Hilda!" He gestured to his missus. "Annette can bake a right nice cobbler. But, Lord a' mercy! That was the best peach cobbler I ever had." Miss Annette and the other grown folks along with Archie, and even little Naomi, chimed agreement. Randolph felt like a prophet-everybody echoing what he was just thinking and all. "Young fella!" It took him a moment to realize Mr. Ervin was talking to him. "You ever hear-tell of a whip snake?" "No sir. Can't say that I have." Cousin Hilda, Cesar and them smiled like they knew all about that kind of snake. Verniece, Archie and Arlene could not imagine what in the world...

"Well sir, once was a time 'round here when there were so many different kinds a' snakes and things, you just didn't know what'chou might come up on." Mr. Ervin shook his head as if it was difficult for him to believe what he remembered. "Whip snakes never did come after you if you were with somebody. No sir. They were too smart for that. But if one of 'em saw you on a path or walking down the road by yourself, he was sure to try to get you."

Cousin Hilda's long porch faced the west. The group sitting there on wicker chairs, one rocker and a lawn chair, could see the sun sinking over Arjays. Mr. Ervin had not yet described the whip snake, but whip and snake and sundown conjured something Randolph was not sure he wanted to know about. At the same time, he would have gone crazy if he didn't hear the rest of the story-or as he perceived it, history. He braced himself.

"Let me tell ya... One day, come to think of it, was bout this time of day, I was takin' a shortcut through the woods between the Methodist church and our house. Randy, you know where I'm talkin' about don'tcha?" Randy felt a little chill run through him. "Yessir."

"I was a young fella about Archie's age. I was trying to get home before dark, cause you don't know what's likely to grab hold of you out there when you can't see your hand before your face."

Randolph was sitting on the floor near the edge of the porch. Without knowing it, he inched back until he was tucked between Mr. Ervin in the rocker and Miz Annette on the lawn chair. "I heard a kind of wailin' sound." Mr. Ervin paused to purse his lips and blow a haunting-one-note whistle. Mr. Mason bolted erect in his chair, startling Randolph. "Well I'll be! Can you believe I'd almost forgot? That's exactly the way a whip snake sounds. It sorta gives you warning the way a rattler does with its rattle. Yessir."

Mr. Ervin leaned forward in his rocker. "I looked over my shoulder and there come a whip snake. Did I tell you how it moves?"

"Naw sir."

"Well, the whipper is about six foot long. He kinda slides along on his tail so, when he catches you, he can spit in your eye. His venom blinds you, then he can take his time and whip you to death."

Randolph's arms were wrapped around his knees so tightly he trembled from the tension. He thought it was from the chill that rushed up his spine. He was scared-he was thrilled. He wished Mr. Ervin would shutup-he couldn't wait to hear more. "I took off runnin' fast as I could. Now, I knew cause my papa had told me, you can't out run no whipper. He can sit up on his tail and scoot along like greased lightning." Randolph placed his hands against the floor to steady them.

"The reason I was running was that I knew if I could find a ditch before that rascal caught me I'd be safe. Well, he was gettin' closer and closer. And by golly he woulda had me but I finally saw a ditch. Just when that ol' whipper was about to strike, I jumped across the ditch."

Randolph thought the porch sounded like the moaner's bench, the way everybody carried on about Mr. Ervin's story. Most said stuff that let him know they were glad it was him and not them. Archie didn't say a word. That was his way of making believe that cause he had turned seventeen the tale didn't make him no never mind. Arlene asked Mr. Ervin if that really happened to him. Naomi, sleeping on Arlene's lap, stirred but didn't wake up. Cousin Hilda was laughing and shaking her head. "I declare, Ervin. You're gonna scare young Randy to death." "No mam. I ain't scared."

Mozzelle chuckled. She was the only one who didn't pretend to believe Randolph's denial.

Mr. Mason sat erect in his chair again. "Ervin, when you mentioned jumping over that ditch, you reminded me of another kind of snake that used to be in these parts. I don't know if any of them are still around. But did you ever run across or hear tell of a hoop snake?"

"I never did see one. But I sure did know they were 'round here."

"Well, one day I was coming up from the spring with two buckets of water...Lemme tell y'all what a hoop snake is. Like a whip snake, it's cold black. The difference is, you can't get away from a hoop snake by crossing a ditch. The reason folks call it a hoop snake is that when he takes a notion to go after a body, he puts his tail in his mouth and makes a hoop so he can roll like a wheel. Anyway, I was comin' up the hill from the spring and I spotted one. He just about had his tail in his mouth. So I knew the son of a gun was about come after me. I waited 'til he got his tail in his mouth. Then I threw one of the buckets of water at him. Water splashed on him but the bucket missed. Now it was plain as day I had made him mad, his eyes got right red and gleaming. I threw the other bucket of water and it went right through his hoop. His eyes commenced to look like hot coals. I took off up the hill. He came rolling after me. As I live and breathe, that confounded redeyed devil was rolling faster than I was running. Not only that, but I was gettin' tired. I knew it was no use, cause sure as Carter makes little liver pills, he was gonna catch me. Just before he rolled up on me, I saw a heavy stick laying on the ground. I picked up that stick and waited for him to get close enough that when I swung I couldn't miss him. Sure enough, he got close and I swung with all my might. That old wretched thing's tail flew out of his mouth and he went sailing a ways back down the hill." Mr. Mason paused to laugh at himself. "Lord! I took off so fast up that hill, won't no way he was gonna catch me. I didn't even bother to look back. I just kept gittin' up."

* * *

It was dark enough now, blinking fireflies filled the night. The vehicles were parked in the barnyard where the cornshuck had taken place. Randolph reflected on today's cornshuck and the very first one he could remember.

It was just after his fourth birthday. Gladys had recently left for New York and cousin Hilda had moved back home.

Randolph missed the times he and Gladys had spent in the house. He didn't know Hilda who had been teaching school up north. At first he did not realize that this lady who was so nice and gentle to him was Gladys' mama. When he did learn that they were mother and daughter, he noticed that they had the same peach skin. Nobody else he ever saw looked like them.

At that first cornshuck, Randolph tried hard to be the first one to finish shucking his little pile. When he was not, he cried. He cried just like he did when Gladys wouldn't let him touch her where he wanted to. She took pity on him and let him have his way. Now, when cousin Hilda saw him crying, she let him have his way just like her daughter had. She said he was the winner of the corn shuck.

From the time up in Gladys' room to the day he cried and cried until Elmore let him put Jack next to him for the photograph, Randolph Wilford used crying to get his way.

Elmore made it so hard for him, it came to Randolph that he was getting too old to get away with that stuff. That was the first time he remembered making a promise to God. He prayed in his head that if The Lord let Jack get in the picture he wouldn't cry to get his way no more.

Far as he knew, he kept that promise. And that was way back when he was six.

Cesar and his wife drove off in their Chevrolet coupe. Mo and Miz Annette got in the cab of Mr. Irvin's Ford pickup. Arlene, Naomi and Randolph climbed in the back with Verniece and Archie.

They were crossing the creek when Randolph looked down at the shallow stream, then he looked up into the thick woods fanning by. Something 'nother took a hold of him. He promised The Lord that he was gonna try his level best to not be scared the next time he came down this dark road on the way to catch the school bus.

* * *

When Mrs. Merriweather chose Randolph and Henry Hill to do what she called a "scene' from a play," Randolph could tell that she thought she was giving him the better of four roles. She knew that he had a good memory. She proudly gave him the part of the King which had the most lines. He was surprised that she did not notice, as he did, the part she gave to Henry was better than the part of the King. Henry's part, the Jester, had fewer lines but they were the best lines. Why couldn't Mrs. Merriweather see that? Without having any experience with drama, Randolph could see itright off. Anyway, he was more grateful than disappointed. Mrs. Merriweather rehearsed him and Henry along with two other boys until the Friday afternoon of the performance.

Early in the scene, the four characters, the King, the Jester and two Attendants intercoursed; the two Attendants exited stage left. The Jester-played by Henry, and the King-played by Randolph, were left alone center stage.

"Jester, now that we are alone, I must ask you something I have long wished to know. Tell me, Jester, where goest thou nightly?" The baritone sound of his own voice pleased Randolph's ear.

The Jester posed like a little red rooster. "Where goest the candle flame when the breath, which is its life, quits it? Out!" This voice was resonant for Randolph as well. It too was his own.

'That line-Oh! That line,' "Where goest the candle flame

when the breath, which is its life, quits it? Out!" It was the reason Randolph had wanted to be the Jester instead of the King. He had not gotten his wish. But here, he not only got to play the part of the Jester, but he was still the King as well. Mrs. Merriweather was dead set on him playing the King. Ok. Now he was playing both parts.

Most of his dreams were either confusing, fuzzy or night-mares. Now and then, though, Randolph Wilford had a dream that was clear like spring water and just as satisfying. He got out of bed looking forward to his morning chores.

He had accepted that grandma was dead and he couldn't do a thing about it. So, he could feel good about not having to take out her slop jar.

In the back of his mind, Randolph was mindful that he had promised God he would no longer be scared when he walked to catch the school bus. He kept the thought back there. He wasn't gonna let it reach the surface before its time.

The morning was clear. Bessie was not fretful like she was on cloudy or windy days. Randolph stroked her neck when he put the chain around it.

> I am climb-ing Ja-COB'S ladder
> I am climb-ing Ja-COB'S LAD-DER
> I am climb-ing Ja-COB'S LAD-der
> SOL-dier OF the... Cross

He was sure the cow enjoyed his singing. She was wagging her tail like a dog.

At the bottom of the path, Randolph stopped for the cow to drink from the baptising pool. While she slurped, he dipped a drink for himself from the spring. Their spring had the best tasting water around. But it tasted even better when he drank it from the tin cup that hung on one of the posts supporting the tin cover.

On the far side of the blackberry patch Randolph lashed Bessie's chain to a lone pine.

* * *

Since grandma died, he used the extra time in the morning to chop enough kindling for the supper fire. When he gripped the handle close to the axe-head to split chunks into thin strips, he thought of the word, faggot.

He always used that word if he was talking about a creampuff. Back in D.C. he looked it up when he found out his buddies were using it for homosexuals. He didn't know how long the other guys were using the word for something different than he used it for. The dictionary said, faggots were twigs used to start fires; they burned easily. The second definition was a term the English used for cigarettes. Finally, mama's 1938 edition of the Winston's Dictionary said, "faggot" was an offensive word used to describe a male homosexual.

This morning, Randolph remembered that the most difficult thing about learning to read was understanding homonyms by knowing the subject. While he daydreamed, he took the faggots to the kitchen wood box then, went upstairs to get his book bag.

After, looking back to see if the weathervane was spinning (it was not) he resumed his reverie until he crossed in front of the church on his way to catch the bus.

Hundreds of times, Randolph reckoned, he had come down to the road in front of the Baptist church. Hundreds of times, he knew for certain, he began to be scared right here between the church-on one side and aunt May's empty house on the other. This was the day he was gonna change all that. He had promised The Lord that he wouldn't be scared no more. Besides, he was sick and tired of acting like a fool. Everybody knew there was no such thing as haints, ghosts and stuff.

He was deep into the sloping turn toward the creek. That feeling he knew so well was creeping into his chest and shoulders. "Get off me!" His voice rang down through the dell. He examined himself and the air around him. 'Randolph!' He thought, 'That was good.' It was good because he had never dared let his voice be heard down here. He listened for a moment to be sure. Naw. The dark did not seem to be bothered by his words or his echo. He knew better than to think he had got rid of fear just like that. At the same time, something different was happening to him; real thought crowded out imagination. There was never a time when Randolph did not know that his fear came out of his fool head. It was just that he didn't seem to be able to control his imagination.

"Alright now. Alright." His steps were as ginger as ever. He took care of that. His strides got longer and his arms swung easy. He remained careful not to make like everything was copacetic; he still had not reached the creek bridge...didn't matter what he told himself, it was when he was on that bridge that he usually felt like his heart was gonna leap out of his chest.

A few steps from the bridge, he put all of his energy into watching what went through his head. Nothing else about himself entered his focus. His shoulders tightened. His chest, stomach, spine and butt locked up, and his thighs, knees and feet near 'bout cramped.

Three steps onto the bridge Randolph heard what sounded like a hundred little critters scatter. Every part of his body that he had ignored, splattered in as many different directions as the unidentified night crawlers down there in the creek. Randolph screeched and lept straight up into the air.

"Gotdamnit!" His dissappointment with himself erased every bit of fright. "You stupid motherfucker!" He was squinting and gritting his teeth when he got up to the turn on the far side of the creek. Through body, intellect and sense memory, he knew that relief came at this point. Every time he got a little way from that damn creek, he sighed, and breathed easy. The worst was over. Even a fool like him wouldn't hurt himself one single step further.

In the turn-half way up the hill-he was still trying to figure out why somebody would do what he kept doing to himself. "WHAT!" To his right, Randoph heard a clicking sound like the claws of a squirl or a rat or something running on pavement. He had been in those woods lots of times. He knew good and well the ground in there was rich black earth. He fixed his eyes across the drainage ditch and waited. Before he could anticipate, a purple stream-a mist-came out of the bushes, down into into the ditch. Randolph pictured it reaching the bottom where he could not see it. Sure enough, the purple mist came up on his side of the ditch and continued-hugging the ground-toward him. "Oh-Lord!" He wasn't scared. What he felt was more like wonder.

From the moment the sound first reached him, it clicked a

steady rhythm out of the woods into the ditch and now... Randolph froze. He did not dare take another step and put his foot in the purple stream. He stared down. Still clicking, it floated across the tips of his sneakers. A warm sensation surged up through him. He thought he must be in the middle of a fairy tale, or in heaven, or... It was all over.

The purple mist, the clicking sound were gone. Randolph's body continued to feel warm. He stood still in the middle of the dirt road. He reflected on the pavement sound, the mist. Randolph Wilford had witnessed... a miracle?

> I am climb-ing Ja-COB'S ladder
> I am climb-ing Ja-COB'S LADDER
> I am climb-ing Ja-COB'S LAD-der
> SOL-dier OF the... CROSS
> E'vry rung gets high-ER HIGH-er
> E'vry rung gets high-ER HIGH-ER
> E'vry rung gets high-ER HIGH-er
> SOL-dier OF the... CROSS

Because that portion of his morning trek took longer than it ever had, the yellow vehicle of his delight, made more yellow by the rising sun, came from up toward Arjay's at the very moment Randolph arrived at the T. He had decided not to say anything about what happened to him. He didn't expect that anybody would believe him anyway. But the real reason he was not going to tell the other kids was that he had no idea how to. He got on the little school bus and acted like it was just another day.

Chapter Six
The Gingerbread House

He had thought about it any number of times. But he had never thought to ask what was back down there. He knew why too. Randolph had never asked R.J. what was down the road behind his store because R.J. was white. He wasn't scared of white people, he just didn't feel right around them. They lived in the same place as the colored folks. Still, they might as well have lived overseas somewhere. Randolph had felt that way since he was six years old.

Back in Washington, when he started the first grade, it came clear to him that white people lived close but far away. Their schools were as different from the colored schools as poor folks' houses were from Chester Burns'. When he saw Calvin Cooledge High, with its archery range and a tennis court, something changed for him. Nobody had said a word. They did not have to. White people were foreigners right here in the U.S.A. When he couldn't avoid talking to them, he had to kind of shift gears. It was like getting directions or the time of day from a stranger.

Randolph had looked down that road a hundred times thinking that was where the sawmill was. R.J. said "Naw. The sawmill is up yonder." He pointed up the road toward Reverend Esterbrook's house. That bothered Randolpph a little bit cause he didn't want to let go of his assumption. He didn't have time to bother with that though. "What is back down yonder?"

"Well-suh, straight down the road, as the crow flies're a couple a' colored families and one white 'n. But half way down, you'll see a mule path that kinda veers off to the right. If'n you follow that, you'll come to a little bitty house. An old colored lady called Mattie Cable lives in it. You don't wanta go down that path."

Randolph almost missed the path to Mattie Cable's house. He slammed on the brakes and slid around in the road.

The path was longer than he had anticipated. He thought about giving up and turning back. "Oh!" He saw a stream of smoke rising beyond a patch of woods in front of him. The closer he got to where he saw smoke, the narrower the path became. It was almost not a path anymore. He got off his bike to walk. Soon, he was into a thicket and could hardly see. Leafy branches brushed across his face causing the kind of tension in his neck and shoulders that he felt when he was by himself in the dark. He didn't have time to get good and scared-the path opened onto a clearing that was a small patch with sun scorched grass and weeds. A little brown house sat back of the yard. He stopped and kicked down the kickup stand. In his mind, what he saw was somewhere between the Gingerbread house and the witches hut in Hansel and Gretel.

"Howdy!" She was a little snaggletooth-old woman about the same color as her house. The gap in the front of her mouth reminded Randy of himself. "Come in and make yourself at home."

Before he was inside the one story cabin, he had settled on Hansel and Gretel's witch. The old lady was leaning on a crooked cane and her voice sounded a lot like the half dry-raggedy yard he pushed his bike across. "It's right nice of you to come by t'see old Mattie. What's your name?"

"Randolph, mam."

"Your last name's mam!" Mattie laughed loud at her joke. Randolph laughed cause she cackled just like a little old witch. "Sit down and make yourself comf'table. You hungry?"

"No mam." "Aw, you must be a mite hungry. You've been riding that bicycle for a while."

"No mam, I'm not hungry." He saw that the shack had two rooms and there was more shadow than light. But he could see that the place was dusty like grandma's attic. "Could I have a glass of water?"

"I'll do better than that. Go on, sit yourself down. This time he sat in one of two chairs. The one he chose was a straight back wicker. He figured the other one-a rocker-was for Miz Mattie.

"I was just making myself some hot cocoa. Don't get many folks come calling back down in here. I'll give you a nice cup of hot cocoa and a piece of my wholecake. That sounded pretty good to Randolph. Now that he thought about it, he was kinda hungry. His mouth watered. He turned on his chair to take a closer look. There were not two rooms after all. The place was more like a room and a half. Here in the kitchen he saw a cooking stove, a little table and an old-looking cupboard. On the other side of a wrinkled, gray curtain, he could see a bed and a beat up old dresser.

Randolph took a quick third look around the kitchen. He had completed his scan before he realized he was checking to see if the old lady had one of those big black pots like witches and cannibals have. The thought brought a wide gap-mouthed-grin to his face. He smiled even wider when it came to him that his grin must look like the one Miz Mattie had worn since he got here. In a way though, this old lady reminded Randolph of cousin Hilda. She was small and brownskin; cousin Hilda was tall and lightskinned. But both of them acted like they knew what they were about. "You always lived down here?" "Lord, no. I have lived in a lot of places-New York, Crestville. I lived in a lot of places. Once I was in Paris for a spell." A look in her eyes made Randy know she took a quick trip back to Paris. "I liked that." She laughed to herself. "Yes Mr. Randolph, I liked that."

He reckoned she must be about grandma's age when she died. Somewhere in the pit of his reasoning he concluded that grandma had got weary and took to her bed but this little woman got weary and took to a cane. She had put the crooked cane aside once they came into the house. She moved around holding onto the table and the backs of the chairs. Randolph was taking a liking to Mattie Cable.

She put a saucer with a chunk of steaming, buttered wholecake onto the table. "Here you are young man. The cocoa's about ready, I'll have that for you in a minute." Something took hold of his attention. What is that smell? Randolph sneaked a sniff of the wholecake. That wasn't it. Whatever it was, it filled the room and pushed everything else out of his mind. The smell got worse. Randolph couldn't remember a stink like this one. He turned to his imagination to try and get it out of his mind. One time cousin Ames-God rest his soul-told Randolph and Lucille that folks in China ate thousand year old eggs. They must smell like this. The odor was turning his stomach. "I gotta go. I've got a stomach ache." "Alright son." When she didn't discourage him, Randolph knew what the smell was. He let that insight rest where it was until he could get out in the air.

"Come visit me again Mr. Randolph!" He was already on his bike, heading for the bushes. "Yes mam. I sure will!" Randolph did not bother to walk his bike through the thicket. He didn't mind the leaves lashing across his face. In fact, it was like they were whisking away the stink. He reached the wider path beyond the patch of woods. Now! Now it was alright to finish his thought. "That smell...That smell was a witch's fart."

He got to the wagon trail, the stench was still lodged in his nostrils. He rode zigzag back and forth across the grassy island between the tracks. No help. The witch fart hung on.

R. J. and two of his buddies sat on soda crates in front of his store. Randolph shouted "Hey," in response to their greetings. He had no idea he had seen or heard them. Normally he would have smelled the gas that sweated from the two pumps. But he was oblivious to it all.

At the T, just before he turned onto the Cedar Grove road, Randolph accepted that he would not get shed of that smell until he ran into something that outweighed it. He relaxed and pedalled along in near peace.

Cousin Hilda's house looked something or 'nother like glory when he got to it. He had no notion of stopping there, but the very sight of that wide porch and pink curtains through the window did not let him ride by. He kept thought in the shadows until his favorite relative opened her door. "Why, look whose at my door! Come on in child. It's so good to see you." Her bright-peach face and cheerie how-do-you-do filled the air around him with the smell of honeysuckle and roses. "Hi cousin Hilda." If it was up to him, he would come and live with this peachy lady. She never failed to make him feel like little David playing his harp or one of those InkSpots' songs.

The familiar pink and gray bedroom on the right and the blue and gray living room to his left, grabbed hold of Randolph and gave him a soft squeeze. Words came to his lips but he caught them before they got out into the hallway. "I love you!" dissolved in his mouth like butterscotch. He swallowed it.

"Why, look at that smile. I hope it means you're as happy to be here as I am that you came." Randolph knew that she did not have to say stuff like that. It reminded him that when he was little, grandma and them talked to him that way. He got used to it just like he got used to the ice-clear taste of the water from the spring. Hilda ushered him into the kitchen where she always seemed to hang out. "Sit down Randy." She rubbed her palms together in a way that looked like slow-fluttering butterfly wings. "What would you like?" It was no accident that Hilda asked a rhetorical question. Her intention was to have her young caller name one of the goodies he had come to expect when he visited her. She well knew that she would have it on hand or be able to throw it together. Randolph sat still and tried to figure out what she was getting at. Ever since he was real small he had enjoyed figuring out what grown folks wanted him to say. After what he'd just gone through, he didn't have the spunk to be playing around. "Tell ya the truth, cousin Hilda, I'm not that hungry." "Oh! Randolph." She feigned hurt. "How can you break an old lady's heart like that?" They shared a laugh. At that moment, boy and woman-wanted to stop time. As it was, they extended the moment until joy was drained from it. "Tell you what young man." She went through the pantry door. He sat at the kitchen table straining to hear her. "I'll make something suitable for a fine young fellow who is not very hungry. How does that sound?" There was no need to wonder what in the world she was talking about. The young and not so young dreamers were engaged in child's play. The goal was not to make sense but to have fun with their visit.

Hilda returned to the kichen with a bunch of watercress she had taken from a crock. She mixed it with raisins and walnuts, she put her finger to her lips. "Shhh. I'm not done yet." A laugh burst from Randolph.

Hilda took a chicken breast from the stove warmer and crumbled it off the bone into the salad. She slid the bowl across the table to Randolph. "There." She then took a dish towel from the oven handle. Randolph was tickled again to see her wipe her hands and sit down, across from him. He could almost hear her think, 'I'm gonna watch you enjoy what I fixed for you. I know it's good.'

He dug in. "Good Lord! Cousin Hilda, you're right." When he complimented her, neither she nor he remembered that she had not actually expressed her presumption.

"When you were teaching school in New York," Randolph did not concern himself about talking with his mouth full. He knew Miz Peachy would not mind. "did you...Did anybody ever talk about a man called Eugene Chen?"

"Hmmm. Eugene Chen, you say?"

"Yessum."

"No, Randolph... Can't say that I ever did."

One of these days he was gonna have to go back down to the gingerbread lady and ask her if she ever heard of Eugene Chen. He chewed and thought and salivated. Hilda reveled in the pride of knowing how to weave delight from whole cloth.

* * *

The sun spread light all over-across the fields-up and down the roads and shined hot rays through the leafy branches above the hollow. Randolph felt as full of light as the day around him. He had no notion as to why he had not a care. All he knew was that nothing disturbed him. Nothing scared him. Nothing clouded his peace.

He had spent two hours over at Archie's before Mozzelle's call rang across the woods next to the Methodist church and reached the barnyard where he and his buddy were pitching horseshoes.

He mounted Susie Q. dreading the the whipping he was surely gonna get when he got home.

Mozzelle was waiting on the side porch when he pulled into the driveway. Her hands rested on her hips making her broad shoulders look straight as a board. "You know you're gonna get a whippin' don'tcha? Get yourself out to the hollow'n bring me a hickory." She didn't have to say it. Randolph was gonna head for the hollow without being told to. All the way back here he had been scared of the impending whipping. But when he pulled into the yard and saw Mozzelle standing there like she was Sunset Carson or somebody, he felt every bit of his worry run off him like rain from their tin roof.

The sunlight that had already made his bare arms black as coal now warmed them. The afternoon heat even touched his shoulders; it had penetrated the short sleeves of his blue denim shirt. It felt good. Randolph felt good. While he concentrated on how he had, of a sudden, entered something-or-another like Glory, he had been plaiting together three-long-green hickory switches-too ripe to break while Mo gave him the good whipping he deserved. Why he was braiding these thin branches together, Randolph did not know. He just knew to let himself be. The few times in his years that a part of himself told him to get out of his own way, he had not questioned it.

He had kept Mo waiting a long time while he braided the hickory. He stepped out of the top of the hollow, she was still standing in the same pose on the side porch.

Randolph got close enough for her to see how he had made this new kind of switch for her to whip him. Mozzelle smiled. Looked like she was proud of her young nephew for having made a real fine hickory. It was right smart of him.

Stuff was rushing through Randolph's mind like the time he almost drowned in the Potomac.

Mozzelle made him look bad every time they worked tobacco with Mr. Ervin and them. "Make haste, boy!" It wasn't enough for her that she was the best stringer around. She would grab the three or four leaves of 'bacca' from each of the handers and whip the twine around them like nothing. "Make haste, boy!" Every time she shouted at him, he flinched. When she loaded the three foot stick with bunches on each side, Mr. Ervin would lift it off the cradle and tote it inside the tobacco barn to rack it up. Randolph, being the least experienced, the youngest and a daydreamer, handed slower than Verniece and Archie. He knew that Mo was trying to make sure he didn't make her look bad. But that did not make sense. Why would she think that he would be as good at this as somebody who's been doing it all their life. She wouldn't let up though. "Make haste Randolph!"

Last Sunday some woman from midway was down here visiting with Mo in the living room. Out of nowhere, Mo called out to him. He was up in his room reading a Black Hawk Comic book. "Randy! Saaay, Randy!"

"Yeah!"

"Come down here'n go out in the back yard an' kill a pullet for supper." Now, she knew good and well that he ain't never killed no chicken. He couldn't say anything though-that would sound like he was sassing her. He came down and went out to the back porch. He sat on the top step trying to get up the gumption to kill a pullet. He knew it didn't make sense that he was always the first one to grab a drumstick but was too sqeamish to ring a spring chicken's neck. He sat there a while watching the several hens and two pullets pecking at anything they saw in the dirt.

"RANDOLPH!"

He wanted to say, 'Aw, hush up!' "Huh?"

"You killed that chicken yet!"

Here Mo was, making him look bad again. Why'd she take a mind to use him to show off to her friend?

"Naw! Not'chet!" Randolph clinched his jaw. He was just gonna have to take a whipping, he sure wasn't gonna kill no chicken.

Next thing he knew, he was out in the hollow getting a hickory so that Mo could whip him. The woman from Midway was still in the living room. Mozzelle was gonna whip him in front of company.

There Mo was, standing on the porch with her hands on her hips. Randolph handed her the switch, from the yard like he always did. It was like he thought she was going to change her mind before he came up to take his medicine. "Boy. You better get'chourself up here!" He didn't protest as he sometimes did. His confusion about not hesitating to eat chicken but refusing to kill one made him almost feel that he deserved a whipping. He mounted the porch and gave her the switch and turned his face away. Mozzelle grabbed hold of his left hand with her's and flailed away with her right.

It wasn't all that bad. She struck him across the back six or seven times. Randolph didn't jump around. He kept his crying just above a whimper. He wasn't gonna make it worse than it was with the Midway woman listening in the living room.

While Mo was down in the yard ringing a pullet's neck Randolph checked his bare arms. He found two welts on the right one. There was one welt on his left arm from him turning toward Mo when he thought she was done. Her final swing made that one. "Take this pullet's head and throw it out yonder in the field." Randolph wanted so bad to tell her to take it out there herself.

Half way out between the cow shed and the orchard, he hurled the chicken head as far as he could. Then he checked his overalls to make sure he had not gotten any blood on himself. One day he was gonna fix Mozzelle. She kept making up reasons to whip him. And, as if that wasn't bad enough, she acted like she enjoyed making him look bad.

Mozzelle was standing there on the side porch with that, 'You're a good hickory maker' grin still on her face. When he was in the hollow braiding the three green switches, Randolph had been off somewhere away from his mind. Here, at the edge of the porch, he knew who what and what for. He handed Mo the perfect hickory.

"Now, get'chourself up here."

"You must be a damn fool!"

Mo's satisfied grin turned into a kind of 'What'chou say?' grin. Randolph did not give her time to say anything.

"My mama stopped whipping me when I was ten. I told her I was gonna be a good boy. It didn't make no sense for her to keep whipping me the way she was doing. I'm older now, and I still ain't bad. If my own mama stopped whipping me back then, you can stop now. I ain't wearing no more whippings."

Like somebody who didn't have right good sense, Mo cackled, "You shiny eyed rascal you. You're crazy!"

He didn't care what she thought. He wasn't kidding. He wasn't gonna wear another whipping when he didn't do anything. Naw, he wasn't gonna wear no more whippings period. He was a good boy. Wasn't any need for her to keep beating on him like he was some kind of animal.

Mozzelle tossed the perfect whippping switch into the yard. "Go over to the woodpile 'n chop some kindling. Can you do that!"

"Yeah Mo. I can do whatever you say..." He almost added, 'long's you don't try to whip me.' He had good enough sense to leave well enough alone.

* * *

Mo was in the kitchen shelling peas. At the chopping block, Randy had trouble seeing the kindling he was splitting. He was crying because he had decided on the spot that if Mo ever tried to whip him again he would run off into the woods. He would sleep with the haints if he had to. He was tired of her beating on him.

"Lord! I'm glad that's done." Mo tiptoed out to the back porch with pea shells cradled in her apron. She eased down the steps and released the green hulls onto the ground. The chickens hopped up and down pecking at one another to get to them. Mo went back up the steps without looking toward the chopping block. For his part, Randolph pretended not to know she had come out of the house.

Back in the kitchen, Mozzelle put a chunk of fatback in the pot of field peas. She had planned to make cornbread next, but her fingers were stiff from shelling the peas. It had been a while since that had happened. Truth was, she felt a little stiff all over. When that mannish rascal commenced to call her a fool she got a quick flash.

She did not think of papa all that much since he passed, over fifteen years ago. She was scared to death of her daddy and didn't care who knew it.

It had to have been late Summer-persimmons were ripe. To this day she didn't know exactly what Ruth had done. But Mo saw her come running out of the house and take off across the field. Papa came out a couple of moments later with his shotgun. He took off after Ruth. He ran into the woods behind his second daughter. 'Lord a'mercy! That old man was crazy. An' he was mean's a rattle snake.'

Mo remembered praying that papa wouldn't kill Ruth.

A little while later, papa came out of the woods with Ruth right behind him. Neither one of them said a word. Ruth never would tell Mo what had happened. She sure wasn't gonna ask papa why he got after Ruth with his gun. A few months after that, Ruth turned eighteen. She upped and took her nappy-headed-tomboy self off to Crestville and never lived at home again; not even after papa died.

Mo never noticed before today, but Randolph kind of favored papa. 'He ain't as mean as papa was... Lord knows he's just as crazy. Ain't no tellin' what that boy's liable to do.' Randolph startled her by appearing with a load of kindling in his arms. He ignored her flinch. He put the faggots in the wood box and went back out to chop some cord wood. Mozelle watched her nephew who had come to be right strapping from farm work. She was not a bit ashamed to admit to her self that she was scared of him now.

96

Randolph drove the double-edged axe into one chunk after another. This was his favorite chore next to milking. Milking the cow made him feel clever; chopping cord wood made him feel powerful. He wielded the axe-over his left then his right shoulder. He was not at all aware that he had instilled fear into his aunt.

* * *

The sound rang out in every direction like it was meant to. The way the rope held back against his tug on it, seemed natural, too. It wouldn't have felt right if it was easy to ring the bell that called folks from far and wide to the house of The Lord.

He had figured out why their house was right there at the end of the churchyard. The picture of granddaddy's uncle Paul had hung in the back of the pulpit ever since he could remember. Grandma was looked up to as an Elder, no other woman was, and Elmore, when he was home, was Secretary and Treasurer. Still, it wasn't til chocolate Santa Claus-cousin Ames told him that Paul had been the "Founding Pastor" that it commenced to dawn on Randolph why the Roebucks were hot stuff in the Cedar Grove Baptist Church. That was why he, barely in his teens, had the privilege of ringing the bell for Sunday Service.

When Mozzelle first gave him the assignment, they discussed what would be the right number of times to ring the bell. "I always rang it seven or eight times 'fore I got tired." Mo knew good and well what she was doing. The minute this mannish rascal heard that she got tired after any number of rings, he would want to show that he was strong enough to do more.

Randolph would do his chores, and before getting into his sunday duds, he would stroll down to the church and ring that bell ten times. The final few tugs were hard; his arms would be a little stiff. He would jump up and grab hold so that his weight did the work. With each big-iron clang across the fields and hollows, a resonance hummed through him. Surely the Spirit was moving in his soul.

* * *

Arlene and Naomi stayed at Willie's mama's house most of the time. Randolph was tickled to death that they had been here in the house four or five days now. Naomi was eighteen months old and seemed to be just as crazy about him as always. She was talking a little bit. Sometimes she surprised you by saying something like, "Cracklin bread." Randolph was reminded that Arlene had taught him to read when he was four. For the first time, he remembered that she taught him the alphabet even before she broke his tricycle and made up for it by introducing him to the magic of reading. He decided to teach Naomi more words. Arlene had used her old Second Grade Reader, he hoped to use as well but could not find it. Naomi's first vocabulary lesson was vocal; it took place on the back steps. Randolph and she threw kernals of field corn to the cackling chickens between each word drill.

Jack and Flossie took turns chasing the yardbirds, they must've been jealous of them. Naomi giggled as if she understood what was going on. To Randolph, it seemed natural that the child should understand; for as long as he could remember, it had bothered him when grown folks treated him like he didn't know what was going on just because he was little. The older he became, the more certain he was that they had been wrong to take that attitude.

"Hen!" He pointed to a checkered, plump layer. "Hin!" Naomi mimicked. "That's close. Not 'hin,' hen!" Naomi caught on right off. "Rooster!" "Rooster!" she repeated perfectly. For the better part of an hour, teacher Randolph and pupil Naomi engaged in their call and response. They went back and forth between words and interplay with the chickens and the dogs.

The following day, Arlene, Naomi and Willie went back to Willie's mama's place. Randolph hoped they would come back soon so he could teach Naomi new words. He also wanted to get to know Naomi's father, Willie. The man was so quiet. He had even less to say than Gregory.

* * *

They walked pass the double-deck storage barn. It stood on the left between the house at the top of the hill and the tobacco barn, halfway to the creek. Every time he passed the bright-unpainted planks-all put together and tall, Randolph damn near burst open with pride. He had helped Mr. Ervin and Archie build it. "Yeah!" He was proud that he actually worked on a real life building, although it was hard to believe that he really had. Sometimes things, the storage barn was one of them, were like something out of one of his dreams-he was not always sure which was which.

The first time he and Archie went down to the swimming hole, Randolph had let his buddy walk a step or two ahead since he knew the way. These days though he walked right beside Archie-his head almost bumping against his shoulder.

They passed through a pea patch without taking notice. When they got to the watermelon patch though Randolph's mind filled with it. First of all, cause it was a watermelon patch. Second, cause Archie had told him that not long ago, Mr. Ervin took notice that somebody was coming into his patch during the night to steal melons.

"One night papa took his 12 gauge and hid in the pea patch. Sure enough, several white boys come creepin' into the watermelon patch." Archie said Mr. Irvin didn't say a word. He just pointed the shotgun down toward them and unloaded two blasts of rock salt. He knew to pack the shells with those big old grains that would not do much harm but would burn like the dickens. *"Two of them boys, there was six of 'em, commenced to screamin' like banshees."*

You could hear the creek when you got close to the woods at the bottom edge of the melon patch. Randolph kept his breath shallow so he would hear that sound. Just when it seemed maybe the water was gonna be still and quiet today, the babble poured into his ears somethin' a'nother like a hollow xylophone song.

They were out of the narrow strip of brush quick as they got into it. When Randolph could see the flowing creek, the sound mallots on wood to raindrops on a window; it gave him gentle shivers.

Three or four snake doctors buzzed around the edge of the water-looking-for-all-the-world like little bitty helicopters. Because those dragonflies were hanging around the water, Randolph guessed snakes had to be somewhere about. It would have put the fear of God into him to know that in folklore the snake doctor was so called because it was believed to sew a snake back together if somebody cut it in half like he sometimes did.

Because Randolph did not know this and was confused by the name snake doctor, he started calling the doggone things "whirligigs."

The deepest part of the creek was three feet down and so clear, you could count flat river rocks on the bottom. The two boyst took off their clothes and stood on the edge of the creek allowing the afternoon sun to make their naked bodies good and warm before they went into the cold water.

One of the few things Archie had learned from his little buddy was to stay underwater long as he could when he dived in. Although Randolph's lungs near 'bout busted, he always stayed under until he saw Archie come up for air.

Randolph never told Archie about the time he drowned in the Potomac. He had held his breath forever before giving in to a hacking and coughing attack that even in eleven feet of water, made his throat burn like fire until he went into a trance and saw a bright light.

He probably would have told Archie about it except that he would also have had to admit that Dupont, who was Archie's age, came in to save his ass.

Randolph came to the surface panting and grinning like a cheshire cat, celebrating that when they came to the swimming hole, he got his chance to best Archie.

"You can't beat me at nothin' else."

"I don't need to."

Archie gave him a curious look then splashed water on him.

"Look a'yonder!" Before he looked, Archie knew what Randy had spotted. "Like I told you before man, if we don't bother that moccassin, he ain't gonna bother us. Let him stay on his side an' we'll stay on ours." Archie was right. Like the last time they saw the water moccasin, it stayed on its end of the creek. Randolph kept his eye on it anyway. The snake stayed over yonder, its head stickin' up in the air. Randolph tried to see if he could catch that ol' brown thing looking at him. After a while, he decided the moccassin wasn't studyin' him.

* * *

It wasn'r easy to stay away from Reverend Esterbrook's. Listening to the man preach was one thing. But every time Randolph rode into that barnyard he could still hear, "Goddamn you mule!" And he wasn't gonna ever get over the way Holly called him nigger in front of R. J. and the other guy.

A way to avoid the preacher's house was to ride his bike on something like a paper route. He would start out with a stop at Arjay's to get a soda or a Baby Ruth or something. Then, he would go back down in there to Miz Mattie's where he would stay until she offered him something to eat. He would tell her he wasn't hungry and doubleback to cousin Hilda's.

By the third time he had visited the snaggle-toothed lady's gingerbread house, he knew that she was gonna always look like a little brown witch. She wasn't scary or nothing, Randy just didn't like her cooking. But she made him laugh.

"Well! Mr. Randolph, you took it upon yourself to come down and see me again."

"Yes mam." He reflected her snaggled-tooth grin right back at her.

The last time Randolph came back down in here, he forgot to ask Miz Mattie about Eugene Chen.

He crossed his fingers while convincing himself that because she had been to New York and even Paris, she had to know about the man whose name he knew from daddy, but nothing else.

"You ever hear-tell of somebody called Eugene Chen?"

Mattie was sitting across from him in her tiny living room.

"What did you just ask me child!" This was the first time Randolph remembered catching her off guard. "I asked you if..." "No, no. I heard you. Where in the world did you ever hear 'bout Eugene Chen?" "My father..." He choked up. Although Randolph had thought about daddy now and then, he had not spoken of him since the day he broke down in Second grade when they sang the line, 'Land where our fathers died.'

"One day when my sister and I were playing Chinese checkers, my father said that name."

"When did Conny pass?"

"When I was six."

"Well, let me tell you young man, your father was one fine man."

"The old guy on the shortcut in Midway said... 'scuse me, I ran into a man in Midway who told me the same thing. He said daddy was really something"

"He did" You remember his name?"

"No ma'am."

"Doesn't matter. The fact is, after they made Conny Wilford, they broke the mold. To tell you the truth, I don't know that much about Eugene Chen...I knew some folks when I was in Harlem..."She interrupted herself. "You know about Harlem do you?"

"Yeah, yes ma'am. That's in New York."

"Good boy. During my time in Harlem I knew folks who knew stuff like you want to know about-and let me tell you, that curious mind of yours is going to lead you to learn a lot about this old world. Take my word for it."

"Rob Roy told me I was gonna be a poet one day."

"Did he really? Well let me tell you, Rob Roy used to write books before he started delivering the mail. So, if he said you're going to be a poet, he knows what he's talking about." Mattie saw the light of curiosity in the boy's eyes-the same light that identified him to Mozelle as a 'Shiny eyed rascal.'

"All I know about Eugene Chen is that he was a colored fella from the Island of Trinidad. He wound up living in China and became the Foreign Minister to Sun Yat Sen. Sun Yat Sen was the George Washington of China." "Mr. Sen was the first President of China?"

Mattie felt a satisfaction run through her that had been absent for so long she hardly recognized it. "Yes. Sun Yat Sen was China's first president. But his family name wasn't Sen. Chinese family names come first. So, if somebody is called Sun Yat Sen, you call him Mr. Sun. Yat Sen, is his given name. Or as we would say, his first and middle names." She looked into Randolph's eyes until they lit up with comprehension. "Ok. So Mr. Sun was the President and Eugene Chen was his Foreign Minister. A foreign Minister is like...like our Secretary Of State-like George Marshall, our Secretary Of State. You with me?"

"Yes mam." Of a sudden, Randolph missed his father. He wanted to tell him he finally found out who Eugene Chen was.

"Eugene Chen was a Negro from Trinidad who wound up as one of the most important men in China." She cuddled the pride that knowledge brought like a precious cherub.

Randolph wanted to ask where Trinidad was. He knew better. "Leave it alone!" They say. "Don't mess with it."

He swung onto his bike Durango Kid style as always. Usually the image in his mind was the gold mine over the hill or the cattle ranch beyond the valley where that cowgirl lived that he fancied. Today Randolph rode away from the good witch's gingerbread house looking straight down through the center of the earth at China. He saw Eugene Chen standing in front of a pagoda with a bunch of Chinese men and women. Mr. Chen sure did favor daddy.

The ride through the brush onto the wagon path stayed outside his reverie. He turned the corner at Arjay's without seeing two white fellas sitting on a bench behind the gas pumps. He reached the T still planning to stop at cousin Hilda's. When he was half way between the T and her house, he knew he couldn't stop anywhere. He had to go straight home and run up to his room.

His mind turned to the book about Dorie Miller. Before he read that book he always thought of Moby Dick when far off places filled his head. Dorie Miller was a Negro...that sure was a lot more like him than Ishmael.

Randolph knew that soon's he got to be familiar with him, he would be all the way in China, in the person of Eugene Chen.

He pedaled hard past cousin Hilda's driveway-down the short grade and straight away to the top of the creek hill. He leaned his weight forward over the handle bars so that his face was flat against the wind blowing up from the creek.

JUST REMEMBER PEARL HARBOR

He was Dorie Miller singing into the breeze.

JUST REMEMBER PEARL HARBOR

Randolph/Dorie sang at the top of his voice-swinging that anti-aircraft gun from side to side.

JUST REMEMBER PEARL HARBOR

By the time he got close to the creek bridge, he had shot down more Japanese Zero's than he could count.

JUST REMEMBER PEARL HARBOR

* * *

He neither kicked down the kickup stand nor leaned Susie Q. against the oak. He let the bike fall.

When he got up to his room, Randolph sat on the side of his bed. "Daddy..." His call was a whisper, the crying made no sound.

* * *

Although, at first, Randolph wondered how come Gregory hadn't gone off to New York with Mozzelle, it didn't take him long to stop thinking about Mozzelle altogether.

Gregory would sometimes stay away for three or four days at a time. Even before Mozzelle went away, he was staying out all night when he took a notion to. Mo didn't say nothin' so Randolph took it in stride. These days, everything was just peachy. Arlene, Willie and Nadine came to stay at the house. The good thing about that was that Randy had the chance to play big brother to two year old Nadine. As time wore on, Arlene and Willie would stay out all night. Every now and then, they stayed away for two or three days. When they were away, Randolph was not only big brother to Nadine. He had the chance to play papa.

"Want some more Irish taters?"

"Uh huh."

He went into the kitchen to scoop and scrape the balance of the potatoes from the bottom of the big black skillet. As proud as he was that he prepared makeshift meals for Nadine, Randy was overjoyed at the sight of her when he came back to the living room and looked at her sitting at the card table in front of the radio; he had unfolded it for them to have breakfast and listen to hillbilly songs. There she sat all dressed up like a little brown doll. He had bathed her and dressed her in what he later would learn was her Sunday clothes-a brown dress trimmed in yellow frills at the hem and around her chubby upper arms. He paused in the doorway. Nadine was as happy as he was-her hands rested on the peeling pasteboard table. She smiled at his return with their plates of taters. Randolph was always tickled by a bright smile. The brown-eyed smile of his little cousin-through her bright first set of teeth-lighting up her round chocolate cheeks, made him know that he was a good big brother/papa. "How come you sittin' there grinnin' like a cheshire cat?" He knew she did not know what he was saying. At the same time, he knew that she, like he had at her age, understood the intention.

* * *

Randy went down below Arjay's to see Miz Mattie. She wasn't there. That was ok, he was gonna go by cousin Hilda's next anyway. He rode back up to Arjay's and drank a Dr. Pepper before going on to cousin Hilda's. When he was pedaling up her driveway, the feeling came over him that you get when something tells you there's nobody home. Cousin Hilda did not own a car. So, nothing was missing from the driveway. The shades were not drawn. The front door was closed, but she kept it closed all the time. There was just a stillness about the place that he couldn't explain. He could feel it.

Sure enough, like Miz Mattie, cousin Hilda was not at home. The whole day started to feel empty. Randolph could not remember a time when he had visited two different houses and nobody was home in either. When he steered back onto the Cedar Grove road, his legs felt kinda heavy and something or another like a liquid breeze flowed through him. Coasting on the grade and straight away between Mr. Mason's house and the creek hill-Randolph felt like he had put on weight.

Just above the turn onto the drop down to the creek was a long curving slope up to a little house where Mr. Bill and Miz Aretha lived. Randolph had not been up there in months. When he could, he passed by here without taking notice that the house was even there. But because a queer feeling had come over him, he turned onto their driveway.

Before Cesar caused Randolph to realize he could read. Even before Arlene taught him the alphabet and how to read a little bit, Mr. Bill, next to grandma was the one he looked up to the most. One of the reasons he looked forward to coming back to Cedar Grove was to see Mr. Bill. That old man, with skin like shiny black clay, would let Randolph ride along side him on his buggy seat and steer the mule. He told him stories about what Cedar Grove was like back when he was a youngun. Mr. Bill was the first one to make him think he would someday be a preacher; all of this when Randolph was just three years old.

Not long after he came back down to Cedar Grove, three years ago, Mr. Bill took Randolph for a ride on his new wagon. He had new mules to go with the spanking new vehicle. It had seemed near 'bout like old times to Randolph.

They got back to the house and unhitched the mules. Randolph was tickled to death that he was back down the country. Miz Aretha gave him some roasted peanuts out of the oven. "Careful now. They're still hot." Randolph tossed the few hot nuts back and forth between his cupped hands. Each time they landed against one palm, he felt a hot pinch before he tossed them back to the other. It surprised him that it took almost no time before the nuts were cool enough to shell and eat. "Lord! These taste so good Miz Aretha." Miz Aretha was a short round woman. She was as lightskinned as Mr. Bill was dark. She was even lighter than Gregory; she had bright gray eyes and had freckles around her nose.

Randolph had barely finished the first hand full of peanuts before she gave him another. He went through the same ritual. Mr. Bill came into the kitchen with his corn cob pipe in his hand. "I don't know how come I can't find my tin of Prince Albert." "Bill, the last time you couldn't find it, it was in there on the table next to the Victrola." "Aw hush woman, you don't know what'chou talking 'bout." Randolph stopped shuttling the peanuts and let them sting his palm and watched Mr. Bill leave the kitchen.

He was seated at the table, Miz Aretha stood to his left next to the stove. He looked up and saw her cheeks-freckles and all, blood-red.

"How come you take that shit!" On it's own, her right hand flew up across her breast. She had instinctively cocked it to give this smart mouth rascal the back of it until she noticed the earnest

look in the boy's eyes and froze where she was. She relaxed. "Oh. You know how men are." Randolph nearly said. "No mam, I don't." 'Leave it alone. You done said too much.' For a split second he wondered if she had heard his thought.

"Where am I going?" While he reflected Randolph had gone part of the way up to Mr. Bill and Miz Aretha's house. After what happened back when he was eleven and Miz Aretha said, "You know how men are," he had paid close attention to 'how men are.' Before that, he had based his thoughts about married folks on his own household. Grandma, mama, Mozzelle and even Arlene were women who would not dream of being talked down to. As a matter of fact, the only member of the Roebuck household who took mess off anybody was Gregory.

He turned his bike around and coasted back to the road and pedaled all the way down across the creek bridge and up through the turn-past aunt May's empty house and the church. He did not stop pedaling until he got home. He was mad at himself. Didn't he remember?

He had gone over in his mind how Mr. Ervin, Reverend Esterbrook and them treated their women. It did not take him long to feel, hear and see every one of them talking to their wives the way grown people talked to children. Mixed in with his own resentment of being talked down to was that stuff. He had not let himself take it all in. He had good feelings about those men just like he did about Mr. Bill. Now that he thought about it though, they were not that different from the bullies he hated so much.

"I love mama and Mo. But when I think of it, toward younguns, they were kinda like that too. But he had made mama and Mo stop whipping him. How come those other women didn't make their men stop treating them like they did? He could tell that he was starting to blame the women for the way the men acted. He couldn't shape in his head why he shouldn't do that although he intuited that it was wrong. He knew why he always took up for boys at school who couldn't fight; it was the same reason Durango Kid, Red Rider and them took on gunslingers who bullied sarsparilla drinkers.

* * *

'Where'n the world're my dogs?' Randolph's thought had a country twang as it sometimes did when he looked out across the hollow. He could only see trash and trees in front of him. But his mind and his gaze floated down through the woods, past the spring and blackberry patch-up through the fields that rose all the way to Arjay's as the crow flies.

For two days he had either stood here by the trash pit or over near the back porch and tried to imagine that Flossie and Jack were somewhere between here and yonder. "HEARR FLOSSIE! HEARR JACK!" He felt weak inside. Today and yesterday were the first times he ever called the dogs and they didn't come runnin'. He yelled their names out across the trees and fields at the top of his voice that echoed back to him and gave him a lonesome feeling deeper than the one he felt when he turned up the radio so Little Jimmy Dickin's voice would come out of the house and whine across the hollow.

I'M JUST A PLAIN OLD COUNTRY BOY
A CORNBREAD LOVIN' COUNTRY BOY
I RAISE CAIN ON A SATURDAY NIGHT
BUT I GO TO CHURCH ON SUNDAY

A belief that he could will Jack and Flossie home, went limp. He walked over to the porch and sat on the bottom step. "I'm not gonna cry..."What's that...?" He sniffed the air in front of him. Whatever it was he smelled, it wasn't in front of him. He turned his head over his shoulder and sniffed again. It came from back there. After a moment, he knew it couldn't be coming from the house or the porch. He knelt down beside the steps. The smell was coming from under the house; he crawled under the porch to one of the stone pylons. The smell rushed up his nose. "Pew-ee!" He pushed air out of his nostrils. "Pew-ee!"

As a little boy, Randolph used to crawl up under here when nobody was lookin'. He couldn't remember when he last crawled into the dark under the house.

The stink was almost strong enough to keep him from doing it now but...he crawled toward the thick part of the dark and stench knowing what he would find. The smell was all around him like a creek of funk.

About halfway under the dining room-a little to the left, he saw a patch darker than the rest of the darkness. "Oh Lord!" He couldn't make out what the dark lump was... didn't need to. "Oh Lord!" It was one of the dogs. It was too dark under here to see which one it was. He scanned the space under the kitchen and pantry, nothing. He looked straight ahead at the space under the rest of the dining room, nothing. To the right was a small space under the hallway. Beyond that, the ground rose up close to the living room floor. Whichever dog it was, to his left, it was the only one under here. Randolph crawled back out into the light and fresh air.

Behind the chicken coop was a spade leaning against the wall. His shirt was wet enough with sweat that it clung to him. He fixed his mind on that. If he allowed himself to think about what was under the house, he would not be able to go back under there.

He pushed the spade ahead of him while his eyes got used to the dark again.

He edged the spade toward the dead dog so that he could force it into the dirt beneath the carcass. It was hard to grip the handle and push it at the same time, his hands sweated so. "God give me strength." He pushed-wiped his hands on his shirt-pushed and prayed and wiped his hands again. When he was about to give up, Randolph felt the shovel slide under the dead weight. "Thank you Jesus."

He pulled slow so the body of his pet wouldn't slide off.

In the light, he glanced at the load just long enough to see that it was Jack. He did not look again until he had dragged him over to the wood pile. He gulped air to refreshen and to bolster himself. The dog was on its side, dried foam caked on its half open mouth. That sight nearly made Randolph sick. But he saw that Jack's stomach was gaping. There were what must have been hundreds of white worms crawling over and around one another, his own stomach churned. He kept wiping sweat from his face. When he touched his forehead his hand was shaking. The churning in his gut erupted into a strean of puke he was able to stop at the back of his throat, the stregnth came from the collective voice of old folks, "Ya gotta be strongwilled." He heard and trusted it.

Jack's coat-fluffy and white when he was alive, looked stiff and yellow. The only white thing now was all those little bitty worms crawling around in the big hole in his stomach.

Randolph took stock of himself. He wasn't sweating any longer. His hands were steady, his mind was clear.

The maggots were spilling over the edge of the spade. He would have to find something bigger to haul Jack down to the bottom, back below the cow shed. He had not thought of burying the dog down there, he just knew he was going to.

A sheet of tin in the trash pit was plenty big enough to hold Jack's body. When he came back to the woodpile to dump the dog onto the sheet of tin, Randolph started sweating again. "Oh Lord! Oh Lord!" He didn't let himself quit until the carcass was on the makeshift sled. Some of the white worms spilled in the dirt and mixed in with chips. He shoveled them onto the tin next to Jack.

When he got beyond the cow shed and was pulling the sheet down the slope, Jack's body and the worms slid down toward his hands. He lifted the edge of the tin in time to avoid having that whole mess get on him and drive him crazy. The sweat across his forehead itched like the dickens; he couldn't take a hand off to scratch. He was caught between distraction and the neeed to buck up; need won out.

It was easy to dig a hole, the bottom was an old creek bed. It was almost fun thrusting the spade into the soft sand.

Before he buried the dog, Randolph got down on one knee. "Gracious Lord! Take ol'Jack on home. Let your countenance shine upon him..." He was too tight to recollect anything more from the many prayers he had heard. It was alright. He knew it was the thought that counted.

Randolph put Jack in the hole-tin sheet and all, it was his casket. He shoveled the sand over him. "Ashes to ashes, dust to dust."

With the spade across his shoulder, he headed up the slope with the satisfaction of having done what he was suppose to. The hill was steep but it was a short hike. Still, before he reached the cow shed, he felt tired-weak. He sat down in the grass and put the spade down.

It came to fourteen year old Randolph that he had known that dog since he was two years old-just about all his life. It filled him up that Jack had been his good buddy. Of all the dogs they ever had, it was Jack... tears burst from his sudden sorrow.

Randolph Wilford had cried any number of times in any number of ways. This time he cried in a brand new way. He thought of daddy and grandma. Cousin Ames and Trixie. His voice drifted through his saliva-down to Jack's grave. "Lord! I'm tired of crying!"

Before his pain could swallow him all the way up, he felt something behind him. Flossie was standing half way between him and the cow shed, wagging her tail to beat the band. "Where you been all this time, girl! You sure are a sight for sore eyes." She came close to let him pet and hug her soft fur until his crying stopped.

* * *

With all his galivantin' around Randy didn't get a lot done. On the way up here he noticed that the grass back of the house needs to be mowed...better get it done before Mo comes home from New York.

From the orchard, you look across the drying corn in the garden; then across the road to the Methodist church sitting back there in a glade.

The long narrow shape of the orchard he stood in, the garden next to it and the dusty road before the white clapboard church cross yonder, reminds Randolph of a bowling alley in Bethesda, Maryland. 'I forgot I used to set pins.'

The tips were little more than nothing. By the time he bought a tuna sandwich on toast with potato chips and a pickle, the pitiful amount of money was gone. But every night when he and his buddies took the streetcar back to D. C., he was happy as a sissy in a C.C. Camp.

This orchard, lined with apple trees, plum-peach and plain-peach trees, black muscadime vines and one pear tree, was like one of those lanes. So was the long narrow garden. The road was the last bowling lane. The church-with a thicket of dogwoods on both sides, was the snack bar. He stood there enjoying what he had conjured until he got his fill.

The nostalgia rode from the corners of his mouth-down through him until it joined gravity beneath his feet.

Feeling light, Randy turned and walked up the island between the rows of fruit trees. Buzzing above him was a pair of blue wasps 'doing it' in flight. They reminded him of how it used to drive him crazy when Jack and Flossie would do it down behind the Baptist church.

Across the the lespedezas patch above the orchard, there was another memory. Beyond that field of green weeds-was a house he was in once, only once. That day, Archie took a white girl named Kitty through the kitchen door and did it to her under the back steps. Randolph had been left inside to watch Kitty's baby brother. When Archie and Kitty came back into the house holding hands, they were both giggling. Kitty's eyes were like morning dew. "Good God Almighty!"

Her family moved-Randolph couldn't remember where Archie said they moved to. He wondered what she must look like now. He pictured her with her plain gray dress hanging over her titties and hips; she looked near 'bout grown.

Won't nothin' to write home about, doin it to a girl. He, himself, ain't never done it with a white girl, but he sure usto have him some colored girls.

Three years in Cedar Grove this time, Randolph ain't had one single girl. It confused him that back when he was small, girls thought he was cute. They not only let him have his way, they made sure he did. Now they seemed to get mad if he looked like he was even thinkin' about puddin'.

'Shit!' That sure hurts.'

Chapter Seven
New Awakenings

It was like a dream. Randolph had come in here looking for that clearing of moss where Arlene used to help him read while they waited for Rob Roy to bring the mail. Each time he found the area, he was made to accept that it was over grown with weeds and saplings. He came in here every now and then anyway as if he could sneak up on the quiet green bed of moss before the years could catch up to him.

This time, he came across a little moss clearing that looked like the one he remembered, but he was not able to pretend he had gone back to four years old. A trick-memory took him instead to the middle of a December day when he was eight years old.

Randolph, Dupont, Satchel, Ames and Henry were up in Maryland near the swimming hole they called Beaver Dam. They had made like they were hunting for Christmas trees; they didn't have hatchets or anything to chop nothing down. The truth was, they were making an excuse to roam around in the fields and woods. Randolph saw several white boys coming over a rise. Maybe it was that he had not seen young white boys since he and his first buddy, Stephen, used to beat them up going to and from the colored school-maybe it was because Satchel and Dupont had boxing gloves that he and the others put on and paired off every night in Dupont and Sachel's basement; Randolph had gotten to be a pretty good pug-maybe today he felt a little bit like going for bad-maybe he was just a little crazy as he sometimes was. Whatever the reason, he started yelling stuff at the white boys. "Hey! Soda crackers! What you sissies doing out here?"

"Y'all lookin' for some poke salad to feed your mamas?" Dupont and Ames tried to shut him up. They each asked him if he'd lost his mind. Maybe he had, cause he just couldn't stop. "I ain't beat the shit outta a white punk in a long time. Come on down here, lemme go upside your head!"

"Randy, shut the hell up!" Dupont meant that if Randolph didn't shut up he would kick his ass. Before anything else could be said, the white boys were right up on them. There were seven. And every one of them was bigger than Ames and Dupont, the biggest of Randy's boys.

The biggest of the big white boys had bulging muscles like Dupont. He wasn't as tall as a couple of the other white boys, but he looked stronger. His boys called him Shank. Randolph could tell right off that they didn't call him Shank because of the Bowie knife in a scabbard on his hip. He got his nickname because his left arm ended about half way below his elbow.

"What'chou sayin' smartass?" Shank drew his dagger and winked at Dupont before going for Randolph. He threw Randolph down and put the blade close to his neck. "Who the hell you think you're talkin' to!" Randolph wasn't all that scared. He saw Shank when he winked at Dupont. But nothing about what was happening made sense. When he was six and seven, he and Stephen had beat up white boys any time they took a notion to. A couple of the ones he punched out were almost as big as these guys. The boys he and Stephen beat up all had a soft kinda way about them. Shank and his boys weren't anything like that. They had a look about them that put him in mind of outlaws in cowboy movies.

Although Randolph had seemed to be half crazy-and was-when he yelled at these guys and acted the fool, he did so based on everything he knew about white boys. He was messin' with this bunch partly to show his own boys that you could treat white boys any way you wanted to-they were punks.

Here he was, his ass in the grass, and this motherfucker, Shank was treating him like he, Randolph Wilford, was the punk. And all his boys were standing around looking dumb. Worse, all the white boys were giggling at him. And even worst than that, Dupont was laughing as if he was takin' sides with the white boys.

"Tell me you're sorry you fucked with me."

"I'm sorry!" Randolph heard his voice say that even if he didn't mean it. He just wanted this whole thing to stop so he could go about putting it behind him. "Now, promise you ain't gonna ever mess with another white boy in your life." That did it. Randolph's hurt and shame rushed from his eyes and dripped out of his nose.

"You can cry all you want to punk. You had no business fuckin' with us."

"I'm sorry! I swear I won't fuck with y'all no more!" He didn't care how bad he looked or sounded, he just wanted to make this stop.

Dupont finally stepped forward. "OK. That's enough. He said he was sorry."

Shank stood up and wiped his sweat and Randolph's tears off his dagger blade. He was grinning and winked at Dupont again. He looked down at Randolph while he put his weapon in its scabbard. "I wasn't gonna hurt you. I just wanted to teach you a lesson." Randolph looked away from Shank. He couldn't stand somebody puttin' a hurt on him. And as if it wasn't bad enough that this white boy had made him look like a fool, Randolph had been wrong about white boys, to boot. It was even worse than finding out that learning the multiplication table didn't make learning other stuff any easier.

Every time he was wrong it hurt almost as much as getting his ass kicked. Shank and his boys walked away laughing and joking about the fun they'd just had.

"Randolph, what's the matter with you? Why'd you start stuff with those white boys?" Dupont's question gave Randolph an unexpected release. "Goddamnit! I don't know." Of course he knew; he thought he was gonna give his buddies a show. But once he got goin' he couldn't stop. That was the part-the crazy part-he didn't understand.

Sitting here on the moss, Randolph almost broke down. He did not feel sad about the memory of what happened with Shank when he was eight years old. In fact, that had slippd back to where it came from. What he was all bound up about, happened yesterday-up the road a piece from the mailboxes.

He still went over to play with Holly every now and then. But he never really got over the time he called him nigger in front of R.J. and them. One day, coming from Holly's house, he took the shortcut past the cemeteries. He saw two white boys his size playing in their yard. Their house sat back from a little crook in the road between the graveyards and the mailboxes. Randolph had seen them before. He never had a notion to do anything more than

115

wave and say "Hey." Today though, the two boys asked him if he wanted to come and play with them. He rode into the yard and they played for a little while. After that, they commenced to play together in the boys' yard near 'bout every day. Henny and Herman turned out to be twins.

After a week or so, the three boys got to be close buddies. Miz Talmadge, their mother, would call them around to the back door to give them graham crackers and milk. This was turning out to be a real good Summer. Randolph could admit to himself that he did not like Holly all that much no how, now he had the twins to play with. They were real friends cause they were fourteen like he was. Miz Talmadge was nice too. Another thing, Henny and Herman talked in a way that sounded like they were comfortable talking in different kinds of ways, like he did.

The twins and their mama would sometimes talk proper, they sometimes spoke, country like Mo and them, sayin' stuff like 'directly,' 'commence,' 'make haste' and other down home words. They also spoke in another kind of country...hillbilly country. "Yessiree! the Good Lord willin' and the crick don't rise."

Herman and Henny had a real gone sayin' they used when something went right like hitting the rubber ball across the road or winning at horseshoes. They would say, "Hot damn! I'm in the catbird seat now." Randolph didn't know what a catbird seat was, but he surely knew what they meant when they said that.

Since the day they yelled out to the road asking him to come into the yard and play with them, Randolph was in the catbird seat. Sometimes he wondered why he never had any white buddies before. His mind didn't sit down on it, the thought would just run through now and then.

One day the three boys were playing tag out in the yard. Miz Talmadge called the twins to the back door. Randolph noticed that she did not call all three names the way she always did. He didn't pay it much mind though. By the time they got around to the back steps, he could smell the Graham crackers.

"What'chou want nigger?" She wasn't kiddin' neither. Randolph looked her right dead in the eye'n she wasn't smiling-not one bit. He grinned at her anyway. He couldn't think of anything else to do. "You heard me Sambo. What'chou want?"

Either Henny or Herman said "Yeah nigger, what'chou want?" The Randolph Wilford who was in touch with his pride-the boy who had learned when he was six years old not to take no shit, would have shot back, "Fuck you soda cracker motherfucker!" He surely would have noted that Miz Talmadge meant to hurt him. He would have added, "Fuck your mama too." Then he would have glared at the twins, waiting for one or both of them to break bad. That was what Randolph would have done if he was in touch with himself. The Randolph standing here at the foot of these white people's back steps hearing what he had to believe inspite of everything in him, was one of his dreams or that he had lost his mind; this Randolph couldn't say a mumbling word.

He found himself moving toward Susie Q. parked in the front yard. He felt like...he didn't know what or how he felt. Truth was, he came close to one thing after another. He almost felt hurt, he was close to feeling lost. The two feelings bumped up against one another and pinballed off rage. Self pity tried to inch in there but a confused numbness pushed everything out of the way.

Randolph mounted his bike Durango Kid style as usual. Nothing else was usual, though. Bouncing off the back fender, the seat and the back of his head was stuff like "Tar baby!" "Monkey!" "Beadyhead nigger!" What got his attention more than the names he heard was the voice of Miz Talmadge yelling after him as if she was a youngun like her two boys. 'What kinda grown woman would be carryin' on like that?'

The sound of Rob Roy's T' Model coming down the road made him picture the little mail truck passing the Talmadge house. It wiped all the shit away and Randy's thoughts came clean as he anticipated mail from mama, maybe a letter from Lucille; she hadn't written in a long time.

By the time he got up off the moss and walked out to the mailboxes, Rob Roy was chugging to a stop. The old man's crinkly, sparkling blue eyes made Randolph think of Santa Claus like always. "How'do young feller."

"How'do."

* * *

Day before yesterday, Mozzelle wrote she would be home sometime next week. Yesterday, Randy did the grass between the back of the house and the orchard. It had grown so tall he had to cut it down with the scythe before he could mow it. Today, he was doing the front and side yards. Before he got started, he did what he had done a number of times since Mo went to New York. He closed the front door, opened the side windows and the back door then tuned the radio to WNOX out of Knoxville, Tennessee-it came in loud and clear. He turned the volume high as it would go. The twang and whine of good ol' country music drifted out those windows and that door, down the hill across the hollow, blackbery patch and up the other side where Randy imagined it reached all the way to Arjay's two gas pumps and circled back to echo off the hollow and back up to his waiting ears.

SHE'S MY HEART'S BO-KAYYY
SHE'S MY HEART'S BO-KAYYY
I PICKED 'ER FROM THE FIELD OF LOVE ONE DAY
I LOVED 'ER THEN
I LOVE 'ER STILLL
CROSS MY HEART I ALWAYS WILL
SHE'S MY DARLIN'
SHE'S MY HEART'S BO-KAYYY

Randolph pushed the mower forward four beats, pulled back two then pushed forward again in rhythm while he sang along with Little Jimmy Dickens in whooping-hillbilly-twang. He placed a girl in his feelings without picturing her in his mind. His 'heart's bouquet' was an amalgam of the girl in the song and the one he longed to possess someday soon.

SHE'S MY HEART'S BO-KAAAY
SHE'S MY HEART'S BO-KAAAY
I PICKED 'ER FROM THE FIELD OF LOVE ONE DAY
I LOVED 'ER THENNN
I LOVE 'ER STILLL
CROSS MY HEART I ALWAYS WILLL
SHE'S MY DARLIN'
SHE'S MY HEART'S BO-KAAAY

The whir of the push mower blades was in perfect country harmony with Randolph and the singing star on the radio who presented a clear picture in Randolph's mind. As the thin whine of

118

his voice rang out across the hollow, Randolph saw a short, slim, sandy haired man with red freckles and shiny white teeth.

Listening and imagining, he dang near ground up a turtle in the blades of the lawn mower before stopping just short of the yellow speckled-brown-shell of the creeping creature. "Hey fella. How come you're crawling right in my path?"

His hand barely spanned across the shell as he moved the turtle to an area he had already mowed.

In perfect time with the return of his attention to the radio, Randolph's favorite hillbilly was strumming into his hit song that sounded for all the world like the jump music sung by Colored stars on that same radio station at night. It was "The singing Ranger," Hank Snow. Hank Snow had a voice about as mellow as Bullmoose Jackson's or Bing Crosby's. He didn't have a twang; his words were smooth. The song was, "Im moving on." It had a railroad chugging bounce that made Randy want to break loose.

THAT BIG EIGHT WHEELER ROLLIN' DOWN THE TRACK
MEANS YOUR TRUE LOVIN' DADDY AIN'T COMIN' BACK
I'M MOVIN' ON... I'LL SOON BE GONE

The guitar strum was a rumbling lope.

MR. FIREMAN WON'T YOU PLEASE LISTEN TO ME
'CAUSE I GOT A PRETTY MAMA IN TENNESSEE
KEEP MOVIN' ME ON... KEEP ROLLIN' ON

The Singing Ranger had Randolph trying to do The Hucklebuck on the green grass of Cedar Grove on that bright afternoon. He duckwalked up toward the garden and back toward the mower, movin' on.

I'VE TOLD YOU BABY FROM TIME TO TIME
BUT YOU JUST WOULDN'T LISTEN OR PAY ME NO MIND
NOW I'M MOVIN' ON... I'M ROLLON' ON

Randolph's hands were back on the handle pushing the mower full forward-half back, in time with the music.

BUT SOMEDAY BABY WHEN YOU'VE HAD YOUR PLAY
YOU'RE GONNA WANT YOUR DADDY BUT YOUR
DADDY WILL SAY
KEEP MOVIN' ON... YOU STAYED AWAY TOO LONG
I'M THROUGH WITH YOU, TOO BAD YOU'RE BLUE
KEEP MOVIN' ON

"Hot dog!" His hands were free again, swinging in rhythm to his duckwalkin'-hucklebuckin' clod hoppers. Movin' on.

* * *

Today is the last Saturday before Mozzelle was to come home. If she were here, Randolph knew, even if he'd finished his chores, he would have to hang around til she thought of something to keep him busy. He might have made her stop whipping him but she still did her best to keep him from going off somewhere to play.

One Saturday a few weeks ago, Randolph mounted his steed and rode up to Midway to watch a ball game. This might be his last chance to do it again so, he'd better git to gittin'. He made sure the front and back doors were shut before he hopped on Susie Q and headed up the road. When he passed the mule track, leading to Archie and them's house, he was reminded that Archie had moved back home from Durham. Randolph was also reminded of one day when he accompanied Verniece down to the church where she practiced piano cause she was gonna play the following Sunday.

"Lord!" That girl near 'bout drove him crazy the way she sashayed about in her gingham frock-making her nineteen year old hips and titties lay up against it- something'another like watermelons and cantaloupes in a croaker sack. "Good God A'mighty!" He sat on the front pew looking at her back while she played, "Nearer My God To Thee." Randolph felt ashamed-he knew it must be a sin to think...rather, to feel what he was feeling. But he gave himself release by recalling that he had told the Lord he was going to keep all The Commandments except the Seventh one.

Once guilt was cleared from his mind, the hymn Verniece was practicing might as well have been, "Embrace Me My Sweet Embraceable You" or "Just A Kiss And A rose."

120

One time, a bee had stung Verniece on the shoulder. For a minute, Randolph saw her in just her skirt and bra. He was standing behind her, she didn't know he was there. 'Oh Verniece!' The sight of her smooth brown back made him imagine she and he were husband and wife-she was undressing to climb in bed with him. Now, as she played, he could see her soft shoulder blades move beneath her pale blue frock. It got into him to unbutton his fly and pull his peter out. Good sense resisted to no avail; Randolph just whipped it out, then pretended to be asleep.

Verniece practiced the song three times before she turned on the piano stool to look at her young friend. Without hesitating, she, in a sense, dragged him down the hill and dipped him in the cool water of the baptizing pool. Verniece accomplished that by saying, "Randy! Wake up and put your private in your pants before you catch a cold."

His memory made him cringe with embarrassment before he jerked his mind away from Verniece all together and pumped hard to get over the little hump just before the mailboxes-the cemetery road.

Mild exertion supplanted his reflection before breath came easy and he coasted downhill toward the Kennedy's place near the bottom and kept his attention on pedaling up to the top of the next hill.

* * *

Far back's the young cowpoke could remember, he fancied living in the big white house of Chester Burns' with it's gables and running water.

A week ago, Gregory borrowed Mr. Ervin's pickup to carry a new heifer up to the house with the long driveway, before you reached Chester Burns's. Gregory explained that the young cow needed to be mated with a bull before she could give milk. Randolph near'bout fell out of the truck when Gregory opened his yella mouth and said, "Folks call it animal husbandry." He had specks of brown tobacco stains on his teeth; it wasn't the speckled grin that bowled Randolph over, it was that Gregory knew a big word.

Randolph anticipated seeing that 'Duel In The Sun' ranch house up close. He had always wondered who lived there. When they turned onto the long driveway, it occured to him that he not only was gonna find out who lived in the house but he was gonna see a bull do it to a cow. "Hot dog!"

The farmer as it turned out, is named Odell Burns. Gregory said he wasn't no kin to Chester Burns. He was a tall skinny man with a thin mustache above thin pale lips.

Odell had a thin voice that sounded exactly like Randy expected it would-cousin Hilda's voice sounded like she looked, peachy. This man, who was the color of straw, had a voice that sounded kinda like that.

Randolph took a liking to Odell until, when he was leading the cow off the pickup, he said, "Greg. You don't want the boy to watch while the bull is mounting the heifer, do you?" Randolph looked at Gregory, it was clear as day he didn't care if "the boy saw the bull mount the heifer." But it was just as clear that Gregory wanted to seem like a good Christian man which everybody-near-and-far-knew-damned-well-he-was-not.

"I most certainly don't... Randy, go on over yonder over that rise. I'll call you when it's alright to come back."

Randolph could have said, 'I see chickens, dogs, bumble bees...hell I done seen birds flyin' in the air, doin' it. How come..." He let it be.

Forty or fifty yards away, beyond the rise, he cursed himself for not saying something. He soon realized though, he could crawl up almost to the crest of the little ridge and see all he wanted to. He did crawl the few feet in time to see a massive bull mount the young cow being held still by the two men. He had not known what to expect. When he saw chickens do it, they kinda fluttered for a minute and went back to pecking in the dirt like nothing had happened. The first time he saw birds flying through the air doin' it, they just looked like they were stuck together. When dogs did it, he always got the feeling that the male dog was taking pussy from the female-it was exciting, even though it made him uncomfortable.

When that big ol' bunch of muscles got up on his hind legs to mount the plump heifer, it was like seeing for the first time how God created thunder and lightening. Something mighty was happening. Randolph felt himself get hard against the ground

122

underneath him. "Damn! Damn! The bull made him think the whole county rumbled. He grabbed onto the grass with both hands, laughing at himself for acting like he didn't have right good sense. His laughter didn't drown out the sound of the heifer mooing like he used to hear Bessie do when he was milking her with a gentle stroke. "Damn! Damn!

The bull got down off the cow and Randy saw his dick-lookin' like a rhinoceros horn dripping goo.

That was a magic kind of memory. It was one of those things he had seen yet wasn't really sure he had. He pedaled by Chester Burn's big house. That house wasn't ever going to mean as much to him after what he had seen in Odell Burn's barnyard.

He coasted down the second hill toward the gulley that he thought of as the halfway point. There was a farm to his right. That farm was like farms on every road he traveled. He did not recall seeing anybody go in or out of the house or barn or plow the fields. This farm, and all the ones like it, might as well be in picture books.

In the gully after the next hill, Randolph passed the spot where he had seen the curious looking, square-shaped-brown-and-yellow-snake. Sometimes stuff he saw and did every day was, like the farm back there, something or 'nother like a fairy tale. A thought of the Garden of Eden flitted through his mind. He did not remember that a similar thought went through his mind when he saw the snake that day.

* * *

The dirt road ran into the blacktop at the crest of the last hill-Midway showed a bold face with a series of red brick buildings-Midway School. Like the Colored school he was headed to, this school for whites went from First through Ninth grade. It wasn't like his school in any other way. This White school did not cause Randolph to get mad or envious the way Calvin Cooledge High School back in Washington did. Maybe that was because this school didn't have a tennis court, a swimming pool and archery range like Calvin Cooledge. Maybe it was because he had just gotten used to White schools being a lot better than the ones Negroes had. Every time he went by, he did try to imagine what it must be like to be a student there.

When he turned Susie Q. onto his schoolhouse road, a little light went on. Somewhere down there where his lamp drew its fuel, he sorta knew, he wouldn't trade the white clapboard, "Midway School for Colored Children" a quarter mile ahead, for nothin' in the world. That feeling made him commence to giggle.

* * *

Folks crowded around the ballfield making a racket. The game was about to start or had just started. Randolph leaned his bike against a tree. "S'cuse me." He had bumped into somebody... didn't get a good look at who it was because he was looking at a young woman in a white dress with big purple flowers on it. "Lord have mercy!" Given his druthers, Randolph Wilford cottoned to what he thought of as 'Hershey colored girls.' But sometimes he saw a 'Bit O'Honey with eyes like crunchy peanut butter that made him have to breathe hard to keep from falling over. The woman in the flowered dress was one of them. "Lord have mercy!" Much as he wanted to keep ogling the woman, he was pulled away by the voice of William Pinkett who ran Midway's only Colored barber shop. "PLAY BALL!" Mr. Pinkett was still adjusting his umpire's mask when he barked the order. Randolph worked his way into the part of the crowd along the first base line. Voices-grown folks and a few children-seemed to be saying stuff that didn't have much to do with baseball. The Blue Jays were up. The other team was the Cardinals; both were local teams. They were in different leagues and played each other twice during the season.

That was all there was to it for most onlookers. For the real fans though, there was a heap that didn't meet the eye. For one thing, the winning team had bragging rights-if one team won both of the interleague games, they could talk trash from early Fall through the Winter and into the following Spring-not to mention, "Them little fast girls runnin' 'round here." Randolph had actually heard a woman explain that to a girlfriend during one game.

David Hill was on the mound. He had two strikes on the Blue Jays shortstop. "STRIIIKE THREE!' Before Mr. Pinkeett's bellow faded, Randolph shouted to no one in particular. "Ha! That ol' boy didn't even see that fast ball!"

On his way to the bench, the boy turned to look at the plate the way a stumbler looks back at the ground for the pebble-or whatever it was-that tripped him. Getting no satisfaction, he looked down at his shoes the rest of the way back to the Blue Jays' bench.

David Hill was a tall broad shouldered seventeen year old with light skin and steel gray eyes. He stared down the Blue Jays' batters and struck out the side. Randolph was elated. It wasn't that he liked the Cardinals anymore than he did the Blue Jays, he just happened to know David and liked him because he sometimes came down to Cedar grove to visit.

David walked with long sure strides from the mound. He soaked in cheers from all around. Support from behind the backstop and along both base paths was typical at home and home games. Most of the folks had relatives or at least a friend or two on each team.

Randolph took in the crowd while the players switched sides. He looked around to find the woman in the flowered dress. She had disappeared. That didn't stop him from enjoying what he did see and hear. Across the diamond from his spot, half way up the baseline, was a woman who was a sight to behold. She was wearing tan gabardine slacks and a yellow blouse with a ribbon collar tied in a bow under her dimpled tan chin. Barely visible, in the shadow of a wide brim straw hat, Randy saw her white frame-shades. Talking to the decked out woman was a heavy set dark complected man in light blue overalls who took swigs from a pint Mason jar between words. Randolph's eyes slid up to third base to start a sweep down to the backstop and around to his side of the diamond-all the way up to first base.

Everybody seemed to be with somebody. He kept scanning the loop between first base on his right and third base, across the infield. He hoped he would see the woman in the flowered dress again. He did not expect that she would give his young ass a look that would encourage him, or even a friendly grin. On the other hand, he could not help making himself expect something even less likely; that she would wink at him. But she was not even still out here...Like a mirage, the purple flowers and tan face pushed into the crowd along the third base path. She must've been coming back from one of the outhouses. Through happy eyes, Randolph looked her over again. This time, he decided what had been chunky peanut butter eyes were shoo-fly-pie eyes.

She saw him looking at her. "Damn straight!" He knew good and well she did. Nothing in the woman's demeanor gave the slightest hint that she knew Randy was anywhere in the county. In his mind though, she saw him looking at her. He kept an eye out for a sign from her while the Cardinals came to bat. Their short, skinny second baseman hit a hard line drive and wound up with a double. Randolph got a kick out of the fact that there the guy was, standing on the very base he played. The next two batters struck out.

David Hill, was not only the Cardinals' best pitcher, he was their best hitter too. He stepped into the batter's box and on the first pitch hit a high fly ball that carried all the way into the yard of the Dew Drop Inn across the road beyond rightfield. The boy who had been on second base came around to score. Big yellow David trotted around the bases with a look in his gray eyes that said, 'Aw., t'wern't nothin'. The Cardinals scored a couple more runs before making the third out.

In each of the next five innings, Randolph sneaked peeks for a sign from the pretty woman in the flowered dress. There still was no indication she even knew he was there.

In the bottom of the seventh, the first two Cardinal hitters hit fly balls that were caught. After those two outs, they scored six runs. One of the Blue Jay outfielders, who was also the manager, called time and came in to change pitchers. Randolph saw all the folks along the third base line looking toward his side of the diamond. He couldn't see who or what they were looking at until a guy came out of the crowd bunched up near first base.

"It's Archie!" Randolph nearly said out loud. 'Where'd he come from?' His next thought was to wonder if Archie was the new pitcher... 'Naw. He ain't no pitcher.'

Archie headed straight for the mound. Randy actually spoke this time. "Well, I'll be damned." He watched and waited. The manager called the catcher to the mound. He said something to him and his new pitcher. Then he returned to his center field position. Randolph felt his body twitch-he took a few deep breaths. He kept taking breaths to keep clinging to hope. It was hard. Concern for his friend had grabbed hold of him.

Archie finished throwing warmup pitches. Randolph was gasping; he bounced on the balls of his feet to keep control of his nerves. Archie threw lefthanded. Randy had never noticed that his buddy was a southpaw. "Wow!" Not only was Archie left handed, he threw side-arm. Randolph had not seen a pitcher throw like that. It looked funny.

Maybe the first guy to hit against Archie was baffled by the way he threw, he struck out on three pitches. Randolph turned his attention away from his own nervousness. Taking note of the rest of the crowd, he was proud that Archie had them in the palm of his hand.

The second hitter to face Archie struck out too. "All right now, sidewinder!" The woman's voice sounded husky-like a sexpot in the movies. It had to be who he thought it was. Sure enough, when he looked across the field, he saw the woman in the flowered dress waving at Archie. You could tell that Archie saw her as well. You could also tell he was comfortable with himself.

Big David stepped into the batter's box. "Striiike one!" So far, so good. David grinned as if to say, 'Yeah. You got me on that one. Come on, lay another one in here.' He dug in to show Archie what for. "Striiike two!" David stepped away from the plate. The umpire dusted it off. Archie walked behind the mound and squirted spit between his teeth. Both guys got back in place at the same time. Randolph felt a tingle run around his torso and dance across his back.

"Go 'head on sidewinder!" Her smoky voice added another kind of feeling. Randolph wanted to jump and shout like getting happy in church. David settled in and squinted at Archie who squinted back and went into his windup. He hurled that sidearm-submarine pitch that, because of how it was thrown, rose up on the batter. Big Dave saw the ball come into his wheelhouse. You could've seen his eyes get big from a mile away. He swung like won't no way he could miss-he didn't.

Archie turned around against his will. By the time he looked toward the outfield, the ball was landing across the road beyond the centerfielder.

"That's alright sidewinder. That's alright!" The woman's sexy voice held off Randolph's disappointment until some guy yelled. "Don't turn back now country." Randolph didn't like the way the man called Archie "country" like there was something low about country folks.

Before his resentment settled in, everything speeded up. The next batter singled up the middle. The one after him, beat out a bunt.

"That ol' country boy cain't play no ball!"

"Git 'im outta there!"

"Give it up sidewinder!"

Randolph waited for Miss pretty to give 'Sidewinder' some support; he heard not one word from her. Archie bristled as if the taunts had made him mad enough to want to show them what he could do. He threw the next hitter a curveball for a strike. But his second pitch hung over the plate and the batter sent it sizzling above Archie's head for a base clearing double.

"It don't mean nothin' Archie!" It occurred to Randolph it might have helped his friend if he had not been too shy to yell something before now. Archie stepped back off the mound and 'slouched like a question mark while he had stood straight like an exclamation point a few minutes ago.' Randolph's clever thought momentarily eased the pain of watching Archie look like he wanted to go somewhere and hide.

Again! "Git back on that mound country boy an' take your medicine!" When Randolph heard that, he knew damn well if it was him out there he would either yell, "Fuck you!" Or he would at least get back on the mound and do his level best to strike out the side.

He had admired Archie for knowing how to bale hay, plow fields and anything a body would want a good farmer to do. Hell, Archie even did it to white girls. Out there on the ballfield though, he got that ol' hang-dog look punks and cowards get when things go wrong.

The centerfielder/manager came in to take his pitcher out and give somebody else a try. He took the ball without looking at Archie who kept his own head down and walked through the outfield and disappeared beyond the schoolhouse.

Randolph looked for the pretty woman with the sexy voice. He knew she was probably the only one who might feel as bad about Archie as he did. She had gone with the wind.

"Humph!" The bike felt a little heavy when he lined it up to mount. His legs were near-bout numb. Randolph was not studyin' how he felt, his thoughts were trying to make sense of the way Archie didn't show grit-Archie whom he looked up to in a lot of ways.

To the main road, past the white school, down to the country road, his thoughts were just snatches.

Along the dirt road from the Colored schoolhouse Randy had to be careful because a hotrod was liable to come barreling down through there like a bat outta hell; on the highway, there was so much traffic he had to keep his wits about himself.

Here on the Cedar Grove road, you could hear a car coming a half mile away, he could let his mind roam free.

Notions came and went without grabbing hold of his interest until an image of the storage barn he helped Mr. Irvin and Archie build from the ground up, came into focus. None of the farm work, including learning to chop wood and milk the cow real good, was as satisfying as being allowed to do carpentry along side them.

He hammered and sawed, used the level and measured lengths and widths just like they did. When he made a mistake, Archie showed him the right way.

Randolph was right giddy recalling how they layed the floor then put the first sidewall together on the ground and pulled it up, propping it up until it was nailed against the frame.

Every bit of flexibility was back in his legs, up the hills and down through the gullies. During his reflection on the weeks it took to build the two story pine building, only one car interrupted the flow.

Archie, the master builder, was the star of Randolph's technicolor movie that was, for all the world, a lot like Noah building the Ark. But this time, Randolph was there, and his buddy Archie guided him along the way. A few weeks later, all four walls had been erected so that the second floor could be laid. Then the roof was set.

Randolph's memory drifted down past the tobacco barn through the pea and watermelon patches to the creek. In the cottonwood shade, snake doctors, butterflies and wasps floated and buzzed above the boys while they dogpaddled on their side of the swimming hole-away from the water moccasin.

'Why were they dogpaddling?' They were dogpaddling because when Randy tried to teach Archie the Australian crawl, he resisted.

Susie Q. rolled along like a new bought buggy-he had greased her good, just yesdiddy. At the top of the last hill, near the mailboxes, Randolph was struck alert. He had seen Archie's refusal to do the Australian crawl as a way to let him know that there was no way he was gonna allow him to teach him something; big boys didn't learn from little boys...It wasn't that at all! Archie learned about farm work from Mr. Ervin because he had no choice. If he did not do what his daddy told him, he would find hinself gettin' up off the ground. Yeah! Archie quit school soon's he turned sixteen, didn't he? He wouldn't learn any more than he had to while he was there, either. "Just 'C' me through." He used to say. Then, soon as he came of age, he was "through." He even learned to drive because he had to. "Yeah!"

Unlike many such moments, this one didn't come through a haze of intuition, but through the stark clarity of reason. For the first time, an answer grew in a row he himself had plowed.

* * *

Ruth and her friend Lil, looked about the same as when they spent a week here a few years back. When Randolph thought of it, that was the last time Lucille had come to Cedar grove. He laughed-thinking how much his big sister hated country life. She didn't like the creepy crawly things, the toad frogs, the snakes and lizards. Lucille was especially scared of bees and hornets-a bumble bee stung her that Summer. Poor girl near 'bout went crazy-spinning around-screaming and crying. Randolph was just as scared, watching her jumping so that her dress flew up and he could see her spindly ashy-knees knocking against one another like they were gonna break in two.

Yeah, she swore she was never gonna come down here again. She kept her word by convincing mama not to make her come again. After that Randolph had come down here by himself every Summer until he finally came to stay.

Lil was real brightskinned. She didn't look white like Gregory. She was a different kind of brightskin. If Lil looked like anybody, she kinda looked like the folks who ran the Chinese Laundry back in D.C. And she was pretty as a picture. Her black wavy hair was short with bangs hanging over her forehead. When she smiled, her milk-cow eyes smiled right along with her lips. Both Lil and Ruth were shorter than Ruth's two sisters-mama and Mozzelle. Mama and Mo were good looking women; kinda chocolate versions of cousin Hilda. Ruth though was hard looking. With her close bobbed hair and side of the mouth way of talking, she put both Randolph and Lucille in mind of the prizefighter Beau Jack. She may not've been pretty but Ruth was really nice to the children. So was Lil.

Randy and Lucille talked about how much nicer Ruth and Lil were than Mozzelle and mama. There was no question about that. The children could say things in front of them that they wouldn't think of saying in front of Mo and mama. They could even say damn or hell around Lil and Ruth. And both the women gave the kids lots of candy and stuff and didn't order them around. Randolph and Lucille once tried to decide which of them was nicer. They finally agreed that Ruth was real sweet, but Lil, because she was so pretty, was their favorite.

One Saturday when grandma, Mo, Gregory and Arlene went off to town to do the week's shopping, the two younguns were left at the house with Ruth and Lil.

"Randolph!" Lucille's whisper was almost too loud to be a whisper. She added, "Shhh! Come here." Randolph followed her into the hallway between the living and dining rooms. Lucille pointed to the stairway. Whimpers and pants came from the space under there where Randolph used to go when he wanted to think. At first, he ignored the sounds of Ruth and Lil doing it. He could only feel resentment that anybody else was using his space for anything at all. Then it hit him that Lucille was staring at him wondering why in the world she did not see the reaction from him she expected. He let go of resentment and came back to the sounds rising through the stairs. Both children covered their mouths to smother giggles they could not control. Ruth's head peeked around from the closet. She was grinning the way everybody, at any age, recognizes as admission of guilt-no shame though. "What are you children doing in here? How come you're not outside playing?" Lucille was thirteen, Randy was nine. Usually Lucille would have taken offense if somebody talked to her as if she and Randolph were equals. But she was, at this moment, just as stymied as her little brother.

"Y'all want some honey bisquits?" The two kids were relieved, as intended, to have something they could respond to. "Yeah," came in hurried unison.

On the edge of the front porch, they licked the residue of melted butter and honey-bisquit crumbs from their lips and fingers. When all the tackiness was gone they wiped their hands on their clothes. Then, they returned to what came before the bribe.

"You see the way Ruth looked at us?" Randolph went ahead and answered his own question. "Didn't she look like the cat that ate the canary?"

"She sure did!"

They knew that Lil and Ruth were girlfriend and... girlfriend. They had once caught the two women kissing in the pantry. At the time, Lucille had told Randolph that she was surprised to see two women kiss like that. She had long known about men who were "funny." But, she told him, she did not know that women could be that way too. Randolph nearly burst with joy. He was so glad that for a change Lucille didn't know something before he did.

If Lucille could only be down here now to see the way he looked at Ruth and Lil and the way they looked at him. She would share those looks too. There was a kind of smile and wink and giggle all-in-one-and nobody was smiling-winking or giggling. It was just a way of saying through that look, 'We know something nobody else knows. And we ain't gonna say a word. It's our secret and that's that.'

Like the time before, Ruth and Lil didn't stay but a week. They hugged him long and hard before they went back to Crestville. When they were gone, Randolph was reminded of how much he missed cousin Ames and his dog Jack and grandma. And he wished Lucille was here.

* * *

It was the same kind of clearing Randolph had been in before. And the old man in the fedora looked familiar. Even though they were out in the woods, it was like there was a window pane between them with a crack running down across the man's face. At first Randolph thought it was a scar. But the crack ran all the way from the upper lefthand corner of his vision, down to bottom right. A young woman stood in front of the man. Her back was to

132

Randolph, didn't matter, he could tell from her nappy head it was Ruth. The man had an old timey shotgun slung under his arm. The girl shifted her weight. Randolph saw the old guy wagging his finger in her face. "You're gonna turn eighteen directly. Soon's you do, I want you gone from here. No bull-dike's going to live under my roof. And when you go 'way from here, don'tchou darken my doorway ever again. If you do, I swear before Almighty God I will shoot you on sight."

Randolph knew Ruth was crying by the way her shoulders shook. "I would've filled you with buckshot today, but I had cooled down by the time I caught up to you. Follow me back to the house and remember, soon's you turn eighteen, you better be gone from here." The old man pushed Ruth aside and started walking toward the cracked window pane. He did not seem to see Randolph on the other side of the glass. Randolph tiptoed into the brush to hide anyway. The old guy walked out of the woods with Ruth following him. Neither of them saw Randolph.

On the back porch washing up, and at the kitchen table eating fried strick 'o lean, bisquits and eggs, he felt like he was close to getting a hold on the dream.

"What's on your mind Randy?" Mo had only been home since a week before Ruth and Lil came down from Crestville. Randolph told her he was just thinking about stuff. He didn't tell her about the dream, she might think he was 'bout half crazy. "Mo, I'm real glad you're home." He was changing the subject but he was telling the honest to God truth. This was the third time he had told her he was glad she had returned. The first two times, he added that he had missed her. He could tell she was pleased to hear that because she got a right peaceful look in her eyes.

Some mornings, Randolph would go through the living room so he could walk from the front porch wall, all the way around to the pantry wall. For as long as he could remember, turning past the bay window at the corner of the living room then again at the corner by the rain barrel, was an adventure.

Just feeling a little nervous about what might be around each bend gave him a teeny tiny chill. Today, he got a bonus on his way through the living room. On the wall, between the front door and the radio-phonograph-combination, was a portrait granddaddy had sat for before he died, and before Randolph was born. The painting was in a horse collar frame. The glass on the picture had always struck Randolph cause it had a crack running down across it.

While he was dreaming last night, he didn't once connect the cracked pane in the portrait to the one in the woods. He stopped to stare at grandpa. He had a Mexican bandit mustache and he was wearing a fedora hat and a necktie. The picture cut him off at his chest. "Why didn't I see that it was granddaddy in my dream?" He did not ponder for long. Taking the detour through the living room delayed getting to his chores as it was.

During the hike from the front-to the side-to the back porch, he mixed the thrill of each corner with the wonder of life and where he would take the cow to graze for the day.

What Randolph did not consider-could not, was that had he not been scared to tell Mozzelle about his dream, she would have learned what happened between her sister Ruth and papa. She would also have come to realize that her nephew had a queer ability to sometimes see outside here and now. On the other hand, maybe it was just as well that he did not know to consider and that Mo did not learn.

* * *

Rain and dark clouds depressed Randolph, except when he was up in his room listening to the staccatto drone of raindrops on the tin roof. Summer rain was like dark before dawn; what came after made it all worth while.

Unlike the perfume of honeysuckle or the robin-red-breast scent of a fresh sliced orange, there was a smell that followed a hard shower on the the green fields and dusty roads that folks and storybooks never said a thing about. It seemed like the leaves and blades held their breath while the drops fell-and the dirt lay down until the sun came curling around a dark cloud. They and the bees and butterflies, hiding out of sight, burst out into a smell of clean. Clean! He never remembered nor thought of it except the times when he was out on the road or standing in the grass after rain stopped. The sky was half gray-half bright. The air just above the ground where his nose couldn't miss it, smelled brand-spanking-new-clean.

He walked slow, pondered and inhaled the after rain the whole way from his driveway to the mule path from the Mills' house. "Hey Randy!"

He had not seen Archie coming toward the main road.

"Hey Archie. Whattaya-say?"

"Looked like you was way cross yonder somewhere."

Randolph wanted to tell his buddy what he had been thinking...feeling. Yeah, he wasn't thinking, he was feeling. He realized that right off, cause there wasn't no way he could have told Archie or anybody else what had hold of him. "Just daydreaming."

"Goin' to the mailbox?"

"Yep."

"Me too."

Randolph felt the heft of Archie's voice and his full-head taller height. Archie's near grown presence reminded him of how bad he still wanted to become a man.

He hadn't thought about it much since that day, but the notion of becoming grown brought his mind back to the sight of Archie on the mound. "Sidewinder." A picture of the pretty woman wearing the white shades went through his mind like a gust of wind. "Done any pitching lately?"

"Shoot! I cain't pitch."

"What'chou mean?" Randolph had allowed himself to forget how badly Archie did that day. He glanced at the house to his left. Kitty the white girl Archie did it to used to live there.

"I let them ol' boys talk me into goin' on the mound'n makin' a fool outta myself."

Archie made him so upset, Randolph forgot all about Kitty. "What the hell you talkin' 'bout? You can pitch. You didn't make no fool outta yourself!"

"You don't know nothin' 'bout pitchin'. So just shut up."

"Who you tellin' to shut up?"

"You."

"Fuck you."

"Say what!"

"You heard me. Fuck you!" Archie stopped. "I dare you to say it again." "Fuck you! Fuck you! Fuck..." Randolph felt Archie's fist where his next word was gonna be. It hurt enough that he rubbed his lips expecting blood to be there. No blood. He threw a left hook knowing this old country boy didn't know half as much about pugging as he did. The blow surprised Archie more than it stung him-coming from the side of his vision. Randolph was dancing-bobbing and grinning. "That ain't nothin'. Wanna see what else I can do?"

The same pride that made archie give up on becoming a pitcher made him summon the grit to throw a haymaker that almost knocked Randolph on his ass. Randolph caught his balance and threw a three punch combination-left-right-left to the ribs and another left hook to the jaw. He knew immediately that, pretty as his punches were, they were only like three hits from a house fly and just made Archie madder. "You had any white pussy lately?" The question caught his big buddy off guard, but it was loud enough to tickle him. "What'chou talkin' bout boy?" Randolph threw a play jab into his chest. "You know what I'm talkin' bout." Archie took the time to finish his laugh. "Naw. Not since Kitty and them moved up the road a piece."

They walked in-step like a near grown and a less grown pair of soldiers on a parade field. The flare-up was history. "Where they move to?" "Somebody said they moved to Richmond, Virginia."

The two boys were relaxed enough to feel winded from their brief set-to. Each isolated and caught his breath.

Archie was satisfied that he had just won a fight for the first time in his life. Randolph, when Archie wasn't looking-touched his jaw that was a little sore. He accepted that even though he had beat bigger boys than himself when he was little, he could not do the same to a youmg man now that he was a teenager; that hurt even more than his tender jaw. "You sure hit hard." It had not been his intention but the admission siphoned the bitter taste clean off his tongue.

Old man Rob Roy chugged to a stop at the mailboxes at about the same time as Archie and Randy got there. "Hydee-ho!" That little old man always found a way to come up with a cheerful howdy. With those crinkly blue eyes, and the blue veins babbling like creeks on his pale, skinny arms, he still gave Randolph the candy cane feeling of Santa Claus and 'The First Noel.' "Hydee-ho!" He and Archie chimed in unison. Pale Rob Roy and the the two blackskinned boys were a sight for sore eyes standing there on a country road grinning like cheshire cats who didn't give a whit about nothing except being neighborly.

136

Chapter Eight
Phantasmagoria

The last time Randolph was up here in his room at eight o'clock, was two years ago when he had the mumps. He took pride in staying up until ten like grown folks.

The dining room was warm, soft and sweet with the brown and yellow scent of banana pudding. Mo finally got around to making it again. While she was up in New York, Randy had thought about it and concluded that everything he missed about his aunt; playing Pitty Pat or checkers, her tickling laugh when she wasn't showing the mean Mozzelle, her surprising bits of knowledge...all of it fell short when he remembered the smell and taste of her banana pudding. Even the deep, cream colored baking pan that was chipped at the corners, added to the something 'nother like Glory, taste.

Mozzelle was a 'sho-nuff' cook. Her chicken and dumplings was mouth watering. A couple of times she made an orange layer cake. The citrus tang was so doggone good Randolph felt guilty about his pleasure.

Yet and still, Mo's banana pudding was the the only something to eat he ever got whippings over. Back when he was little, they didn't make banana pudding. Grandma, Mo and them didn't even have bananas around. All of a sudden a couple years ago Mozzelle started baking that crunchy-creamy dessert with the toasted meringue on top. Randolph liked bananas. He liked vanilla wafers and custard. He liked the topping on lemon meringue pie. All those did something to him that was a lot like the feeling some girls gave him-he didn't know which-a-way to turn.

Banana pudding! Mo would bake it, then she would put it in the ice box to cool and set. After the first time Randolph followed the aroma to the freezer and sneaked a spoonful, he found out that as long as he dipped in there before the dish set, he could smoothe it over so you couldn't tell he'd been in it. That would have worked just fine if he'd stopped after one or two return

137

trips. But he couldn't control the urge to coms back time and again until there was a hole too deep to smoothe over.

Mo whipped him after the first time. She explained that it didn't make sense for him to go into the icebox knowing that if he just waited a little while he was gonna get some of the pudding. "It even tastes better after it sets." She made all the sense in the world. But for some reason, he was not able to wait. The second time Mo made banana puddiing, she wound up having to give him another whipping. After that, she kept him in the living room- playing cards or talking so he wouldn't get out of her sight.

Tonight, she cooked the dish for the first time since she got back from up the road. Sure as Carter made little liver pills, Randolph got into it while it was cooling.

"Mo. I know you're not suppose to whip me no more. But it's wrong for me to get into that pudding before it's ready." It took a minute for him to say it, but say it he did. "So I won't run from you if you want to whip me. I had no call to act like somebody who ain't got right good sense." He stood in front of her expecting she would send him upstairs to get one of Gregory's belts.

Mozzele was wearing a head rag as she often did. Tonight was the first time though she put him in mind of Aunt Jemima.

She put her hands on her hips-her shoulders squared. "Lord have mercy! Boy, I don't know what's gon' come of you." She squeezed her eyebrows together and her shoulders sagged. Randolph had to listen hard to hear her say, "Naw. I ain't gonna whip you."

The naked bulb hanging from the bedroom ceiling was an eye sore. Randolph would just pull the cord to turn it on then, ignore it. Tonight, a candlefly flitted around the light.

Randy studied it to figure out why the damned-fool-moth was doing that. It kept flying too close and you could see and smell its singed wings. It kept bumping up against the bulb. The moth finally stayed close long enough to stick to the hot light. A tiny flame flashed and the bug fell to the floor. Randy picked up the charcoal chip by what was left of a wing, walked to the window and threw it out into the night.

From then on, it was easy for him to wait until a banana pudding in the ice box was ready to be messed with.

Word about the singing Carter boys had been around for weeks now. Near 'bout everybody in Cedar Grove was in the prayer meeting. Outside the church a minute ago, anticipation was so loud you couldn't hear yourself think.

Wilson was seventeen, David was nineteen. They looked like twins; that was how Randolph thought of them, 'the Carter twins.' Reverend Snow had them seated in the pulpit along with preachers. Like most preachers and deacons seemed to, the Carter boys wore black suits. Word was, they weren't just good singers but they could preach too, both of them. It was the singing though that Randolph looked forward to. There was nothing in the world he liked more than good old gospel singing.

Blinking dots of light, from more lightning bugs than he could count, came through the open windows. All the firefly dots were echoed by the chatter of crickets, like thunder to ligthtning.

Before he came inside, Randy felt a breeze sneak up under his short sleeves, he saw a big old moon, the big dipper, milky way, and all the stars from all the songs on the radio hung in the sky to celebrate the night. He was gonna finally hear the singing Carter boys.

Reverend Snow usually had a wide white grin in his big-coal-black face. Tonight, that grin was wider and whiter than ever. He thanked the choir for their soul stirring rendition of "Leaning On The Everlasting Arm."

The choir was good alright. But it was the way the whole church joined in that made the song run around and inside Randy.

The Carter boys sat there in the pulpit for the whole forever that it took for the preahers-there were three of them in all-to take turns gospelizing and eliciting shouts of praise from the gathered throng. Collection was taken and Finally...

"Brothers and sisters of Cedar Grove, y'all're about to receive the blessings that folks up in Midway have had the pleasure of getting every Sunday for a long while now. You know, sometimes I forget just what the old preachers meant when they used to tell us, 'The Lord works in mysterious ways.' Did y'all see that sky out there, feel that heavenly breeze? GREAT GOD ALMIGHTY!" The church-about half full-raised its voice up and it bounced around in the unpainted rafters. Randolph could tell, and everybody else knew it too, something or another was about to commence to happenin'.

Reverend Snow was a big solid man who was getting old. But right now he seemed like somebody younger than Randolph. Out of his wide grin came a sound that was for-all the world-like an outright giggle. "I reckon you-all can tell just how happy I am to let'chall hear these two young men!" The Carter boys were on the edges of their seats. Randolph could see that they were as anxious to get started as the congregation was to hear them.

"Cedar Grove! Without further ado, here are the Carter brothers!" Both the boys started to get up. They looked at each other and sat back down. One of them gave the other permission to go first. Randolph figured it was the older boy David giving his younger brother Wilson the go ahead. It was just a guess-didn't matter none. Like his brother the boy who stood first looked to be a couple inches taller than fourteen year old Randolph. But their frames had the heft of full grown men. This made Randy envy them rather than try to compare himself to them.

"Thank you Reverend Snow. My brother and me keep you in our prayers amd hope you keep us in yours." He looked around the church and kinda cackled. "I don't know about you church, but I feel the Holy Spirit in this place tonight!" The lean-brown-singer-preacher from up in Midway had entered whatever state he needed to be in. A big old candle fly flitted about his face several times. The Carter boy didn't pay it one bit of notice. He skipped down from the altar still making the cackling sound. Randolph wasn't sure he would be able to stand it once the guy actually started singing.

> LORRRD! KEEP MY BOD-EE STRONG
> LORRRD! MAKE MY SPIR-IT STRONG
> LORRRD! FILL-ME-UP! WITH YOUR LOV-ING JOY

When the Carter boy chanted that last line, Randolph knew that he was not only starting to sing, the guy was making up his own song right there on the spot. His supplications were for God to give him what he needed to find the words and melody he needed in order to commence to sing his praises. "Oh Lord!" Randy heard himself whisper.

> I WANT THE LOVE OF MYYY GOD TO COME INTO ME
> I WANT THE LOVE OF THE ALMIGHTY TO PASS INTO THIS
> CHURCH TO-NIGHT

The organist added chords to the melody coming through the young man's voice; the mixture sounded to Randolph like orange, lemon and honey. Her fingers pressed and her feet pumped the organ so that the sun-fruit-tart filtered through the warmth of a honeycomb.

The rest of the congregation felt it too. Some rose to their feet. Others were bouncing on the edges of their pews. "Oh Lord!"

LORD DO YOU HEARRR MY PRAYER
LORD ONE OF YOUR CHILDREN IS CALL-ING ON-YOU

Wilson-if it was Wilson, not David-sang his plea in a way that Randolph understood. The wail was so much like his own pleading when he was little and wanted one grown person or another to give him surcease.

The organ player, who was from Cedar Grove, played as if she and that pretty-voiced young man did this every night. They had never met.

DO YOU HEAR ME JEEE-SUS
JEE-EE-EE-EE-SUS

A youmg woman who was standing-clapping in spastic rhythm fell to her knees screeching. Folks around her tried as best they could to calm her. They themselves were barely in control.

Sweat dripped off the Carter boys chin. A deacon offered him a hankerchief which he refused.

BE WITH ME JEE-EE-EE-EE-SUS
DO WITH ME AS YOU WILL OH LORD
TAKE MYYY HAND
TAKE MYYY HEART
TAKE EVERY-EVERY-EV-ER-Y PART OF ME
LORD I LOVE YOU SOOO

Looked like half the women in the church were doing a sanctified dance and crying out the name of The Holy Ghost. Randolph was so full of The Spirit that he whined and cried like he had never done before.

The other Carter boy who had come down to the altar apron to cheer his brother on, commenced to singing in a voice of lemon and orange just like the one already filling the church. The one who had the congregation beside itself sat down at the piano to accompany his brother-in blood and in Christian joy.

LORD YOU LIFTED ME FROM-OUT THE MIRY CLAY
LORD YOU-YOU MADE ME WHOLE WHEN MY SOUL WAS
A-SUNN-DERRR
LORD YOU BECAME MY GUIDING LIGHT WHEN I WALKED
IN DARKNESS

Randolph wondered who-what and why-when he realized he had for the very first time got to his feet in church service. All his life it had seemed not right for a youngun to showout before The Lord. These young men from Midway had made it alright. "ALRIIIGHT!" He did his own little dance before he felt self concious and sat back down. "Alright!" He whispered from his pew.

The whole time, Reverend Snow had been jumping out of his pulpit chair to prance about, then sit back down. When both the Carter boys held forth at once, he stood and remained on his feet. For a moment Randolph was surprised that the first Carter boy could play piano as well as sing like the dickens. But then a deeper sense informed him. Of course, it was Devine inspiration.

"Alright." 'All things are Possible through God.'

"All-riiight!"

The brothers sat down together on the piano bench to play and sing.

GIMME THAT OLD TIME RELIGION
GIMME THAT OLD TIME RELIGION
GIMME THAT OLD TIME RELIGION
IT'S GOOD ENOUGH FORRR ME

The hymn was familiar enough that the congregation would normally have joined in. The sound coming out of the mouths of the brothers was such that the folks of Cedar grove were content to just listen.

IT WAS GOOD FOR MY DEAR MOTHER
IT WAS GOOD FOR MY DEAR MOTHER
IT WAS GOOD FOR MY DEAR MOTHER
IT'S GOOD ENOUGH FORRR ME

142

Earlier, each of their voices had evoked for Randolph, citrus and rich honey. In two part harmony, the sound of the two boys's combined spirits was somethin' 'nother like a gospel echo off the spring, baptising pool and blackberry patch coming off the hollow, blended in with the tang and sweetness. On the edge of their notes was the ancient gospel exclamation, "Angels singing and joy bells ringing in Glory. " Randy had forgotten that the honey in the mix came from the clear syrupy moan of the pump organ until he was reminded. A pill box, straw hat worn by the organist fell to the floor behind her organ bench. She did not know it had flown off her head. Randolph saw that and knew, she too was possessed by the Devine spirit.

> IT WAS GOOD FOR MY OLD DADDY
> IT WAS GOOD FOR MY OLD DADDY
> IT WAS GOOD FOR MY OLD DADDY
> IT'S GOOD ENOUGH FORRR ME

Everyone in the church older than six or seven was put in mind of at least one relative who had gone on home. A few of the elders wiped away tears.

> IT HELPED ME LOVE MY JESUS
> YES IT HELPED ME TO LOVE JESUS
> IT HELPED ME LOVE MY JESUS
> IT'S GOOD ENOUGH FORRR ME

The boys sang and played and switched back and forth between the piano and skipping about and singing. Congregants waved fans in the air-cheered the boys on-shouted praises to The Almighty and wondered at it all.

> GIMME THAT OLD TIME RELIGION
> GIMME THAT OLD TIME RELIGION
> GIMME THAT OLD TIME RELIGION
> IT'S GOOD ENOUGH FORRR ME

* * *

Back outside the clapboard Methodist church, Randolph discovered that his white dress shirt clung to his body. He had not known he was sweating. Folks gathered around the Carter boys-touching them, praising them. You could see that they were humble and uncomfortable about being given credit for what The Lord had wrought.

Randolph noted the the hum and chatter of people-crickets-blinking lightning bugs, swirl and become cacophony in the night somethin' a'nother like the Howard theater back in D.C.-the place dark, only music stand lights.

Stars filled the blackness with pleasure that smothered all thoughts of the ordinary. A zephyr brushed about his body com-summating what had been, what was, tonight.

* * *

It wasn't hard to imagine Jack Richard bringing his mule to its knees with a left hook. Mr. Jack... Mr. Richard... didn't have bulging muscles like Jersey Joe Walcott although he did have a kind of boiler plate forehead and square jaw with drum-tight-skin like the heavyweight fighter. Maybe that was why his lean muscularity convinced you he had the kind of power that could drop a five hundred pound animal.

Mozzelle had allowed Jack Richard to hire Randolph for the day. There was nobody Randy knew who was as full of surprises as Mo. She didn't seem to want him to have fun, but when it came to how much neighbors paid him when he was hired out, she really looked out for him. Mr. Ervin used to pay him a dollar a day; Mo told Randolph to demand two bucks a day. When Jack Richard approached her, she said, "Since you only want him for one day, you're gonna have to give him three dollars." "That's fine with me, Mo." It was not lost on Randolph that his aunt had never asked for one red penny of his earnings nor told him how to spend it.

Jack and Randolph spent the day 'Bringing in the sheaves.' Randolph thought of reaping wheat in those words because it made him feel both intelligent and christian. He was also tickled to finally spend time with someone whose sinewy limbs were like his own and whose height and built he could expect to replicate when he grew up.

144

The two didn't talk much while they worked. For Randolph's part, he would have had a lot more to say, to ask of the strong man whose company he felt honored to be in. The problem was, he could not decide how to address him. The man had two first names. Randolph could have called him Jack. After all, he was younger than Mr. Ervin and them. At the same time, he wasn't young enough that Randy could call him just plain, Jack. Mr. Jack didn't fit somehow. The thought of saying Mr. Richard seemed out of the question...maybe because the only grown folks he called by their last names were teachers or preachers. It didn't occur to him to ask Jack Richard what he should call him.

The young farmer had a reedy but melodic voice that Randolph enjoyed listening to while he pitched hay. He tried to figure some way to get Jack Richard to say more. No matter how much he strained, he couldn't think of a way to bring him out.

Jack Richard made it a point to compliment Randolph on being a "right smart worker. You ain'y like your friend... what's hte name, the Mills boy?" "Archis?" Yeah, that's the one. He's right sorry, no account." Before Randy could work up resentment that his buddy being called sorry, Jack Richard continued. "Them that's up the road ain't no better. All them Mills boys're sorry; evr' one of 'em."

What Archies brothers were like, Randolph didn't know. But it bothered him to hear his buddy Archie beibg called, sorry. At the same time, it didn't bother him enough to take his mind off the fact that Jack 'left hook' Richards said that Randolph Wilford was right smart; not sorry-no account like the Mills boys.

Among his other bits of coversation, this impressive but still not very familiar man, asked when Myra was coming home. Randolph didn't have time to conclude that Jack Richard must cotton to his mama before that reedy voice softened to a hymn-like tone. "Son, your mama is one fine woman." 'Say what!' rang around inside Randy's head like his skull was a D.C. school lavatory until it came to him that Jack Richard didn't mean fine in a Nellie Lutcher, "Fine Brown Fame, kind of way. What the farmer was trying to say was, Myra is a fine upstanding woman.

They reached the close of day, and although Randolph figured out the truth of what the man had said about his mother, a resentment or whatever it was, lingered as if Jack Richard had been insinuatin'.

No matter what that flip-flop feeling meant, Randolph Wilford had no intention of trying to make sense of it. He let it float around in the shallow part of his well while he told Jack Richard what a pleasure it had been working with him today. He actually managed to begin his brief speach of manners with, "Jack."

The man had given him that license by bringing up mama.

* * *

He rode Suzy Q. out of the driveway. It hadn't rained in several days-the road was hard, dry and a layer of dust rested on the surface.

Randolph had no idea he was grinning. He only knew that-like he'd heard a wino say back in D.C., He was "Happy as a sissy in a C.C. Camp." Although he had no idea what a C.C. Camp was, like so many other sayings he kept hearing as years went by, this one rang right through him like church bells on a Sunday morning.

He made sure the back wheel was beyond the little gully between the road and the driveway before he brought one of the pedals all the way up and threw every ounce of his weight onto it. The pedal went down hard and fast-spinning the back wheel. He did the same on the other pedal and was able to spinoff five times before he gained too much momentum to do it again. Now he knew he was grinning-from ear to ear-a burst of dust had flown in his wake with each spin. He had done something, "Cool as a fool in a swimming pool-reet peteet and gone."

A lot of things tickled Randolph, orange popsicles, banana pudding and a whole heap of stuff like reading good stories and comic books about boys he could identify with. Above these things, was sentimental music and stuff that made him laugh. Spinning off gave him a thrill like those things. "Damn straight!"

Chapter Nine
A Faint Light

Breath came hard and dry. He was not as tired as he was stirred up. The shovel flew out of his hands and landed under the porch.

"Cousin Hilda!" She came to the open back door and talked through the screen. "What're you all worked up about?" "I saw a snake out on the road!" "What did you do with the snake?"

A half smile-curious smile-told him she had something behind that question. He answered her straight... cousin Hilda wouldn't fool around, she would let him know what was on her mind. "I cut him in two and threw one half to one side of the road then threw the other part of him to the other side." Hilda knew well the old myth about a snake crawling back together and biting its attacker. "How many snakes do you reckon you've killed in your life?" Randolph did not have to ponder, he pretty much knew. "Three, maybe four." Hilda opened the screen door and steered him past the pantry to the kitchen table. "I made a blackberry pie yesterday. Would you like a slice and a glass of milk?" Randolph's mouth watered. He swallowed before forcing himself to be calm. "Yes maam...yes, please."

"You're a well mannered young man." She uncovered the pie sitting in a cake dish on her sideboard. "Do you think you can handle a fair-sized piece?" "YES MA-AM!" They both laughed.

Hilda waited until Randolph relaxed into his pleasure. "Anybody you know ever been bitten by a snake?" He chewed and swallowed before answering. "No mam. Can't say that I have." Both Hilda and Randolph knew that he was bright enough to guess what she was leading to. Further, for different but complementing reasons, they also knew that they were about to share the kind of moment that they had on previous occasions enjoyed and not forgotten.

" 'All the animals in the forest are Mine and the cattle on thousands of hills. All the wild birds are Mine and all living things in the fields.' "

"Is that from the Bible?"

"Sure is. It's from one of the Psalms. I don't remember which one." Randolph took care to only speak between mouthfuls. "Would you please say that again?" He scooped up a spoonful of crust and blackberry. Hilda adjusted to the rhythm of his eating.

" 'ALL THE ANIMALS IN THE FOREST ARE MINE.' " *She paused...* "AND THE CATTLE ON THOUSANDS OF HILLS.' " *She paused again.* "'ALL THE WILD BIRDS ARE MINE. AND ALL LIVING THINGS IN THE FIELDS. ' " Randolph pondered.

"Take your time-enjoy your pie. Think about what the Psalm means."The blue-black and beige congealed to a delight to swallow. "It means that all the animals are created by God." He wiped the corners of his mouth with his thumb and forefinger. "And He doesn't want us killing them."

"Well, that's kind of what the Psalm means, but not exactly. I mean, if we didn't kill any animals, how would we have meat to eat?" Randolph's eyes widened. "You know something? When I was little and mama and them still raised hogs, I made one little pig my pet." Sadness came over him; he examined it to get some sense of where it had come from.

Randolph had thought the memory was gone for good. It came back now just as heavy as it had ever been.

"I used to go down to the pen everyday to feed him." He spoke fast to keep from crying. "I saw him grow up to be a full grown hog..." Hilda saw his tears coming before they poured out and down the boy's face. She rushed around the table. "Now, now." Her soft way of holding his shoulders was nice enough that he was just as glad he had started to cry as he was embarrassed. "A few days later, I was eating the meat just like mama and Gregory and the rest." He broke out laughing. "And it was good too." They shared an ironic-laughing moment. Hilda pulled a dainty hankerchief from her apron pocket. "Here." Randolph took the hankerchief to wipe his eyes. "It's funny ain't it?" "It sure is. It's ironic." 'Ironic.' Randolph had seen that word and heard it on the radio and in the movies. He was sure he had looked it up. Like any number of words he had looked up, this one did not come clear to him until he heard it in context again.

He returned to the psalm. "I'm confused. I'm not sure what the Psalm means." Hilda sat still until Randolph saw by a curl at the corners of her her mouth that she had come up with something.

"Here's another passage from the Bible. I actually know that this is from Ecclesiastes, chapter 3, verse 1. 'To every thing there is a season, and a time to every purpose under heaven.' "There are times, Randy, when it's right to do something. And there are times when it is not right to do the very same thing." She considered what to say next. "Sometimes you pick corn or peas or tomatoes?"

"Yessum."

"Why do you go to the garden or the orchard and pick vegetables and fruits?" She raised her palm. "Better yet. Why did Gregory kill the hogs?" "So we'd have pork to eat. And that's why we pick fruit or vegetables, to eat." "And you don't go to the garden or orchard unless you want something to eat?" Randolph lit up the kitchen with bright comprehension. He thought, 'I love you cousin Hilda.' He had never heard those words except as a romantic expression. He kept his thought to himself.

"Here. Have another slice of my pie."

"Yes maam. Thank you."

* * *

"You ever walked up to Midway before?" Archie's question gave Randolph the chance to let him know that he wasn't talking to some little kid. "Sure have...lots of times." He had made the trek twice. The two boys were side by side-pace by pace. It wasn't long ago that Randy had to struggle to keep up with his buddy. Archie's growth was slowing as Randolph's was speeding up. He was two inches at most from being the same height as almost eighteen year old Archie.

In Midway, they took the bus to Crestville. This was the first time Randy had been on public transportation since he left Washington. He thought of how different it was to be on the way to the swimming pool at William Penn High school here than the trips he remembered to the Benjamin Banneker pool back in D.C. Some of the sights-A & R Grocery and Roses Furniture store on Main Street were similar. He knew them by sight from driving by them a hundred times with Gregory and them. Back in Washington, the stores had a tactile sense. He had been in a lot of them. They were sort of his stores. The businesses down here were like Calvin Cooledge High School back home. They seemed to be for white folks.

William Penn was in the Colored section of town. The sounds-jump music coming out of cafes-loud laughter. The smell of pickled pigs feet and greens brought back Northwest D.C. But the accents and the low hung sky gave Midway a whole different sense.

The swimming pool was just like the one back home. The creek he and Archie swam in was like the swimming hole back home too.

When Archie would say, "Let's take a dip," he wasn't kidding. They never stayed in the creek more than a few minutes. At first, Randy had thought their swims were brief because of the water moccasin. But they hadn't seen the snake in a while-maybe he died or, 'Maybe he moved to a new neighborhood.' (Randolph tickled himself with this thought.)

The real reasons he and Archie kept their dips short were that Archie only went to the creek to cool off. And he was not a good swimmer. Randolph had showed him how to do the Australian crawl that he had learned at the swimming holes back home. He was so busy taking pride in having taught an older boy something, he failed to notice that Archie did not take to the stroke all that well.

One day when Randolph was settling in, Archie dog pedalled over to him. "Come on Randy let's go up to the water melon patch'n get us a good ol' ripe melon. Randolph's mouth watered.

They plucked a few melons before they found one that had the the hollow sound of ripeness. Randolph watched Archie cut it open-red flesh and black seeds reflecting the sunlight. They each took one half and sat in the richness of soft, brown earth slurping, slobbering, spitting seeds and glorying in the red sweet and the yellow afternoon. Their pleasure was enhanced when they added what had become an after swim ritual. Between placing chunks of wet-sweet in their mouths, they picked up flat stones, leaned first one ear and then the other against the hot dry surfaces to leech risidual water.

"Back in Washington, we used to go across town to Banneker Junior High School. They had a swimming pool.."

"We got a pool here in Crestville."

150

"Yeah?...Scuse me." He had spit a seed that landed in Archie's lap. *"S'ok. You want to go to our pool? It's at William Penn."*

Randolph had heard of William Penn. His uncle Elmore went to that high school.

"Yeah."

Yep, the pool at William Penn looked about the same as the Banneker pool. The swimmers didn't look the same though. Instead of a bunch of little kids, they were big kids, mostly teenaged girls. He didn't think he'd ever seen so many fine looking chicks in one place in his life-Chocolate--blueblack-peanut butter, a lot of them were built up from the ground-filling out their one piece and two piece swimsuits.

"Lord have mercy!"

Archie grinned at Randy's mumbled approval. That was proof that the folks up North didn't have nothin' on the folks down here. "Randolph, this is Estelle Warren. She's a friend of mine." Did Archie really know this pretty yella girl with hair down to her round butt?

"Hey Randolph. Nice to meet you." She had a smoothe voice that sounded like some white woman on the radio.

"Nice to meet you too.."

Archie and Randolph moved on. Randolph forced himself not to look back at Estelle. It was hard to keep his face forward. In order to take back control of his mind, he dived into the pool and stayed under water until he was half way across the pool. He came up panting but refreshed. After a breath, he went back under.

The chlorine smell didn't bother him like it once did. Today it was pleasant nostalgia. 'A time for every purpose under heaven.' He laughed, water rushed into his open mouth. Even the taste of chlorine didn'y bother him. He came up still laughing. "What's so funny?" Archie had dived in. "Nothing." Archie was too busy staying afloat to question him further.

The boys stayed at the William Penn pool a lot longer than they had ever stayed at the creek. The creek didn't have no girls.

Randolph remembered an event when he was nine. He thought he had managed to forget all about that day.

She was about his age and she was his favorite shade of brown, creamy peanut butter. When she was treading water, boy's swam underwater to grope her. She would tell them to stop. At the same time, she would giggle. After a while, Randolph got up the nerve to dive under. She was so fine, he couldn't wait to touch her. And, once he did, he was more excited than he had anticipated.

To see if the girl was reacting to him as she had to the others, he popped up above the surface; she was giggling. Encouraged, he dived down and groped her again. She was still seeming to have as much fun as he was having.

Several times, he dived and groped. "What do you think you are doing!" She climbed out of the pool. Randolph could see that she was mad at him. "I thought you liked it." Before she could respond, "You didn't get mad when the other boys played with you." "They didn't keep on doing it time after time like they were out of their minds!" Her voice was strained and pleading. He climbed out of the water and went over to where she stood. "I'm sorry!" "You ought to be!" He stared at the girl. She was cute with dimples, even when she was mad. Like guys in the movies he gave her, "The once over." Her hair was curly-not kinky enough to shrivel from the water. Her body filled out her white one piece bathing suit. He could see why he and the other boys were attracted to her. She looked almost grown.

Moments passed before he realized she was grimacing because he leered at her like she was a '45' DeSota or something. Her look could not be mistaken for anything but disgust.

His mind said, "I didn't do anything wrong."

Her eyes, said, "Something is wrong with you!"

He never went back to the Banneker pool.

The pretty girls in the colorful bathing suits here at William Penn seemed like they were far away from here. Some of them were right in front of him or next to him or right behind him. But they might as well have been up on a movie screen. "You can look but you better not touch." He had not touched a girl since that day at Banneker. Funny, that expression should cross his mind now. Maybe it was finally time for him to realize what was wrong with how he had behaved.

The big boys, including Archie, talked and joked with some of the girls. They knew how to do that. Watching and listening didn't bring Randolph any closer to knowing how. It did give him comfort to expect that by and by he would get the knack of it. He couldn't wait.

After a while, most of the guys and girls who were at the pool when Randolph and Archie got there, had drifted away. It was like turnover time at the movies.

* * *

A block from William Penn, Archie had Randolph wait while he went into a State Store. Two women passed Randolph while he waited on the sidewalk. One of them wore tan gabardine slacks just like the woman he remembered in mama's front yard. Her pants clung to her bottom like skin to a plum-peach. As it did back then, the sight drove him near 'bout crazy. 'Lord! Something about a shapely woman...' instead of attempting to frame it, he just revelled in the way it felt.

Archie came out of the store. Randolph was all set to talk about what it was about women and girls bodies that made him excited when a small paper bag sticking out of his friends hip pocket distracted him. "What'cha got there?" He had already guessed the answer-he wasn't sure. "Half pint of Seagram's Seven." Archie led Randolph into an alley where he broke the seal and took a swig.

"S'that liquor?"

"Sure is. Aaaa boy! Good liquor too."

"Lemme taste it."

"Boy! I can't give none of this to you. Mo would skin me alive."

"How she gonna know?" Archie pondered the question.

"Well, a little bird might tell her. Anyway, you too young to be drinking." For a moment, Randolph was stumped. Then, he had a brainstorm. "Didn't we come to Crestville together?" Archie gave him a confused look. Randolph did not give him time to think. "Didn't we go swimming together? How come all of a sudden I can't do what you do? We're together. We're buddies ain't we?"

Archie wagged his head side to side. He started to say something but wagged his head again. "Your daddy's dead, right?"

153

"Yeah."

"You swear on his grave, if I give you a little sip, you ain't gonna tell Mozzelle?"

"I swear t' God and hope to die!"

"Here. Just take a little bitty sip, now."

"Whew! That taste like fire!" The words were barely out of Randy's mouth before Archie nearly busted a gut laughing. He caught his breath. "Some folks call it fire water."

"Lemme have another sip." Randolph did not like the taste of the whiskey, he only wanted to show Archie that he could drink it down like somebody who knew what he was doing. Archie intuited exactly what Randy wanted to do. "Here. Don't be no hog, now. Just a little sip." Randolph took another swig. It wasn't easy but he managed to keep from showing that it burned his throat.

What happened after the second sip, Randy did not know. His next awareness was of being alone on a strange street. He wasn't scared, he just wondered where Archie was. There were people walking by-talking-laughing. In his next awareness, he realized another blank period had come and gone. Something magical was happening-this going in and out of knowing. It did not bother him that he couldn't tell where he was or what was going on. Every time he came around, he felt like things were normal except there was a veil between him and the people and storefronts he saw. He was in the middle of it all without being part of it. Then, another period of nothing.

The final time he came to light, it was to the sound of Archie's voice. "Where the hell you been!" The question and concern were funny to Randolph. Through a giggle he said, "I don't know. Where the hell have you been?"

"Oh Lord! I done made you drunk!"

So that was what caused the magic-he was drunk. His trip into 'wherever' was coming to an end; he was almost all the way back. The veil was gone-Archie's sharp tone broke it up like something in a cartoon-blown to smithereens. "That was funny."

"Maybe it was funny to you. You near 'bout scared me to death."

"I don't mean funny, funny. I mean it was strange. It was like I was in another place there for a while."

Archie studied him. "You alright now? You still drunk?" "Naw. I'm ok." "I went into the drugstore to get a pack of gum. I thought you was right behind me." Archie allowed himself to laugh. "I reckon I was wrong." They both laughed. "Boy, if you ever ask me for a drink again, I'm gonna bust you in the mouth." Both boys continued to laugh. Archie was laughing at the obvious, Randolph was laughing at how, in a queer kind of way, his excursion had been exciting.

Chapter Ten
Waiting for Tomorrow

It was just after dark when Gregory came in the back door, ducked into the kitchen and gave Mozzelle a good evening kiss. Then he came back into the dining room where Randolph was churning butter. "Hey, Randy." "What'ya say, Greg."

In his own quiet way, Gregory usually treated Randolph like an equal, like he was grown. Other than that and being able to practice country talk with him, Randy didn't have much to do with his uncle by marriage.

After Gregory went by, Randolph wondered why he never did any of the chores around the house. It did not occur to him that Gregory spent all day working at the sawmill-that was his big chore. Still, reason told him, everything was as it probably should be.

He continued to roam around in his head-partly because it was his nature to do so, partly because every rotatation of the churn crank was more difficult than the one before. The clabber slowly turned to butter and grew more difficult to churn. Imagining hot buttered cornbread steaped in tart buttermilk, helped him through to the end.

Once when Randolph complained to Mo of how hard it was to make butter, she laughed.

"You see that old fashioned churn in the pantry?"

"The one that'chou had to plunge up and down?"

"Yep. Now you talk about something 'nother that's hard? That was hard. When the butter commenced to get thick, you had to force the dash down through it. With this new fangled churn, you just sit there turning the wheel while the butter gathers around the dash when it's gettin' thick. Pshaw! You're lucky you ain't got to churn butter the old fashioned way."

Randolph was sure she was right. But, 'then was then and now was now.' Still and all, he appreciated Mo telling him about olden times. Since she came back from New York, she did that a lot.

He credited Mo's trip up the road with things being better these days than they used to be. He was partly right. Another thing was that going away for a spell helped straighten things out between her and Gregory. When he pondered the matter further, Randolph's conclusion was that the trip up North had given his aunt time to think things over. Again, he was partly right. Indeed Mozzelle had been able to work things out in her mind while she was away. Her dealings with him though were determined by the bold way he told her not to whip him again. Anytime she reflected on that day, she pictured his sinewy arms and that double edged axe he wielded at the woodpile.

Randolph had not forgotten the day. His memory of it was simply of the way he let Mozzelle know he didn't want no more whippings. Her recollection was founded on her fear of 'that youngun' who, like papa, 'didn't have right good sense.'

* * *

More often than not, Randy and Mo played Pitty pat after he had washed the supper dishes. To keep from getting in a rut, they would sometimes play checkers. This was a checkers night.

When grandma was alive, Gregory would try to win her favor by chatting with her while whoever else was there played cards or checkers. These days, he would sit in the one wicker chair among the stuffed living room furniture and grandma's rocking chair. By Randy's reckoning, nobody ever sat in the rocker since mama 'Went on home.'

Mozzelle and Randolph sat on either side of the card table, setup in front of the radio. From Knoxville, Little Esther and Mel Walker or Ivory Joe Hunter or Dinah Washington crooned Colored music. Randy and Mo would tease one another over their checker game. Gregory sometimes dozed while reading the paper. Even when he was awake and not perusing the daily news, he was quiet as a church mouse. Once it crossed Randy's mind that Gregory might as well have been the sofa, the easy chair, the coffee table or the rocker. "What in the world was that man thinking, sittin' there so quiet?"

Tonight, Randolph was ahead two games to none. As was her wont on the rare occasions when she was losing, Mozzelle commenced to talk about whatever was on her mind. "You like the Carter boys a whole heap dont'chou?" It had been two months or more since Methodist, revival time. Not a word had been spoken about those boys since. But Randolph went along with Mozzelle's attempt to distract him. He knew she was about to reveal something he wanted to hear. "Yessir. Them old boys sure can preach and sing... One of them is down in Goldsboro at the insane asylum." "Say what?" Randolph half wished he could tell his aunt to stop right there. "The oldest boy took to going out in the woods in the middle of the night and bang on an old oil drum out there and sing and preach at the top of his voice...screamed so loud he would wake folks up. They say he coulda woke the dead."

Randy had heard from Archie that one of the brothers went into the woods at night to sing praises to the Lord. At least that was how he chose to hear it. One day he even went into the bushes to see if he could find something metal to bang on and sing. He didn't find anything suitable.

"At first, they say, his daddy talked to him about it and the boy stopped. Just when everybody had forgot all about it, he commenced to goin' out there again." Mo went on to say what a pity it was the Carter boy drove himself crazy loving The Lord too much.

While Mozzelle gave him that bit of gossip, she beat the pants off him at checkers.

"I've had enough."

Mo thought he meant he'd had enough checkers. What he wanted to get away from was her seeming to tell him that it was possible to be too good a christian. He did not want to hear it.

When he passed Gregory sitting there nodding, Randolph wanted to shake him. "WAKE UP YOU HALF WHITE SON OF A BITCH!"

* * *

"Now I lay me down to sleep. And pray The Lord my soul to keep. If I should die before I wake, I pray The Lord my soul to take." Here, Randolph shifted on his knees to get more comfortable. "Dear Lord..." He pondered how to phrase what he was about to say. "Heavenly Father... I hope I'm not being mannish. But I think Mozzelle is wrong about the Carter boy loving you too much. I don't think sombody can love you too much. I love you Lord, with all my heart. In Jesus' name, Amen." He crawled into bed exausted by the knowledge that one of those good christian brothers had been put in the insane asylum. Something was wrong. His daddy or somebody up in Midway didn't understand what folks called "Old time religion." Maybe they had some new fangled way of loving The Lord.

Like usual, he lay there with the intention of reflecting on his day. Like usual, before thoughts could coalesce, he was sound asleep.

Randolph dreamed frequently and had done so for as long as he could remember. Dreams had become like old playmates. He recognized them for what they were; often he was able to control their outcome. If he had indigestion from eating too much watermelon or cake or any heavy food, he could expect to have a nightmare rise up from his knotted stomach in the middle of the night.

The flight route was above where he had walked with the old guy when he missed the bus and had to walk home from school. Randy looked down on a slow motion home run that sailed from the ball field over the school house into the woods.

When he reached the road where the old man lived, Randolph banked left in order to fly pass the old man's house, over the junk pile and to the Cedar Grove road. He sailed over the house alright, but when he neared the junk pile, he stalled and fell toward the the tin cans, broken glass and the jagged edges of auto parts. He tried flapping his arms to regain altitude to no avail. He was close to the pile and about to crash. It was too late to do anything but wake himself up.

Sweat drenched his face and pajama underarms. He cleared his mind. Why was he able to wake himself but wasn't able to swoop back into the air. Sometimes when he stalled and fell towards the ground he could flap his arms until he soared toward the sky again. While he attempted to solve his dilemma, he heard Mozzelle and Gregory whispering in their room. He didn't hear all that they said, but it was clear that Gregory wanted her to give him a little bit.

160

Randolph folded his pillow around his ears. He had a desperate need not to be reminded that he wasn't doing it to nobody.

* * *

Back in elementary school in D.C. it was different. The sun would be shining through the windows.

Even it it was cloudy outside, the big bright globes hung down from the ceiling. The Sleepy Hollow story about the headless horseman and other spooky tales were scary. But hearing about ghosts and such in a classroom in bright light was nothing like being down here in the country listening to that kind of stuff outdoors around sundown.

Like every year, Randolph and Mozzelle had come over to help Mr. Ervin and them harvest tobacco. The work day was from sunup to sunset.

After Miz Annette fed them supper, Mr. Ervin, Verniece, Archie, Mo and Randy came out to the front porch. Much as he loved Miz Annette's cooking, Randy had hoped he and Mozzelle would forgo supper. That way, they would get home before dark. Here they were with Mr. Ervin adding insult to injury.

His voice was a lot like his looks-thin and wiry. It quavered a little when he spoke. Sounded something 'nother like the spook in his story might sound.

"This was back when me and Annette were courtin'." Mr. Ervin had a junior highschool education. He spoke though like cousin Hilda with a clipped accent and cadence. "I was heading on up the road after her daddy ran me off, it being after sundown. The shortest way to Anders Grove from here was to take the cemetery road. That didn't bother me one bit. I was almost grown and wasn't scared of haints and that sort of thing. To tell you the truth though, every time I passed the graveyard at night, I had to remind myself I wasn't scared.

"I remember one night like it was yesterday. A big old harvest moon was hanging low-pretty as a picture. At first I didn't pay it no mind, but just as I went by the driveway that runs up to the Colored cemetery gate, something 'nother right chilly commenced to blowin' 'round me. My body started to shake, not a lot, just a little bit. Then, whatever it was blowing cold on me, started making a sound like nothing I'd ever heard in my life. It wasn't a whistle, wasn't exactly a hum. I reckoned it was a kinda hum-whistle. That old thing started to work its way around me-whistle-humming as it went-slow at first. I froze in my tracks. And that whistling, humming thing kept moving around me picking up speed and getting ice cold as it went. "

Randolph remembered the morning he saw and felt the warm, purple mist down by the creek. He felt special, he too knew about such things. That didn't keep Mr. Ervin's story ftom being spooky though. Randy fought himseelf to keep from looking around the yard and out into the field to make sure nothing strange, no haints were out there.

"My Lord! I thought I was gonna freeze to death right there in front of the graveyard. All of a sudden, nothing. It was gone. I was myself again, like nothing had happened."

"Papa, did you ever find out what it was?"

"Naw, Verniece. Never did."

* * *

He and Mozzelle were near 'bout to the main road before the secure warmth of numbers left Randolph. The dark settled in and bothered him.

"How come you so close up on me?"

He was not aware that he had eased up against his aunt. "Scuse me Mo." His embarassment did not erase his unease with the dark. 'Damnit man! What kind of Christian are you?' Randolph's thought was loud enough that he took a glance at Mo to see if she had heard it. The minute he did that, he was more embarrased.

They reached the Cedar Grove road-halfway home. "Lord, I can't count the times I've walked from Ervin and them's place to our house." Randolph could have hugged Mozzelle for distracting him from his fool imaginings.

"How many times you walked it at night?"

"Not too many times. But the many times, night or day, are enough to wear out a pair of shoes."

"Know what?"

"What?"

162

"Talking about shoes. Remember the time we were picking blackberries and saw a black snake?"

"Sure do."

"Remember you ran out of one of your loafers?"

Mozzelle stopped. "How come you'd bring that up now?"

"I forgot to tell you." He kept walking so that she wouldn't keep him standing there in the dark. "But one day I was down in the blackberry patch and came across that old loafer. It was half rotten. It was your loafer though."

"Well, bless Pat!"

They were passing the garden. Randolph didn't care if his fear came back now. 'Hell!' They were close enough to home he could hold his breath til they got inside the house.

* * *

The old stump, up a little from the spring and pool, was still solid. Ever so briefly Randolph concluded that this stump had not rotted like another one in his mind because it was next to the path on the church side. The rotten stump rested at the top of the path on the house side. The brief notion made enough of an impression to let him know what he wanted to think. Yet it was lodged too deep for him to hold on to it. He did not fret. What he wanted to think was rich enough that he felt right spiritual. What did not come close to mixing in with his awareness was that he sat on the very stump where one of the Campbell sisters once gave him half an orange to do her first that day-he was four then. The fun the three of them used to have when they came to the spring to fetch water was the memory that made this stump special. Church and hymns and the feeling he had when he got quietly "happy" were a whole heap like what he felt when he either thought about doing it or when he actually did it-at least that was what he thought he remembered about how it felt to do it.

If he had been able to sought it all out, he would have seen that he was unable to wrap it all in one bale because he had been taught-and firmly believed-that it would be a sin to think that his spiritual sense was at all related to his lust sense. Bliss protected him from guilt, allowing him to have pleasure unfettered.

The sun glistened through the silks on top of the cornstalks in a field over yonder about halfway between the nearby blackberry patch and ARJAY'S store. It was the same time of day the first time Randolph came down to the spring to daydream. That was the day cousin Ames had taken him and Lucille down to the mill. Ames' jolly, brown, Santa Claus figure rested on his mind until melancholy set in. Ames was followed by grandma-daddy-the dogs Jack-Trixie- Jabbo and all the snakes he had killed, all in their turn.

He continued to stare at the setting sun through the amber wisps atop the cornstalks, until he began to cry; it was gentle weeping, only deep enough that he could feel philosophical about his sadness that was as much wonder as anything else.

"Lord, Lord, Lord!" The sun turned orange. Randolph pictured Little Robin Redbreast. He had never seen a robin with a red breast. Every one he had seen had a breast the color of that sinking sun. When he was in First Grade, he was taught the colors, red, green, blue and brown. It was during that time that he memorized "Little Robin Red Breast."

When the color orange was made known to Randolph, it confused him. The cause of this and other periods of befuddlement was retention. What he learned cleaved to his memory. If he mislearned, he had difficulty dislodging the error. Jesus was a girl. Randolph must have thought that for weeks before mama (grandma) told him that men wore their hair long in Jusus' time.

The sun was about to go below the crest of ARJAY's hill. Randolph knew that the Earth traveled around the sun. But because it appeared that the sun traveled around the Earth, he had settled into thinking about it that way. He shifted his weight on the stump and wondered where the sun went after sinking below the horizon. "That lucky old sun's got nothing to do but roll around heaven all day."

* * *

An unfamiliar kind of resentment came close to the surface. 'I like your gotdamn nerve, making me hold the end-handle of this chain saw!' were the words Randolph saw from the top of his awareness. He managed to keep them from reaching the level of out loud anger.

Gregory was at the business end of the newfangled tool that Randolph was seeing for the first time. Sawdust was flying

164

into his face off the teeth of the chain rotating in his direction. At first, he was blinded by the fine grains of pine as well as irritated. Like a miracle, tears soon poured out, washing the dust down his cheeks. Every now and then, a piece of wood near 'bout the size of a chip would strike him in the face. None of the chunks had hit him in the eye yet. He prayed that none would.

He kept the prayer from himself while at the same time he let it float toward Heaven. Mixed in with all this was the thought that nothing he could remember had ever made him feel so grown.

When Gregory showed up with a six foot long canvas bag, Randolph played it cool-it was somehow necessary to act like he knew what was inside. Gregory didn't pay him no mind. He unzipped the bag and pulled the tool out. "This here's a two-man chain saw." Randolph saw the 'chain machine' and forgot all about his affectation. "Oh yeah!" "Yep We gonna cut some cord wood. Then we gonna cut up some of them slabs Cesar brung yesdiddy."

Randolph hooked his thumbs halfway up his overall bib. "Ok." He wondered how the dickens the confounded thing worked.. "Well suh! I reckon we'd best git to gittin' !"

Gregory chuckled in a way that let Randolph intuit he was having a flash back to when he himself was a mannish young rascal.

A fair sized chip smacked Randolph in the right eye. It did not put his eye out as he had imagined it would. The eye blinked at the right moment and reminded him of a time when a horse fly flew against his eye. Now, he knew empirically what he was taufgt back in the fourth grade about voluntary and involuntary muscles.

Relaxation came into the discomfort of his station at the steadying end of the chainsaw. As soon as he let himself alone, he became aware of dust in his mouth and nose. He spit. Then he snorted to clear his nostril into his throat, and spat again. 'Yes indeed!' Randolph Wilford was near 'bout grown.

Suddenly the air was clear-the hum of the saw was gone. Quiet gave him space to reflect back to yesdiddy.

Thr two over- full buckets splashed water on Randolph's pant legs. By the time he reached the top of the hill, they were soaked. "Boy! How come you put all that water in the buckets?" Mozzelle shouted from the porch and clucked her tongue. "Don't make sense; that's a lazy man's load." She clucked again and went into the dining room.

Maybe, it occurred to him, he kept overfilling the buckets because Mozzelle kept scolding him about it. No matter, before he could regret that the waterlogged legs of his overalls clung to his shins, a big green Studebaker truck pulled into the driveway. It was Cesar. His truck was loaded down with pine slabs.

Randolph continued to the porch with the splashing pails while Cesar turned the truck around and backed it to the woodpile. He waved at Randy through his rolled down window. Randy wasn't studying him, he was thinking about having to help unload that big load of lumber. Gregory came out the back door. He removed his straw hat to scratch his head. "Well, I'll be!" His voice was raised above the noise of the Studebaker motor. "You said you was gonna bring me a load of slabs. And here you are!" Cesar just grinned and continued to back up toward the chopping block.

Randolph waited for Cesar to turn the motor off and climb down from the cab. Instead of seeing him get out of the truck, he saw Cesar's grinning reflection in the side mirror, looking back at his load. he raced the motor and pulled forward a few feet. Then he threw the truck in reverse and backed up the same distance before slamming on the brakes.

Like the Lone Ranger or somebody, Cesar reared the truck up while Randolph and Gregory stood stunned at the sight of the big green Studebaker hood, six feet off the ground. The load of wood slid-as smooth as anybody's business-right off the truck bed and landed in a neat pile. The cab bounced down against the groung

Still grinning, Cesar climbed out. "Well-sir, Gregory. I gave you my word. And, as I live and breathe, my word is my bond."

The sights and words of yesdiddy floated in his thoughts while he climbed the steps to the porch. He took the wash basin over to the rain barrel to fill it with water to wash the dirt and sawdust off his face and hands.

When he was four years old, learning to read, it was Cesar who told him he was gonna be a preacher. He was still trying to figure out when and how that would happen. But for now, he had looked up the meaning of "bond." Then he vowed that, just like

Cesar, he would grow up making sure that his word was his bond.

Randolph reflected again on what had happened today and yesdiddy. He looked over the buckets on the shelf, out across the hollow, spring and blackberry patch, up beyond Arjay's to the the familiar horizon. "Walking in Jeruselem just like John!"

* * *

'What's different about Miz Mattie?' ArJays had been like always. So were the narrow wagon trail and the path through the patch of woods-lush green leaves still brushed against his face. Miz Mattie's gingerbread house looked the same, but she looked different. 'Oh shit!' Randolph's awakening bolted through his mind. "You got teeth! I mean... your new teeth look good Miz Mattie."

"I was wondering when you were going to notice." She saw a defensive look cross his face. "I'm just pickin' at you son." His smile of relief put her at ease and, for them both, Mattie's windowless kitchen felt full of the sunlight that did not actually penetrate. "Sit down and rest your bones Randy." He grinned, with his mouth closed, and sat at the table.

Glad as Randolph was to see the brown witch again, for the first time around her, he felt self concious about the gap in his own grin.

"Mozzelle and them ever talk about getting you some dentures?"

"When I first lost my teeth, the dentist told us, my mother and me, they would grow back in 'cause I was just nine years old. I guess they're not gonna grow back in after all." He thought for a moment. "I'd better write home and ask mama about it."

Mattie set a box of graham crackers and two cups of milk on the table. "How'd you lose your front teeth..if you don't mind me askin'?"

He did not mind. At the same time, it came to him that it had been a while since anybody had asked-long enough that he could sometimes relax into the pretention that everything was like it was supposed to be. "Well, back home..." Randolph looked into Miz Mattie's eyes. "Back home, I was playing hookie..." He had never before used that euphemism, he'd always said 'cutting school.' "...and playing a game of baseball with a pick handle as the bat. My friend Henry hit a home run and slung the pick handle right into my mouth." While he spoke, he discovered that the incident was far enough behind him, he no longer felt pain when he talked about it. He explained, "I was catching."

Mattie heard the irony in the explanation. 'He sure was catching .' She saw that the boy felt comfortable telling her what happened. That allowed her to suppress a wince when she told him how she lost her teeth. "My front teeth had to be extracted several years back... Umm! These graham crackers are nice and fresh aren't they?"

"Yes'm."

"Help yourself. If we don't eat the lot of them, they'll just stay here and get stale."

"Miz Mattie, you from 'round here?"

"Naw. My home's Waycross Georgia. 'Course I left there more years ago than I care to remember." Randolph tried to imagine how many years she did not care to remember.

"Your home is Washington isn't it?" "Oh. Yes ma'am. I was born in Garfield Memorial Hospital at 13th and Clifton Street Northwest." What led Randolph to give the exact location of his birthplace was the sound of Waycross Georgia. Miz Mattie had cut off his enjoyment of that sound when she asked about his home.

Waycross Georgia. He had heard of that place.

Like a heap of other words and phrases with square sounds; "Rock Creek Park," "Butterbrickle," "Jump down, spin around, pick a bail of cotton," "Back street," "Duke Ellington," "Box cars" and "The Hucklebuck, "Waycross Georgia, danced around in the pleasure corners of his well. "What's Waycross Georgia like?"

Mattie tilted her small head and stretched her mouth imto a contemplative grin. "What's Waycross like? Lord, it's been so long since I left home-I never went back you know-Well, at the time I left, it was a little cotton village..."

A revelation came to Randolph "We never had cotton around here!" He wished he hadn't interupted, "Did you pick cotton as a youngun?"

"I picked cotton from the time I first started walking. Got to be pretty good at it too. When I took the first thing smokin' at seventeen, I was picking over two hundred pounds a day." She looked at her hands. "Cotton bolls, the little white puffs, have burrs

168

underneath. If you don't have good gloves those burrs will cut your hands to pieces. Yessir Mr. Randolph, I sure did pick cotton, a heap of it." Mattie stopped abruptly and jumped up from the table. "Looks like we need some more milk."

Randolph was set to talk about getting sticky tobacco gum on your hands when you work tobacco. But when Mattie sat back down she took him on a train ride to the Big Apple.

"I had my train ticket and twenty seven dollars I had saved. Child, I didn't know a soul in New York. I had an aunt there I'd never seen. It just came to me that was where I oughta be. I must of been grinning like a cheshire cat when I climbed into the Colored car-no more backaches from dragging a cotton sack up and down those rows in the hot sun all day." She looked at Randy. He was in the train with her, anticipating. "I had packed two banana sandwiches and some pecans." (She pronounced it, 'pee-cawns.) That made her sound to Randy like Betty Davis or somebody. "You ever had a banana sandwich?"

"My friend Lincoln used to bring banana sandwiches to school before he moved to Winston Salem. Sometimes I would swap a ham or a peanut butter and jelly sandwich for one of his banana sandwiches."

"I thought that choo-choo was gonna take the rest of my life to get to New York City. We got to... 'PENNSYLVANIA STATION AT A QUARTER TO FOUR...'" Mattie sang the line from, Chattanooga Choo Choo. She had a good laugh, placing herself in the middle of the big city station, in 1923. "You would've thought I had arrived at the Golden Gate. Here I was inside a room that seemed as if it was big enough to hold all of Waycross-ceiling high as the sky. Big signs and lights all over the place. Lord honey, I wanted time to stand still, right then and there!"

She was years ago and miles away. Randolph tried to imagine he was up there-back then with her.

She smoothed the pleats of her black skirt, adjusted her clotche hat, and toted her match box suitcase out onto Eighth Avenue.

The girl from Waycross could not have been prepared for how small she was made to feel by the gray towers-up down and around. The first building to catch her eye was the New Yorker Hotel diagonally across from the station. Before recovering from the mass of that edifice, she looked further up the Avenue and one stone mountain after another loomed toward the Summer sky. More overwhelming than the looming monsters, was the sense that maybe she had made a mistake, coming to this place.

"I tell you young man, if it wasn't for my aunt Maude who I was going to stay with in Harlem, I might've turned around right there and caught the next train back home. Aunt Maudie, they called her, couldn't meet me at the station. They wouldn't let her off from the dress factory where she worked."

"How come you wanted to go back home?"

"It was just so cold... I mean it was the middle of Summer. But being surrounded by all that concrete made me feel like a body would imagine it might feel down in the Grand Canyon. For a few months, I hated New York. Then, and it happened without me taking notice, I was in love with that city... crazy 'bout it!"

"What'd you do in New York?" An involuntary guffaw burst from Mattie. "Well, Randolph, I can't tell you all I did do. Let's just say, for the most part, I enjoyed myself. And I learned a good deal more than I had ever thought there was to know."

Today, Miz Mattie's face was already different because of her new teeth shining all over the place. The look she took on while she led him back to old times made her seem something or other like pretty-not pretty like pretty-but pretty like a dream or a painting in a museum.

Randolph forgot about the gap in his own mouth and grinned as broad as he ever had. The way Miz Mattie had gone about answering him, told him more than he had anticipated-more than he could immediately grasp. She reminded him that like her he was destined to learn more than he ever thought there was to know. He was tempted to ask her to tell him about Paris. That would have to wait until another time; the door she led him to, opened on a wide space. It was kinda like the world that he began to see when she told him about Eugene Chen. The kind of stuff thar needed him to be up in his room by his lonesome.

Because he was afraid that what he needed to cogitate on might get away from him, Randolph abruptly got up and left. He had the manners to apologize although he did not have the time or words to explain.

* * *

"That you Randolph?" "Yeah." He didn't let Mo's voice stop him. He went up the stairs-two by two-hoping she would not tell him to do some chore. At the attic level; 'So far so good.'

The three steps up to the three bedrooms felt as long as the staircase to the landing. "Whew!" Mozzelle was not gonna call him back down. He was free to steer his mind into the shadowy grove filled with thoughts that could guide him into light.

Every time Randolph came up here to his room, he examined it as if he were entering it for the first time. Back in D.C. the bedroom was kind of like in the movies. It was a little room with egg shell walls. This room had faded wallpaper. The ceiling was plain planks like a barn...or Jesus' manger. He liked the way it looked and felt in here. Still, every time he came up the three steps, and walked inside, he had to let the old timey feeling settle over him like new. It was like stepping into history-President Lincoln's log cabin or a hay loft he once climbed up to in a deserted barn.

The trip to yesteryear only took a moment. He glanced up at the ceiling and thought of the tin roof above the slats. In the next moment his gaze reached his library-now twenty books on the shelf he made from a pine slab. pretty soon, he'd have to put up another shelf.

The crunch of the straw mattress was like a weedy hug around his bottom. His mind was cluttered with snatches of pictures and thoughts. It was like one of his dreams of flying; where should he light?

Randolph tried to imagine what it was like to pick cotton. He pictured the balls in the little blue box in the medicine cabinet back home.

In only a moment, he saw the balls on the plant which he imagined to be like a pea vine. He picked one of them...his sense faltered. The cotton ball, unlike a pod of peas or a tobacco leaf, had no weight. He could not feel it in his hand. The picture faded.

After drifting through more snatches, here he was in the middle of the big New York train station amid a crowd like those in the radio show, "Grand Central Station." Everywhere he looked, white people dressed like movie crowds milled about in a New York City way.

Miz Mattie had not given him the details of how she got from there to her aunt's house in Harlem.

He pictured the neon sign outside the 7th & T. Cocktail Lounge in D.C. and he was smack dab in the middle of Harlem. Colored people sat at tables dressed in tuxedos and fox furs, sipping coctails out of long stemmed glasses.

Not knowing the incongruity of it, Randolph heard Glen Miller's "String Of Pearls" bouncing in the background. He did not see himself there. Like in his dreams, he was an invisible presence.

Folks used words like, "Copacetic" and "Marvelous!"

He lay back on the bed-kept hold of Harlem-until he drifted into sleep.

Sometimes Randolph took flight after a running start. Other times, he stood where he was and shot straight up like Rocketman.

It came to him, that's New York City down there.

After sailing above neon cocktail signs and photographs of Duke Ellington, Sarah Vaughn and Louis Jordan in evening clothes, he shut out everything except the feel and sound of summer wind against his face. Only a moment lapsed before another familiar sight appeared below; the Empire State Building. He was about to dive down and land on the its peak when he spotted a crowd.

"Hey y'all! Hey! Look up here!" A throng of facelesss people looked up to see what in the world... "Here! Here I am!" He knew doggone well they were shocked to see somebody flying.

"OHHH!" His voice rang out through mid-Manhattan. His body tumbled toward the concrete sidewalk. "HELLLP!" He got closer to the ground than he meant to before he decided enough was enough. "OH-OHHH!" He sneered at the crowd that now had faces, white faces, only a few feet from his sneer. He yelled "OH-OHHH," again before swooping upward with his arms straight out from his shoulders. "Up, up and AWAAAY!"

Pricks from the straw mattress against his back brought him wide awake.

Before Randolph was sent to Washington at age six to begin school, he had no dreams, at least he didn't remember having had any. Certainly there had been no vivid ones. It seemed that from the very day he got to D.C. he began to have dreams. Many of them were scary, some were delightful, some were sweet. Almost all of them left him confused. Among the most puzzling were his flying dreams. When he awoke from the most hazy, dark, confusing or downright frightening dreams, some security force-living beneath his level of reckoning, joy or fear, guarded him against the thicket of cobwebs he would walk into if he tried to figure out what the blazes was going on. Today it rose to separate him from the confusion that would have surely come had he tried to connect his dream with Miz Mattie's mew York anecdote and his future.

Chapter Eleven
Sometimes a Notion

Arlene and Willie came by this afternoon to drop Nadine off for the weekend. She's four years old now. She has bright chicklet teeth that remind Randolph of Miz Mattie's new store-boughts.

The front porch light comes though the window. Gregory is out there patching an innertube for a Chevie coupe he borrowed from somebody. Mozzelle, who allowed Randolph to listen to 'Gangbusters' tonight, is reading the paper. Some time after grandma died, mo brought the rocker in from the porch and took to sitting in to read the paper. It was like she was taking her mother's place.

A break comes in the radio drama, a Sal Hepatica ad comes on. Nadine is as attentive to the announcer as she is to the show itself.

Randolph studies his little cousin in her miniture overalls. It is not easy to remember the one and two year old he used to mind while Mozzelle was up in New York, and Willie and Arlene were off gallivantin' around.

A flashback of another Saturday night descends on him.

He and Nadine were here by themselves. Randolph had put her to bed soon after Gangbusters went off.

After the child was sound asleep, he put on his denim jacket to guard against the night air. Then he slipped out the door to head off to Midway. Randolph Wilford was no less afraid of the dark now than he had ever been. He also was fully aware that he ought not be leaving Nadine in the house by herself even if she was asleep.

One day, out in front of the schoolhouse, he stood looking down the road where a small building sat on a knoll at the corner where the schoolhouse road and the road to the hardtop met.

The DewDrop Inn was run by the family of a classmate of his. Why his attention was suddenly increased on that day, was a mystery. After that, Randolph stood many a time staring at the corner cafe. When he passed by on the school bus, his fancy would penetrate the artificial brick and tar paper exterior to imagine what that juke joint must look like inside.

Tonight, haints or no, being a good boy or no, he was gonna see what went on in that place-what those grown folks did in there where they drank liquor, smoked cigarettes and played the jukebox.

The air blew cooler against him than air in the sunlight. It was the first time he'd had Susie Q. out at night.

Although the hills and gulleys between Cedar Grove and Midway were mostly sided by fields and barnyards-no woods, the night spooked him a little.

Peddling on an upgrade-his shoulders hunched, Randy saw a farmhousr-all-lighted up. The corners of his mouth slid into a grin. "Hell! Along here, there're more people than haints.

* * *

SINCE I MET YOU BA-BY
MY WHOLE LIFE HAS CHANGED
SINCE I MET YOU BA-BY
MY WHOLE LIFE HAS CHANGED
EV-RY-BO-DY TELLS ME
I AM NOT THE SA-AME

The juke box had a deep bass rumble to it. And it was turned up the way Randolph turned the radio up when he was in the house by himself. The young grownfolks were slowdragging to the smooth voice of Ivory Joe Hunter. The place was near 'bout dark except the Wurlitzer jukebox lights and little lights-red-green-yellow and blue, swirling around the tiny cafe. It was like a smokey Christmas morning.

I DON'T NEED NO-BODY
TO TELL MY TRUH-UH-BLES TO
I DON'T NEED NO-BODY
TO TELL MY TRUH-UH-BLES TO
SINCE I MET YOU BA-BY
ALL I NEED IS YOU-OO

This was the second time in a row the song was playing. Randolph had dropped the nickel in the slot that brought it back. It was kinda like a fairy tale. At home, he had to sit in front of the radio hoping his favorite song would play. All you had to do here was put a nickel in the slot to hear any song on the list. When he first came in, he found a corner and sat on the floor-as if nobody would notice that this mannish rascal was in here. The lights swirled and the voice of Ivory Joe floated over the tinkle of his piano. His voice sounded like his name. It was the color of, and melted in the heat, like salt water taffy.

SINCE I MET YOU BA-BY
I'M A HAPPY MAN
SINCE I MET YOU BA-BY
I'M A HAPPY MAN
I'M GONNA TRY TO PLEASE YOU
IN EVERY WAY-AY I CAN

Ivory Joe Hunter was Randolph Wilford. Every word he sang, all the emotion in his voice, every piano note he played was Randolph telling his someday girlfriend how he felt. That nameless passion from church rose up through him-he wanted to cry. Without warning, Jimmy Witherspoon's powerful voice comes sounding like it's out of the mouth of somebody with a new head cold. It is not hoarse-it's rich, nasal, booming.

There ain't nothin' I can do, nor nothin' I can say
That folks don't criticize me
But I'm gonna do just as I want to anyway
And don't care if they all despise me
If I should take a notion, to jump into the ocean
'Tain't nobody's biz-ness if I do

Next, came the voice of the 'King of the Jukebox.' It was so familiar to Randolph he could hear it in his head anytime he wanted to. There was not a time when Louis Jordan did not have a big hit. Louie played alto saxophone too. Without thinking about it, Randolph heard the wail of the horn and the voice as one, "rockin' and rollin' ".

Now, if you've ever been down to New Orleans
Then you can understand just what I mean,
Now all through the week it's quiet as a mouse,
But on Saturday night, they go from house to house;
You don't have to pay the usual admission
If you're a cook or a waiter or a good musician.
So if you happen to be just passin' by
Stop in at the Saturday night fish fry!

It was rock-in'! It was rock-in'!
You never seen such scufflin' and shufflin' till the break of
daw-awn!
It was rockin'! It was rock-in'!
You never seen such scufflin' and shufflin' till the break of
daw-awn!

*Hoopskirts swung and porkpie hats bopped and bounced,
two by two. The small space of the juke-joint was packed with the
'scufflin' and shufflin' the man sang and honked about.*

IT WAS ROCKIN'!

IT WAS ROCKIN'!

* * *

*Wasn't til he got back past the white school's yard full of
yellow buses reflecting starlight that Randolph himself reflected.
He really had been almost invisible sitting on the floor next to the
juke box. One long lean woman looked down and said, "S'cuse me"
when she stepped on the side of his shoe before she jitterbugged
away. Nobody else paid him any mind. Anyway, he had dared do
something he'd wanted to do for a long time.*

*A warm satisfaction stayed around Randolph until he
reached the top of the hill by Chester Burns' big house. Fifty yards
later, when he turned past the house where the bull had mounted
the heifer... 'What if Nadine woke up and saw that he wasn't
there?' He tried to push the thought away. The closer he got to the
house, the heavier it settled on his conscience. When he passed the
mail boxes on cemetery road and was in the home stretch, he
imagined hearing the child pitching a crying fit. No sooner had he
pedaled past Mr. Ervin's mule path did Randolph really hear
Naomi screaming at the top of her lungs.*

"Oh Lord!" His voice sounded too loud-he looked over his shoulder adding embarssment to the guilt filling him up.

"Oh, Lord!" He did not know why but when he got to the front of the house, he climbed off the bike to tiptoe into the driveway. Nadine was crying loud enough to wake the dead. He could tell that she had cried long enough for phlegm to change the way she sounded.

He let Susie Q. fall next to the tree and ran toward the front door knowing good and well he wasn't gonna outrun his fear and shame. She was standing in the middle of the living room. Randolph turned the light on and saw that her diaper was sagging-wet. Nadine looked up at him. She shocked him and made him cringe by crying even louder-it was like she wanted to make him suffer. He ran to her-picked her up to try and console her. Nadine wailed and gulped air, repeating each wail and gulp on and on.

"Baby I'm sorry! I'm sorry!" He spoke loud, hoping to either console or distract her. Nadine did not let up. Randolph sat her on the couch, knelt before her. "Nadine! I'm so sorry!" She still didn't let up. He grabbed her shoulders and shook her more times than he intended. The child took a breath long and deep. He thought he had injured her. He froze. A gush of sound came from her little body so loud and pitiful that Randolph screamed out his own pain. He could hardly see her through his own tears.

He picked her up again, toted her around and around the room. "Nadine, I'm sorry. I swear 'fore God I won't ever leave you by yourself again." Whether it was his solemn promise or exhausttion, Nadine wound down to a whimper. She hugged his neck and stopped crying all together. Her drenched diaper was around her knees. The front of Randolph's jacket was also drenched. He took off the jacket and put a dry diaper on the child before picking her up again to hug her long and deep.

Four year old Nadine stared up at his distant expression. Gangbusters was over. He looked at her. "You alright?"

"Uh, huh." Her bright smile convinced him that she must not even remember that night. He looked across the room to see if Mozzelle noticed he had been daydreaming. She was still engrossed in the newspaper.

"Want to play a game of checkers Nadine?"

"Yeah! Let's play checkers."

She fumbled for the flashlight on the night table. It was 3:a.m. Normally Mattie did not mind living back down in here where there was no electricity. But sometimes, like right now, it would be nice to have electric lights. She wanted to look in the mirror at herself. After the dream she woke up from, she would be bold enough to face the vanity mirror, lift her night gown and have a good look. How did her body look now-her private parts, at sixty seven?

In Paris, she was once told, "Mah-tee, votre corps est magnifique!" Why, after all these years, would she dream of a man she spent one night with on the West Bank? It must have been thirty five-forty years since she thought of that night... "After all Mattie, it was your first time to have a man, faites cunnilingua." Her face flushed in the dark. 'My lord! I never did get used to that...never did.' Under the embarrassment, she felt her mouth shape into a smile. "OH my goodnes!" She could almost reach back and touch the days when she was young and sometimes a little wild. "Fast," as they say down here."

No need to try to get back to sleep.

The first sip from a cup of buttermilk brought her fully-awake. She had wrapped herself in her old-blue-woolen robe, even though it was, "Warm as toast in here."

"Habit I guess."

Mattie stayed in Paris for a month. Then, back to Harlem. Harlem was home now. And as far as Mattie Wells could see, Harlem would be home from now on. She was able to get the job back that aunt Maude had got her at the dress factory. Aunt Maude, may she rest in peace, let Hattie stay on at her place for quite a spell. "Girl, ain't no sense in you going out there on your own with just a few pennies in your pocket."

There were some really good times in New York-the spea-keasies, the integrated clubs in "The Village," The Renaissance and Savoy and the theaters on 125th Street where she saw Bricktop and Josephine Baker. But none of all that held a candle to the few times Mattie got to go up to the "Big house on the hill."

Madam C. J. Walker's mansion was in Irvington On The Hudson, up in Westchester. "I never got the chance to see the whole place. But they said there were 30 rooms in that big white house. Wouldn't surprise me if there were even more.

She refilled her cup, took a big gulp, folded her arms beneath her sagging breasts and allowed her memories of the times in Villa Lewaro to take control.

After the first two visits to the mansion, she no longer paid attention to the antique European furnishings, (rich white folks furniture) she called it. It was being where she could rub elbows with the Colored stars and big shots that made her feel like somebody.

Although she would not let it rise up from the bogs, still down there was a pride at being able to be on equal footing with white folks too. One time, she had someone point out Enrico Caruso across the parlor. The opera tenor, "With his itty-bitty self," the woman whom she did not know told her, was the one who suggested that Madam Walker name her new mansion, Villa Lewaro.

Mattie took another sip and thought of the very first time she tasted champagne. It was at that great lady's mansion. She laughed so hard she almost dropped her cup of buttermilk.

The stem of the goblet was between her middle fingers while the bowl rested in her palm. She had never been more self satisfied. To any ear that might be attentive she actually said, "Madam C. J. is elegantly attired this evening." Most of those within earshot pretended not to be. After a discreet moment, a gentleman eased up beside her. "Madam C. J. Walker passed on four years ago. Our hostess is her daughter, Lelia." Hoping not to embarass her, he added, "She is the inspiration for the name of this estate... her initials, anyway."

No effort, no matter how well intended, could have Kept Mattie from being as embarassed as she had ever been or would ever be. She kept her mouth shut for the balance of the evening and never visited the big house on the hill again. She told herself, "That's too high falutin' for me. I should've known it all the time." The Harlem dance halls and bars, as well as the clubs in The Village, were more her speed.

Mattie lived in New York for thirty seven years. She frequently attended St. Philllip's Episcopal Church. Once, she was

tempted to go again to Villa Lewaro. Someone told her that a
Colored man named Vertner W. Tandy designed the church as well
as Madam Walker's mansion. She decided it was enough to be
proud that her race produced folks like Mr. Tandy and Madam
Walker.

More important than any of the good times was finding out that her people didn't have to take a back seat to anybody.

Before she caught the first thing smoking to New York, Mattie had believed that Negroes were just what the folks she knew had been convinced they were; dimwitted shiftless good for nothings. She learned in The Big Apple and The city Of Light how much she and everybody else had been lied to.

Somebody somewhere said (it might have even been in Waycross for all she could remember) "Some things you pick up along the way are like chewing gum; you chew on them until the flavor is gone, then you spit 'em out. On the other hand, there are things that stay with you, they never lose their flavor."

She was thankful that as a young woman she was of a mind to travel. Otherwise, 'I would have spent my whole life chewing gum.' Pride flowed all through Mattie because she framed that thought on her own. Not for one moment though did she compare her occasional epiphany with the brilliance of Black folks she met in New York and in gay Paree. "Oh!" It came to her, one of her girl friends later told her that the man who hipped her about the hostess being the daughter of and not Madam C. J. Walker herself, was Duke Ellington. Learning that she had met Mr. Ellington without recognizing him only further convinced Mattie that she was right to stop going up to the mansion. "I won't no Sophisticated Lady." Something else came to her. 'Maybe' she was more in the know than she gave herself credit for. "Nobody's here but me so I can think or say anything I want to." She tilted the cup as if it were a longstemmed glass, and for a brief moment the buttermilk tasted a little like champagne.

* * *

The amber-crust-peach cobbler-aroma, wafted from the oven. This tingling bouquet abetted Hilda's mind in its wool-gathering. That morning she had noted in her vanity mirror a roll of fat around her middle. She wished, in vain, that telephone lines had by now been. 'extended out here to we country folk.' If they had telephones she would be able to ring up her precocious young cousin Randy. With his appetite, he would surely help her dispose of the cobbler that she, 'As things stand, am going to dig into with sinful glee. "Maybe I will stroll down to the pea patch and pick a peck while the dish cools. That will melt away some of the lard I am carrying around."

Hilda had a good laugh at her silly self. One of the advantages of having attained age fifty eight was that she deceived herself far less than in her younger years. Something that did not cross her mind was calling out the side window for Mason to come and join her for a little dessert. Her brother in law, after all these years, would still want more sweets than come from the oven. And it was her fault.

It had been overcast all day. Before, during and after Morgan's funeral it looked as if rain would come at any minute. At the gravesite she was certain that it would finally come-it seemed that more often than not, burials were accompanied by rainfall. But blessedly not a raindrop fell.

A day or so later, Mason came over to comfort her; it was clear he meant to do that and nothing more. The kitchen was full of the scent of peach cobbler that day too.

So many times, Morgan and she had enjoyed their favorite dessert and, without thinking about it, winding up in their bed sweeting, sweeter sweet.

Mason had always favored Morgan. Today, he seemed to be the very embodiment of his late brother. Maybe it was Hilda's memory of an afternoon in the hay loft long before she had dreamed of marraige-let alone to Morgan. Anyway, she and Mason were no more than sixteen-seventeen then, and the sap was rising. Mason was an easygoing fellow who was quite goodlooking in a long-lean and lanky sort of way.

Today, less than a week after she burried her darling Morgan, Hilda intoxicated Mason with her peach cobbler and lured, "Yes, lured!" her impressionable brother in law into the soft comfort of her pink and gray bedroom.

She stared into the wisps of steam rising from the piping treat, now on the sideboard, making her salivate. "Oh well. All in all it was harmless. Besides, I suffered long and hard over it." Anticipation floated on the scent and all but turned regret into nostalgia.

During Hilda's years in New york she was consumed with teaching English to a rainbow of high school students; hoping that she was helping to prepare them for the coming of true integration. On occasion she felt the tug of doubt. "Scat, doubt! You are not welcome here. Racial prejudice will surely end."

To this very day, she held fervently that either jim crow would end or there was no God in heaven. That was the long and the short of it.

Hilda found time for a few romances while in the big city for more than two decades. There was a sequence of four men. She noted that she had covered all but one Borough. "Poor Staten Island." She and her girlfriends enjoyed this bon mot. None of the affairs lasted longer than a year or so. Hilda had the integrity to admit that what passed for love in each relationship was only lust.

Even with hot flashes and night sweats, she said good riddance to her gone away libido. After all, Morgan-God rest his soul-was the only man she ever really loved.

The cobbler bouquet lingered in her nostrils to excite Hilda's salavaries.

Without perpending, "Well, if I gain an additional pound or two it won't be so bad." A saucer, a spoon and ladle were already next to the deep-dish baking pan.

* * *

Ervin was two years younger than his brother, Wayne. Everybody he knew who was the baby in the family was spoiled-if not spoiled, at least allowed to get away with more than their big sister or brother could. Not with his mama and papa; they made allowances for their older boy that made Ervin know, they either thought more of Wayne or less of their baby boy.

184

Both the Mills boys were "cute" according to the girls in the community of Red Hill. But even they made more of a fuss over Wayne than Ervin. It won't no secret; Ervin knew exactly why he always got the short end of the stick. He was dark complected. Well, not really dark, and his hair wasn't all that nappy either-it was soft and thick. The difference was, Wayne was light skinned. His hair was almost straight. He favored grand daddy, on mama's side. Wayne showed the Cherokee blood from that old man.

By the time the boys were twelve and fourteen, Ervin had stopped fretting about how he was treated. Anyway, folks didn't treat him all that bad. They were just nicer to his big brother.

Later on, Wayne went off to high school and Ervin was left at home to help papa with the farm work. He knew dadgum well brother won't no smarter than he was. Truth was, he enjoyed working the fields and tending the livestock. Oh! It was clear to him that darker younguns with nappy heads caught hell. Every now and then, a darkskinned boy or girl would have something about them that caused folks to be nice to them. He never was able to figure out why... Anyway, being made to stay home on the farm kinda made Ervin feel like Brer Rabbit. "Thank you Lord for throwing me into the briar patch."

Ervin got on his knees to slide the half gallon of Schenley's under the bed. He had taken a few sips over the half hour he had it out. He was proud that while he was fond of drink, he was also a man of moderation.

A while back, he lived in Durham. During those years, he was a Prince Hall Mason, known in the Lodge as a man of character. All masons aspired to be, but not many reached 'perfection.' When Ervin decided to take himself a wife, he knew it was time to get back to the soil where he belonged. Wayne, who had introduced him to freemasonry, stayed on in Durham even after he too got married.

"These many years later, brother..." Ervin chuckled at the word brother. (Men in the Lodge called one another brother. He and Wayne would sometimes call one another, "Brother, brother.") Wayne was still up there in the Lodge in the big town.

Ervin was looking back to let let himself catch up to himself because Wayne was about to arrive for his annual visit to go possum hunting and renew aquaintance.

He pondered the two single shot, scatterguns hanging over the door. His was a Blue Eagle. 'Wonder what made 'em come up with a name like that? No such thing as a blue eagle. Of course, they could call that cheap gun anything they wanted to. Wayne's Winchester, hanging just below the Blue Eagle, was called Model 37-simple as that. The polished stock of that gun looked like the ingrained finish on a chestnut wardrobe. Ervin let his gaze rise back up to the Blue Eagle. The stock was solid brown and, no matter how much you rubbed polish onto it, the dang thing stayed dull. Didn't matter none in the end, he had the satisfaction of knowing that he was a better shot blindfolded than brother would be with a magnified scope. He allowed himself a full throated laugh and decided he was entitled to one more swig before he took down the guns to give them a good cleaning.

All in all, he looked forward to seeing his big brother. Oh, Wayne might be a high fallutin' insurance executive up there in Durham, but when he came down here, Ervin was mister man. *'Covet not. Covet not.'* "Anyway, we're about as close as any two brothers I know." He reflected for a moment. "At least those that live as far apart as we do."

Ervin decided he did not need another swig after all. He commenced to take the shotguns down from the racks. He had already placed the bore-rod, patches and a little bottle of solvent on the floor between his chair and the bed.

The Schenleys was wearing off. "Brother and I will have a nice drink and talk about the old days."

* * *

Gregory was 'dead to the world' when Mozzelle swung her feet on a quiet arc to the floor. She tipped through Randolph's room on her way downstairs to to take a bicarbonate of soda. Her whispered voice came out of the dark to her own ears. "Lord! That boy snores louder than a cross-cut saw!" Randolph's ungodly wood-sawing wasn't all that bothered her. Her hand was pressed against a knot in her stomach. "I can't say the second helping of bread puddin' wasn't worth it." The beginning of a chuckle came up short when a blunt pain ran through the knot making her pass wind. "That sure felt good." The expulsion of gas was relief enough that she no longer needed to take a dose of soda. She decided to go on anyway.

Mozzelle wanted to work out something that had been bothering her ever since she came back from up the road. Why she had not had a fling while she was in Brooklyn she could not undestand. That was part of the reason she went to New York in the first place. The Good Lord knew, she had more chances than she had ever had in her life to lay with some man if her heart desired to. For some reason though, she stayed up there for weeks and never let anybody come close to bedding her.

In the kitchen, Mo put a teaspoon full of bicarbonate in a glass of water and stirred the drink while she walked unawares to the dining room table.

"Bustling," was a word she had heard somebody use. When she learned what that word meant, Mo agreed wholeheartedly that New York City-every inch of it-sure as Carter had little liver pills, was a bustling town.

After one gulp of the elixer, she belched what felt like the last of the gas that had been bottled up in her belly.

"Honey, I can't tell you how glad I am you decided to come up here." Juanita had been up here since who knew when. To listen to her talk you wouldn't know that the girl was from down home. It seemed a little queer hearing her new accent... Well, it wasn't so new no more. Folks weren't kidding when they said, 'Time changes things.'

They closed and locked the doors of Juanita's forty nine Ford Fairlane. "Lord 'Nita! I had forgotten how tall you are. Juanita pulled herself up to her full five foot eleven. "Yeah child. I'm a big ol' yella gal."

Mozzelle made herself preen to the fullness of her own five-eight. She thought , 'I can't say you're as big as you are tall, with your nice curves.' She was thinking of her own middle aged spread. 'And you ain't so much a gal no more either.' Mozzelle enjoyed this private assessment.

From Juanita's sixth floor window, the sky blue Ford-with

its chrome bumpers, strips and door handles, looked like a toy. At the same time, the car looked like what Mo imagined folks came up North for.

"Mo! I've decided to throw a little get-together tonight for you to meet a few of my friends. How does that sound to you?" The ring of Juanita's voice off the high ceilings made Mo aware of the space and distance from the dining room to where she stood by the window. Like the brand new car downstairs, Nita's nice clothes and everything about this city, there was something kinda 'too big or nice to give a good hug to. 'Maybe I'll get used to it'-"You would do that for me?"

Juanita was now beside her at the window. "I not only would but I'm going to."

"Well, I'd better unpack my Sunday-go-to-meeting duds." Mozzelle felt a tinge of discomfort, hearing her countryfied expression bounce off the window. Just as quickly, she chided herself for feeling self concious. Juanita smiled as if she intuited her old friend's attempt to get herself together. Nita had always been a good soul.

The Cabernet Sauvignon went straight to her head. Mozzelle had good enough sense to not take another sip until the buzz wore off. Feeling a little tipsy wasn't all that bad though. She just had to make sure not to lose control.

The Dominoes, Clovers, Ruth Brown, The Orioles and Laverne Baker were stacked on Juanita's HiFi. The voices of the ten or twelve revelers blended with the those of Rudy West and The Five Keys.

YOU'VE GOT TO...

WHOOOOO

GIVE A LITTLE...

WHOO-OO-OO

TAKE A LITTLE...

WHOO-OO

AND LET YOUR POOR HEARRRT

BREAK A LITTLE

WHOO-OO-OO

THAT'S THE STORY OF...

WHOO=OO-OO

THAT'S THE GLORY OF LOVE...

The fellow slow-dragged close enough that she had to decide-then and there-whether or not she wanted to get it on with him. He wasn't a bad looking brownskin fella either. In a few minutes Mo realized something was keeping her from giving in to him. Keith was a funeral director; that impressed her. But he had a smell about him... not a nice smell either. Later on, Juanita told her that what she smelled was formaldehyde. "That's what they use for embalming folks."

"Oh Lord! I told him he could call me, here." The word, embalming had congered the image of a corpse laid out in a coffin. Mo couldn't shake it. "Nita, you got to think of some way I can put him off. Lord! I almost... please help me think of something to tell that man."

Mozzelle stared into the antacid residue at the bottom of the glass. Of the different fellas Nita tried to fix her up with, that was the closest she came to getting down to business. 'Maybe I'm not warm blooded like I used to be. Maybe next year when I turn forty, I'll be hot to trot again. They say life begins at forty.' Mozzzelle knew very well, she had never been, "warm blooded." She smiled her way to the ice box to add a little water to the dregs of bicarbonate, drank it and burped again.

The indigestion had led to some kind of resolution? Was that the word? Yeah, that was the word.

* * *

The scent of sweet potato custard-pie was rich and heavy in his nostrils. That tan tingle mixed deep in the shadow of Randolph's breath with the scorched brown taste of roasted peanuts he chewed in deliberate chomps. The back oven smokiness of roasted peanuts and honeycomb aroma of baking sweet potato

189

were familiar like a church bell on Sunday. What informed his awareness, this twilight, was that the goobers Randolph savored and the tater pie glory drifting from the kitchen, were his own doing, beginning to end.

"You sure you want to grow peanuts?" Why was Mo asking him that like she thought he didn't mean what he done told her? Anyway, he'd better let her know he was serious so she wouldn't ask him again. "Yeah, Mo.' She still stared at him like he was playing or talkin' out of his head or something. "Yeah!" He almost added, 'I swear fo' God!' He had better sense than let blasphemy slip out of his mouth though. "I ain't kiddin'!"

"Alright. But it ain't easy. Sit down here." She motioned him to the dining room table where she was shelling peas. "You're gonna have to dry some peanuts until they're fit to sow."

Randolph had told Mozzelle he wanted to grow the peanuts in the field across the road, fifty yards or so down from the Methodist church. " ...Since Gregory didn't plant no field corn over there this year..."

"You don't want to sow peanuts in the whole field. That's a heap of peanuts. Why don'tcha sow some sweet potato slips out there too?' She thought for a minute. "Yep. Sweet potatoes and goobers'll make good rotation crops. Yep."

Randolph didn't break her rhythm to ask what rotation crops were. He could trust himself to find out all about that by and by.

Saliva drooled from the corners of his mouth, as much urged by pride as the smokey flavor of his peanuts. "Randolph Wilford's peanuts... Naw! Farmer Wilford's goober crop."

Bits of farmer wilford's crop sprayed out of his mouth with a prideful laugh. He sat still until he was sure Mo hadn't heard or noticed from the kitchen. He used his shirtsleeve to wipe the crumbs from the table into his palm and stuck them into his pants pocket. "Damn! I almost ruined it." He stilled himself and appreciated that Mozelle had let him eat some roasted peanuts right before supper. She sure was different since she stopped whipping him and went up the road for a while. He leaned back to let the moist smell of the almost done pudding-pie ooze through-his-nostrils-to-his-palate, until he could taste it.

190

'Soon be supper time.'

'What's for dessert?'

'Why, can't you smell that 'tater-puddin' pie in the oven?'

'Oh! Ok, I forgot.'

Farmer, Randolph was tickled by his mental chitchat... Didn't laugh out loud... Just grinned like a cheshire cat.

* * *

Hilda was the only person Mason spent any time with, to mention; and he didn't spend a heap of time with her. If it wasn't for the farm animals, he'd just as soon keep company with himself...Hilda being the one exception, of course.

The locust tree outside the screen of his enclosed porch was bathed in shadow-near 'bout to the top. Mason opened the door to throw out the dirty water from his bird bath. The chipped, hand basin was older than Mason cared to remember, even if he could. Whether he cared to count years or not, he most certainly held on to every detail of the events after they laid brother Morgan to rest.

"Morgan, you were the only buddy I ever had." Mason talked aloud to himself as regularly as most folks talk to family members or anybody who might live under the same roof with them. At one time, it bothered him that he held soliloquy with himself, until it came to him that he was reacting to the old saw, "People that talk to themselves are tetched in the head." At that point, he told himself, "Mason, you'd be tetched in the head not to talk to yourself since you're most always by yourself."

He took a jar of canned stringbeans and corn from a shelf. It was one of several quarts of either fruits or vegetables put up for him by his dear sister in law (who should have become his wife) during last canning season.

"One thing about Summer folks might not think about, a body needn't heat canned goods. "He took a ham from the ice box and sliced a hank.

When he sat down at the table, he saw through the open door, the shadow had slid closer to the top of the locust tree. "Just about dark. Wasn't that long ago, I still got lonesome this time of day." He chewed reflectively on the mouthful he was talking

191

through. "I reckon it's finally made it into my thick head that Hilda ain't only never gonna be my wife, but she's not studyin' me either." He guffawed and did himself proud by catching the half chewed food in his palm. "Still, no disrespect to my dear brother, God rest his soul, she was mine before she was his. I'm not ignoring that she married him...and I'm not pretending to know how come she was to do that. What I do know is that she wouldn't've layed with me so soon after the funeral if she didn't have feelings for me." By now, Mason was eating his supper without tasting it; the sight and feel of Hilda so consumed him.

* * *

Gladys had been in New York nine years before she allowed herself to think about the experience with young Randolph, let alone discuss it with someone. Last year, her closest friend Laverne mentioned having read an article in the New York Post about a child abuse case on Staten Island. The mention of child abuse prompted Gladys to recall the thing she had managed to keep from her consciousness.

Shortly after she decided to leave Cedar Grove, she swept from her mind any notion that she had abused that child. Yes, she had elected to wipe the episode with the boy from her reflective landscape. It was not because she thought herself a pedophile, that was not her sin. What she felt guilty about was the inability to apply discipline to a child when it was required; a sin of complaisance. (She surmised, it must have been that same passive nature that caused her to marry her ex-husband, knowing that she was not in love with him.) Although she she was certain of her conclusion, it would not hurt to be supported by further proof.

When Laverne brought up the newspaper article, she revealed to Gladys something she had not told a soul prior to that day.

She and Gladys became the fastest of friends while attending college. They agreed that what they had in common was having recently arrived at City College-she from the hills of West Virginia and Gladys from rural North Carolina.

After a while, Laverne developed the need to tell any and all secrets to Gladys that she might prove herself worthy of the bond they shared. She wasn't embarrassed to share secrets with her pal that she even kept from her husband of seven years.

"Can I tell you something Glad?"

"You sure can. what is it ?"

"There is child abuse or pedophilia as they call it. But, you know, sometimes what looks like child abuse, is not really what it seems to be." Out of nowhere, doubt arose in Laverne's mind. She was not so sure she should continue. She paused to measure where her friend stood so far. Gladys was distracted by the re-emergence of her own secret. "Don't stop now Verne. Soon's you're done, I want to tell you something along the same line as what you seem to be about to tell me."

Laverene smiled. "Good. Well, as you know, I've got an older brother..." She thought she saw Gladys's demeanor change in a way that indicated she might suspect that she was going to reveal an event between herself and her brother. The expression she imagined on Gladys's face said 'Well, I don't think we need to talk about something like that.' "Nothing happened between brother and me!" She paused until she was sure gladys was with her again. "It was between my aunt Myrtle and my brother."

"Ok. Right!" Gladys reassured.

"My aunt-she was my mother's brother's wife-my aunt by marraige-told me about one time when she let my brother...rather, my brother seduced her."

"How old was he?"

"She said it happened when he was six or seven. Brother was grown and in the Army by the time my aunt told me about it." Laverne thought it curious that Gladys seemed to wear a grin of relief. She put that aside and continued. "Myrtle and I were having a little nip of corn liqour. I'm sure she never would have told me otherwise."

Gladys shifted her weight on the couch where they sat side by side.

"Ok. I can see you want me to get down to brass tacks..." They laughed. "So, According to Myrtle, brother tried to touch her where he had no business touching her. Then, when she pushed his hand away, he started crying as if she had slapped him across the face. Myrtle said she tried to distract him by offering him a Baby Ruth she had on the sideboard in the kitchen where they were. But no matter what she offered him or said to appease him, he just

cried harder. To make a long story short, Myrtle gave in, because it was clear that was the only way she was going to get him to stop crying. Gladys!"

"Huh?" "How come you 've got that silly look on your face?" Gladys had no idea what look was on her face. But she reckoned it must be a sign of finally having confirmation of what she had concluded years ago.

"Child, let me tell you. The very same thing happened to me. It was my little cousin Randolph. And he was only four years old when it happened. He was a sweet child whom I was very fond of. I was stunned. It took me a second to pull his hand away. Then, just like your brother, little Randy took to crying in a way that was so pitiful that after a while, I couldn't stand it." Gladys turned her eyes toward the ceiling and frowned. "You know, Laverne, seduction is the perfect word for it."

What might have also come back stark and clear to Gladys, was the day she slapped the boy across the face for putting his hand up her dress, in her store. That incident remained beyond the border of recollection. Her uncertainty as to whether she would have disciplined him if a customer had not been present, kept it out there. Instead, what did come to her, was that some children-boys and girls, are probably born with sexual cravings. She chose not to try and frame it. Both she and Laverne had learned on the journey they shared through undergraduate and then Masters study of Sociology, to vet first then, opine.

A thought occurred that was both satisfying and decisive. "When grown men do it, Verne, it's recognized for what it is. But honey, if you try to tell somebody that a child seduced you, they'll think you're out of your mind."

"Amen!"

* * *

Every time he was sure he had put it behind him, the memory came back. What happened couldn't be blamed on him. Jack had thought it through and convinced himself that Nan did it all by herself. Hell, he didn't know she was crazy enough to do such a damn fool thing. Jack Richard was not a churchgoing man, never had been. He thought of religious belief, for the most part, as a lot of bullshit. His atheism notwithstanding, Jack did believe in

The Golden Rule. "A man," his daddy always said, "Ought not do to somebodywhat he don't want done to him." And, like his daddy, Jack held firm to the notion that anytime somebody commenced to do you bad, you had to do your level best to teach them a lesson they would never forget. Still, for Nan to give her husband widow's tea, didn't make no sense.

Jack and Mary's neighbor, a quarter mile down the road, was a busybody; that won't no secret-everybody knew it. But busybody or not, far as he could tell, widow James was no liar. So, when she told him that his wife was being bedded by the klansman, Early Potts, Jack believed her right off.

First thought he had was to take his twelve gauge down there and blow that crackerwood's head off. Two days passed while he pondered how to go about getting close enough to kill that son of a bitch.

His plan had near 'bout settled in when he remembered that Early's wife Nan fancied him. He knew that for a fact, he had her in his daddy's hay loft when they were Spring chickens. Since then, whenever she had a chance, she would give him a look that even a little bitty child could read clean through.

Another few days passed-Jack didn't say a word to his wife Mary who didn't surprise him by laying with another man, he had suspected her of whoring around at least twice before. For some reason though, he had told himself he was just being foolish.

Maybe he let it go by so easy, cause in bed, that gal was like chocolate cake and ice cream mixed together in a bowl. Or, maybe he convinced himself he satisfied her so much she wouldn't even think about being with some other man. Didn't make no difference, cause he now remembered talk aeound that Early was bedding Colored women and girls to beat the band. Besides, Miz James was somebody you could trust.

He still said nothing to Mary. He let her go right along like she always had while he asked around to make double sure what Miz James told him was the gospel.

While he wasn't surprised that Mary was cheatin' on him, Jack felt right stupid when it seemed just about everybody in their hamlet knew how his wife was carrying on except him. Didn't matter none, he had figured a way to make things right.

Like near 'bout every woman around, Nan went into

Sumpter every Saturday for goods and supplies. Jack had learned, Saturdays was when Mary sneaked off with that redneck son of a dog, Early Potts. "Alright." That made it easy for him to get to Nan.

Anticipating a secret affair with Nan Potts, tickled Jack all over-not so much 'cause she was white, but because Early was a big to do in the Ku Klux Klan. That he would be paying the sorry so and so back for doing it to Mary, was meat in the gravy.

Jack arranged to have Nan meet him back of the Piggly Wiggly Self Service Store. Sure enough, she showed up and got in the back seat of his four door, Chevy. Jack wore the old chauffeur cap his daddy used when he was alive; papa devided his time between driving a local Colonel, and running his own truck farm.

Nan set her bag of goods on the seat beside her and primped her pretty hair. "We can go to the Colored tourist home, uptown." She didn't have to tell him that. Fellows he knew who courted white gals, took them to that clapboard, former antibellum mansion to be safe from harm. It ran through his mind that Nan must know about the place because... He didn't care, all he wanted to do was even the score.

"Girl, you ain't lost a bit of your looks."

Nan giggled in a girlish way-the way a southern belle who is confident of her beauty, feigns modesty. She peered over his shoulder, into the rear view mirror at her lean face enveloped by flaming curls. "I'm glad you noticed. I've tried to keep myself right decent."

"You sure have!" He winked into the mirror.

They sneaked off to the tourist home a few Saturdays before Nan told Jack that Early had consumption and seemed like he was about to die. A short time later, Early did die. Then, one Saturday, out of the blue, Nan confessed to Jack that the doctors thought it was consumption killed Early, but she knew better. Without being prodded, she just flat out told him that she had given her late husband increasing amounts of white oleander in his corn liquor. It was her task to serve him a nip every night after supper.

"Say what!"

"Aren't you glad I killed the no good cur?"

"Nan, are you crazy?"

196

"Yeah, I'm crazy like a fox." Her red hair was hung down-straight-resting on her naked, sparsely speckled shoulders and breasts. Jack had noticed the new hairdo, and was aroused by the sight of her soft brown eyes and lean face with the flowing flame against each cheek. But, she had gone and ruined everything. Yeah, he had messed around with the thought of killing Early, himself. That was just foolishness. He won't gonna kill nobody over sex. Here, this woman, churchgoing woman...

Jack looked around the room at the pitcher and basin on the cedar dresser, the canopied bed and tuffeted settee, he knew this was the last time he was ever going to be here. He could see by how amusement danced in Nan's eyes, she knew it too, and didn't too much give a shit.

When he was in his teens, mama and papa had been members of the, UNIA. Jack had all but decided to join himself, until he learned that President General Marcus Garvey had said, "We pray to Almighty God to save us through his Holy Words so shall we with confidence in ourselves follow the sentiment of the Declaration of Rights and carve our way to liberty."

As much as he was drawn to The Universal African Legion, the Universal African Motor Corps, the Black Eagle Flying Corps, the Black Star Steamship Line and a host of programs Mr. Garvey had established and/or proposed, Jack Richard could not follow anybody who believed in what to him was a bunch of nonsense.

For years, Jack wondered how he came to be an atheist until it dawned on him, he didn't come to be a non-believer, that was where he stood from when he was knee high to a grasshopper.

Marcus Josiah Garvey's "superstition" kept Jack from being a follower but Negro independence, as he taugh it, made a lasting impression on young Jack. It was his knowledge that there were several chapters of the United Negro Improvement Association in North Carolina that had made him think of that state as a possible place to 'put down his bucket.'

As for Mary, Jack (without saying a mumbling word) sold his four acre plot, house and all, right out from under her. The day the sale was complete, he headed north to the sister state and didn't look back.

Nine years later, here he stood at the window overlooking his barnyard. Ten rod or so, due west, was the back of the Methodist church. Jack imagined his way through the clapboard slats to the pulpit and stopped right there. He pictured the big bible lying open on the dais and the painting of white Jesus on the rear wall. Jack quirked his lower lip; 'All three of them, Early, Nan and Mary, were churchgoing folks. Yeah, he was just as bad as them for playing payback like two wrongs made a right. But he didn't run around acting like butter wouldn't melt in his mouth. Anyway, he didn't start the whole mess.'

Jack turned away from the window and whispered through clenched teeth, "Yall's God sure got a queer way 'His wonders to perform.'"

Chapter Twelve
In the Middle of the Night

Randolph tried to keep cool. All the same, he allowed the thrill of running into Verniece at the mailbox fill every pore.

"What a pleasant surprise, seeing you here." His movie inspired line seemed to give Verniece a feeling something or other like his own. Her lips parted into a grin bright as Brenda Starr's in the funny papers.

'Ain't no sense in stopping now.' He set himself to deliver another line; this one he had saved for a day like today.

Shortly before he moved back down home, Randy had seen a movie about a con artist, The Baron Of Arizona. Vincent Price played the part, his lemon-lime voice stuck with Randolph. When the baron met a girl, he would use a copacetic line.

Now, Randolph said the words to Verniece in a tone he was absolutely certain was the actor's nasal baritone.

"I've known many women. But with you, I'm afraid."

"I'm charmed I'm sure." Verniece replied before extending her hand for Randolph to kiss it.

"While we await the arrival of the mail carrier, would you like me to show you my secret place?" "Secret place?" "Yes. When I was but a lad, my cousin Arlene and I would sit in a clearing in these woods until Rob Roy arrived with the mail. There, on a patch of moss, she taught me to read. It would please me greatly if you would permit me to lead you there and perhaps have a laugh or two."

Verniece hesitated. "My dear," Randolph became another character before she could resist him. "If per chance you doubt my worthiness, let me assure you dear lady, you have nothing to fear."

"No. No, my dear sir, I have the utmost confidence in your high character." She again extended her hand-this time for the gentleman to lead her to his secret place.

Randolph made sure he did not tremble when he took her hand in his. "My dear, your well being is uppermost in my consideration."

Verniece's noonday smile returned. "Of that sir, I have no doubt."

Several times, Randolph had searched in vain for the shady glade where he and Arlene would read from a book she had kept from her elementary school days. Eventually he had accepted that the space had grown over, never to be enjoyed again. Today however...

Verniece walked ahead of him as if she knew where the carpet of green moss was. But she couldn't... wait! The sun was shining like it never had before. But Verniece's frock is soaked and clinging to her coke bottle figure like she just stepped out of the creek; and there ain't no water nowhere for at least half a mile. "Good God, girl!"

She looked over her shoulder, winked and said, "It's special for you honey." Her buttocks-like a valentine wrapped in a wet-pink-pettycoat, flounced in front of Randolph. If he had the nerve, he would reach out and touch her. He didn't dare though. He just followed her, twitching in his skin.

Sure enough, Verniece knew where the secret place was. After a few minutes, they were standing smack dab in the middle of it. She turned around so that they were face to face. The smile was gone. Now, she looked at him like he might be something good to eat. It went through his mind that she must have seen the same thing in his eyes.

Without words, intentions or a single sound, the lithe young woman and sinewy-adolescent boy stripped off their clothes in deliberate ritual.

Randolph had felt himself against his pants or against his bed sheet any number of times. Now, for the first time, he knew the feeling of unfettered erection. Also, he was throbbing at the sight of Verniece's curly, pubic patch. He looked into her eyes and damn near heard them begging him to go on in.

"Good God, girl!"

"It's special for you honey." She gave him the same look she had when she said the same words moments ago. He approached her... if he approached and not she, he did not know. One thing was certain, Randolph Wilford smelled honeysuckle nectar, heard angels singing and joy bells ringing in Glory! "It's special for you honey."

He saw it, he felt it coming. Still, it got there before he was ready for it-the Fourth of July exploded over the furry green moss. A red Cardinal flitted between bursts, followed by a chirping bluejay and a flight of buzzing bumble bees. Stars came before his eyes like when he was punched in the face. But he didn't feel no pain. From head to toe a tingle ran around and through every nerve in his body. It scared him near 'bout to death.

"Lord! Ain't nothin'that feels this good."

Randolph bolted up onto his haunches-darkness around him. "Are you there, Verniece? Are you there?" The room was silent. He lay his head back onto the pillow. A minute passed.

"Yes, honey, I'm here." Her perspiring belly and his melded into one another until Verniece and Randolph were unlike anything either had previously been. They...it, drifted-or soared-into a distance. Everything became soft-warm and brand-spanking-new.

Chapter Thirteen
Tomorrow Dawning

Early this morning, Randy gathered eggs from the coop; one of them was brown. Usually if he came across a brown egg among a small batch, it would give him a little giggle.

Later, after toting two buckets of water up from the spring, he did not examine his arms to give himself a kick at the sight of bulging muscle and sinew.

An hour ago, he chopped a pile of stove wood. The wielding of the double edged axe did not give him the usual satisfaction of being convinced that he was near 'bout grown.

Right now, here on the milk stool pulling on the heavy teets for the evening's milk, there is not a single thought of how it's special to draw milk without either hurting the cow or making his fingers stiff.

When he found Jack under the house, it hurt so bad he was pretty sure that it was the last time he was gonna let something grab hold of him like that. He buried the dog, sat on the little hill behind the cow shed and thought of grandma and everybody who had died. Then and there, he determined he would not allow himself to be that sad again. As far as he was concerned, he had used up all his grief.

Yesterday, Randolph went up to the mailbox and waited for Rob Roy for an hour before giving up. He figured the old man had come down with a cold or something. There were a couple of times when there was no mail delivery because the skinny little man was under the weather.

When he got back to the house, Mozzelle gave Randolph the news. She had heard it on the radio. "The man said, an old gentleman named Rob Roy who had been driving a rural route for over forty years, was run into by a truck carrying a load of lumber..." Mo sat still for a moment to recollect what the announcer had said as closely as she could. "...He said the two ton truck with the load of lumber ran head on into the little A Model Ford that was converted into a pickup-like mail carrier...said Rob Roy was seventy three years old."

Randolph had heard tell of people getting killed in car wrecks. But nobody he knew ever died when they had a wreck. He had even been in a school bus wreck and nobody got hurt. These reflections kept him from accepting the truth of what Mo was telling him.

Today, he did not go to the mail box; he couldn't. Then, a couple of hours ago, he was on the front porch and heard the radio through the window. "They said that the old man was found sitting there with his hands on the steering wheel like nothing had happen. As best they could tell, he didn't have a scratch on him. But he was dead as a doornail."

* * *

The puffs of clouds Randolph decided to take flight through, did not feel either cool or warm. He had never flown through clouds in the past. He had always marveled at the sight of their cotton white against the azure sky. The notion of changing his flight pattern to enter them never occured to him. That the big snowy piles had not a single sense of heat, moisture, cool or dew, surprised him. He thought of the difference between the warm-purple mist across his toes a few years back and the nowhere-no there surrounding his flight through these mists at the base of Heaven. While he drifted in confusion, his eye caught sight of Rob Roy's A-Model sitting in the middle of the cemetery road below.

Without deciding to, Randolph dived straight down toward what turned out to be the skeleton of the mailman's little vehicle-it was a charred-black frame like a burned out house. He hovered over the frame and saw Rob Roy-the blue veins of his pale white hands holding onto the steering wheel. Above his wrists were wooly cuffs-whiter than his hands, still and cold-gripping the black circle that had guided the car over these roads for those many years. The skinny dead man was dressed in a bright red Santa

Claus suit. Randolph was not taken aback, he had always kinda thought of the old fella as Saint Nick bringing goodies into his life.

Rob Roy's face was no longer pale with blue veins-like his hands. It was dull gray the way daddy's face had been-in his coffin; sparkling white chicklet stones of Arlington Cemetary appeared. Unmanageable memory tricked Randy into incorporating the day daddy was buried into his dream of Rob Roy. His manageable mind struck back. Instead of springing awake like usual, after a flying dream, he allowed a calm to come over him. He slept soundly until morning.

* * *

The rising sun came diagonally over the Mills' farm and the small woods and the Methodist steeple to cross the road and enter Randolph's room. He blinked awake. Something was going on. Deep down, there was a quiet stirring that in his thoughts, was a wisp. Even if what happened had come now that he was awake, it would not have been clear. He only knew he was not the same as when he went to sleep last night. What had come to pass, without immediate notice, was the sowing of a seed, the start of a new understanding.

In Randolph's fourteen years, there was just one white person whose death had affected him; back on April 14, 1945, President Roosevelt died. That day lingered with Randolph-in and out of his thoughts. The death was of the man who was the President; not, a president, like President Truman. Franklin Delano Roosevelt was in office when Randolph was born. He thought of Roosevelt as the now and future president of The United States Of America. Consolidating that notion and making it unshakable was the esteem in which the President was held by anybody Randolph heard speak of him. Had ihe word been familiar to him, Randolph would have said, F.D.R. was 'apotheosized.' He was at least a Demi-God. Truth be told, Rob Roy was the very first white person whose death bothered Randolph. President Roosevelt was not a white person, he was, "President Roosevelt."

* * *

Miz Mattie didn't read newspapers. She had a radio, but seldom listened to it. Because Randolph did not know this, it surprised him when she told him she had not heard about, "Poor, Rob Roy!"

"Yes mam, they say he was sittin' there in his mail truck just like he was still drivin' it."

"Lord have mercy! Lord have mercy!" She shook her head several times. "He was a good man." Hearing that familiar phrase made Randolph think that the gingerbread lady meant that Rob Roy was a Christian. The only times he had heard folks say, he was or is a good man, they meant the man was a christian. What Mattie was saying though was that Rob Roy was not like most of the "crackers 'round here."

Reflecting on her choice of words, she was sure the boy mistook her meaning, as indeed he had. That was fine with her 'cause racial resentment was not something she wanted Randolph to hear from her. In her heart of hearts, she wished there was no need for her to harbor such feelings. But the behavior that prompted those hard urgings could not be wished away. She left the thought aside.

"I first met Rob Roy near on thirty years ago. I was walkin' down Main Street in Crestville. Back in those days, Coloreds won't 'lowed t' walk on the sidewalks. But it was one of those days when I just felt right devilish-didn't care what them old..." Mattie caught herself before saying 'soda crackers.' "Didn't mean a thing to me where they said they wanted Negroes to walk, I was gonna walk wherever the blazes I wanted to." She allowed herself a good long laugh. Randolph felt her irony but he had no idea what she was leading to. He did know she was talking about racial pride-the kind that Myra instilled in him and Lucille.

He pictured Miz Mattie strutting along the sidewalk in a print frock with her head held high. A burst of laughter flew out of him and filled the space left over after a guffaw from Mattie's swelled into three corners of the little kitchen.

"Some old sod buster with chewing tobacco drippin' outta the corners of his mouth, commenced to try to push me off the sidewalk. I threw up my hands to keep him away from me. That ol'...' Mattie caught herself again. "That ol' farmer was 'bout ready to put his fist on me when out of nowhere this little skinny man jumped in between us. That turned out to be Rob Roy." Mattie's lips curled into a smile that Randolph had not seen before-it was kinda sad yet pleasant. Her eyes got red like folks' eyes did when they were 'bout to cry. But Miz Mattie wasn't 'bout to cry. She was letting her confusion and anger and desire to change the world and... "I'm acting like a silly fool."

Randolph bit his tongue. He knew she had more to tell him. "Anyway, that sorry rascal who was 'bout to hit me, backed off. He knew who Rob Roy was, I found out.

"Me and him walked to a Colored cafe he knew about. He had a Dr. Pepper, and I had a orange Nehi. We talked about where we came from, where each one of us was raised and all. That's when he told me he done had a book put out; a book of poems. That's why I told you, if he said you would grow up to be a poet, he knew what he was talking about.

"Turned out Rob Roy came from a well to do family. His daddy had disowned him cause he favored Coloreds...know somethin'?" "What, Miz Mattie?" "That little skinny man didn't care one bit what his daddy an' them thought. He wanted to be around as many kind of folk as he could. He told me, that's what we're put on this earth for. Made sense to me. I never saw him again until he started delivering mail. He was a good man."

"He sure was. He used to laugh and kid around with me and my big sister back when we would come down here for Summers."

"You got a sister? Lord boy, I thought you was an only child. 'Say she's older than you?" "Yessum. She's in college now." "That's good. Sometimes I think that if I'd got some college, I might've... Yes indeed, it's right nice that your sister went off to college. I expect you're gonna be goin' to college too?" "I reckon." He pictured Miner Teachers College up on Georgia Avenue, down the hill from Howard University. Having those schools in his mind somehow gave him a feeling of being equal to Lucille and everybody who attended them.

Miz Mattie heated up some left over field peas and strick o' lean. She served it with buttered cornbread and clabber milk. "Miz Mattie, you ever been married?" He wished he hadn't asked her that. He did not think it was inappropriate, it was just that he had no idea where it came from-he didn't own it. "No. I never did get married...never even came close. I don't know why. It ain't like I said to myself, 'girl you ain't never gonna get married.' I just never did." She reflected for a moment. "Reckon it wasn't something that suited me." While she answered him, Randolph realized she was the only old person he knew who never married. He drew no conclusions about it. It simply made him proud that it had occurred to him.

"I 'spect you'll get married someday." "Yessum. I 'spect so." Why was he trying to sound like marraige had never crossed his mind? The truth was, he couldn't wait to have his own wife, his own dog and his own house. "Yes mam, I surely will." It made Randolph feel right clean inside to clear that up.

He used a chunk of cornbread to sop up the last of the pot likker on his plate. During that act of completion, Rob Roy came back to mind; he was one more in a long line of folks who up and went away or died before he knew much about them. The thought that it wasn't fair nearly pierced the surface before he pushed it back down. Such things were The Lord's work; and that was that.

* * *

His arms flapped or rather waved up and down in a gentle motion that did not require much effort. When Randolph flew with an easy grace like this, he wondered if anything in the world felt better. He expected today's flight like the others that gave him floating joy, to unexpectedly dissolve.

Instead, he went into an abrupt descent. He was not concerned. Each time he felt his body falling in a dream, he woke himself before he crashed into the ground or splashed into water.

"Shit!" The clear surface of his and Archie's swimming hole was rushing up toward his face. Why wasn't he able to wake up. His face pierced the creek surface; fear extruded from him inch by inch, while his body slid below the surface.

When he leveled off, there was a big black catfish and several rainbow trout swimming ahead of him. Then, he was all alone.

Next thing Randolph knew, he had breast stroked beyond the length of the creek; no bank-no muddy wall, just an unfamiliar feeling enveloping him...

"Oh!" There was no sunlight although he was now swimming on the surface of the water. No air brushed against his skin. He was in a tunnel or something but he wasn't scared or feeling

*like everything was closing in on him. 'He thought, 'This under-
ground stream seems...' It wasn't as if Randolph had been down
here in it before but he had known it was here.*

*Mozzelle's voice came into the tunnel. The tone was softer
than he had ever heard from her.*

"See? Toldja didn't I?"

*"I remember. I was down here in a dream before. I was
scared then. I ain't scared now."*

He had learned from Mo that the stream that was the
swimming hole ran on underground until it surfaced again as the
creek at the bottom of the hill where the bridge is. "Then," she had
said, "It runs for a bit and goes underground again until it comes
up over yonder at the bottom of the hill between Rev. Esterbrook's
house and the cemeteries."

*Randolph had read the word aquifer in one book or
another. But in his dream-mind he remembered Mo using it to
describe the underground water. "So ya see, an aquifer runs all
the way from way up by Winston Salem, all the way down to South
Carolina."*

*Randolph was 'happy as a sissy in a CC-Camp' being in
this cramped tunnel not having trouble breathing and not being
bothered that there was no light. He stroked along the narrow way
with the cool water running against and sliding to either side of
his tooth-gap grin. He felt its flow glide along his naked body until
it tickled the edges of his paddling feet.*

*When he was little, Randy used to dream that he was in a
tunnel running ahead of a train that was about to run him down.
Here in the aquifer, he was at ease. There was a hint of tightness
around his neck and shoulders, that was all. The memory of his
earlier nightmares kept him from being fully comfortable. Still, it
was a lot better here and now than it ever was back when he ran
ahead of the train. A light appeared up ahead. He recognized it as
the end of the tunnel.*

*Sure enough, it turned out to be the creek down the hill
from aunt May's house. Randy stood up, the creek was too shallow
to swim in.*

"Well, I'll be!" It was a rat or a mole or whatever the blazes it was, and two big ol' bullfrogs skittering from the water into the brush on the creek shore.

"Well, I'll be!" Right there in front of him was the explanation of what had scared him half to death all those mornings when he crossed the bridge above where he stood now. "Well bless Pat!"

The dream faded. But, on his way down to the unawareness of unperturbed sleep, Randolph knew he was leaving the flow at this point because he was not sure he would be able to re-enter the aquifer at the end of the creek without the dark scaring him to distraction or the water drowning him.

He eased into deep-dark oblivion.

* * *

It was the kind of bright hot day that gave Randolph energy and ambition. He coasted Susie Q. down the slight grade of the driveway onto the road where he slowed almost to a stop. Then, he stood up on the pedals and pumped his legs with all his might. A satisfaction ran alternately up through each calf and thigh. Muscular joy increased with the strenghth of every pump.

Thin streams of sweat trickled from his hairline. Puffs of dust squirted back from every spin of the tire and each dust-squirt made him imagine that muscles bulged all over him like a comic book superhero.

The sweat made its way down across his grinning lips as the bike gained momentum until it had too much speed to keep burning rubber. He tried to get just one last ZOOTZ from the back wheel.

"What the hell!"

His body seemed to drop toward the ground. He had a good grip on the handlebars, his feet were planted on the pedals, yet... Next thing Randolph knew, his ass was on the ground. Susie Q. was broken in two.

Yeah. Okay, it was clear, the bike had come apart. But at the same time, it was not clear at all. Bikes didn't break in half like a wishbone or something. He sat there in the middle of the road, the dust settling around him. He stared at the two parts of his trusty steed; in the back of his mind was the awareness that sooner or later a car would come barreling down the road whether or not Randolph Wilford accepted that his transportation, his toy, the thing he loved more than anything that was not living and breathing, was done for. He didn't want to give a shit if a car came or not. He wanted to will away any possibility that if he kept sitting there he was sure as hell gonna get run over.

Common sense ignored his fool mind. He saw himself picking up the two halves of the long wished for prize he had finally gotten for Christmas when he was ten years old.

He toted the front half in one hand, the back in the other and stood in the driveway. For whatever reason, he stared across the road to where his sweet potato and peanut patches used to be. Maybe it was because those crops had come, made him happy then were long gone. Maybe, he was looking over there for a miracle cause he knew good and well no thought was gonna come into his head that would keep the pain out of his body after banging against the road, and out of his heart, from losing Susie Q.

Still, he tried. His focus dove down to his under-mind. Among other things, city apartments and country roads were in that place. He allowed his mental-light to scan about the different indoor spaces and bends along roads where gladness, hurt, joy, sadness and all emotions caused by passing events were stored according to where they might seem to fit. The search was only moments old when he saw Arlene smash his tricycle against the smokehouse that used to be across the woodpile from the chicken coop. She made up for that by teaching him to read. The magic of understanding words on the page, gave him more delights than he could keep count of.

His mind swirled, steadied and returned to right now. On the surface he felt the weight of a boulder the size of a ten-ton-toothache.

Randolph let the two halves of the bike slip out of his hands. His knees lost support and he collapsed to the ground. An overflow of pain seeped out of his eyes, oozed from his nostrils and he sobbed the very way he had every other time a dearly beloved someone or something up and died.

* * *

Dear Mama,

How are you? Fine I hope. How is Lucille? Does she like college? I am alright. Mozzelle and Gregory are fine. I have not seen Arlene, Willie and Nadine in a while. But I'm sure they are doing well.

Mama, when you come down here next month for the big meeting, I want to go back to Washington with you. It has been nice staying with Mozzelle and them. But I think it is time for me to go home. Do you agree?

(It occured to Randolph to remind Myra that his teeth never grew back in; he would like to get dentures soon as possible. He did not. It seemed, one request was enough.)

Anyway, I look forward to seeing you come September.

Yours truly,

Randolph

* * *

When mama died (grandma, mama) and Randolph asked Mozzelle how come cousin Ames had not come to her funeral, Mo made it impossible for him to work his way up to the real question, by saying that Ames was dead.

Randy and Lucille were crazy about cousin Ames. He told them about ancient Egypt and other places in Africa. Maybe it was because he told them stories and sometimes called Lucille, Queen Nefertiti, and Randy, Pharoah Akhenaten, that they never thought to ask him why he never went to church; it surely stood out that he like Gregory, was not a churchgoer. Gregory wasn't all that bright so it didn't seem to mean much that he didn't go to church like all the smart people did. Cousin Ames though, was real smart, still he never went to church.

His chocolate, rotund, late cousin was on Randolph's mind because he was looking out his bedroom window at the night sky. The one time Ames came down here at night, he took the two children up to the orchard to show them what he said was Andromeda. Ames said that the name was Ethiopean. What caught Randolph's attention even more was when Ames told him and his big sister that when they looked into the night sky, they were looking into to the past.

"Look there" he pointed to the East, over the Methodist church, way back past the mountains. "See that light there that looks like a star?" Lucille and Randy looked until Ames was satisfied that they saw the galaxy. "That's Andromeda. Akhenaten, Nefertiti, you are looking millions of light years from here. You know what that means? That means, you are looking millions and millions of years into the past. That light there took that much time to reach us." Ames laughed and the two children could feel the pesence of his gentle girth. "I know, I know, it's not easy to take hold of that notion...don't worry, it will be clear to you someday."

Randolph looked through the window squinting. It was not as easy to see Andromeda, here in July, as it had been that November night up in the orchard. What was easy to see was that Ames was gone forever, and that there was a whole lot of stuff to learn. "And I'm gonna have to learn it on my own."

* * *

He was wearing the same kind of clothes he always wore except the overalls he had on were brand spanking new. Instead of a denim shirt like he usually had on-buttoned up to his neck, he wore a starched-white one, open at the collar. His toothy grin was as new and sparkling white as that store-bought shirt.

As it happened, Myra, Randolph , Mo and Gregory had just come in from the dining room where they enjoyed some freshly churned peach ice cream.

Jack Richard tapped on the screen door and doffed his gray fedora at the very moment the four arrived in the living room. "Why, Mr. Richard, come right in." Mama put on a smile that showed in her eyes and on her lips. And it also, Randolph noted, flushed across her creamy cheeks (not creamy in color like vanilla custard, her skin was dark brown; but creamy like the soft curves of chocolate kisses.)

Sweet as it was, won't no way anybody would've mistook that smile for anything more than a practiced welcome for anyone who might come a'calling. It did not matter that, as mama, Mozzelle, Gregory and Randolph knew, Jack Richard's aim was, to come a'courtin'.

"How'do Miss Myra."

"Well, I'm just fine, Mr. Richard. What brings you out on this fine Saturday afternoon?" Myra, having done with the greeting, looked and sounded like a shopkeeper confronting a loiterer.

Randolph enjoyed seeing mama back the poor man into a corner. He couldn't help getting a kick out of seeing a grown man being dared to lay his cards on the table, the way a hundred girls had done to him.

Jack richard let the screen door ease shut at his back. He shifted his weight from one foot to the other. "I heard that'chou were home for the big meetin'. So, I uh... kinda figured I'd come by'n say howdy." His boilerplate forehead reminded Randolph that Jack Richard really did look like a slim, Jersey Joe Walcott.

Myra smiled again; this time, with condescension. "I most certainly am here for the revival. It was most kind of you to stop by."

Randolph saw uneasiness replace the awkward smile the farmer had worn before he put his best foot forward and had it stepped on. "Well," His face showed the relief of thinking, 'Ok, I can take a hint.' "I done said howdy." His voice was just above a whisper. "So, I reckon it's time for me to git to gittin'."

Jack Richard, who could bring a mule to his knees with a left hook, was made to look right pityful by a woman he had notions about. Randolph felt for him, and was a little bit ashamed of Myra for... well, for acting like a bully. He looked at Mo and Greg. they were staring down at the carpet.

When Randolph turned his eyes back to where Jack Richard had been standing, the gentleman caller had gone beyond the screen. The back of his fedora, his overalls and new bought shirt, sank several inches, as he stepped off the porch to hit the road.

* * *

In the Summer sun, scent of honeysuckle-buzz of wasps-bumble bees-hornets and nameless snake doctors lookin' for all the world like little bitty helicopters, floated on and in the waves of uninhibited voices. Fifty or more worshipers had just spilled out of the Cedar Grove Baptist Homecoming service. Friends and relatives who were reunited on this day, in some cases for the first time in years. Even those who lived up North but made the trek to the revival annually, enjoyed the warmth of renewal.

Randolph, as was his wont, stood among and at the same time he stood apart from the crowd. The chattering congegants gave him community. But the down-home sights and smells caused him to begin to miss the country, even though he was still in Cedar Grove.

He turned his attention away from himself to Mama and cousin Hilda who, having not strayed far from the church door, were physically away from the crowd. The two, in face to face-tete-a-tete, looked like broad shouldered-wide hipped sisters; one, anthropomorphic salt water taffy, the other, deep dark chocolate. Myra was maybe ten years younger than her cousin. But like sometimes with Negro sisters, the main difference in their looks was their color. The thought of his mother's and cousin's complexions was fleeting. It flitted through his mind like the buzzing insects above the mass of folks in the churchyard.

He reflected on the service that had just ended. Reverend Esterbrook's sermon was about being patient when waiting for prayers to be answered. An old man joined church, a few folks got happy...

Randy's reverie closed in on the verse of what he had inherited as a favorite hymn:

Annnd He walks with me
and He talks with me
And He tells me
I am His ownnn
And the joy we share
as we tar-ry therrre
None o-ther has ev-errr
knownnn

The words and melody evoked a colorful glade filled with butterflies and slanted rays from Heaven. Randolph was in "The garden" alone with The Almighty Who addressed him with undefined secrets, never revealed to another soul.

Outside his reverie but in his view, Myra and Hilda held quiet discourse. Hilda glanced at Randolph and remarked that it was difficult to fathom that only what seemed like yesterday, he was a baby arriving here in Cedar grove for the first time. Myra heard her cousin's reference as it was intended. Yet, the memory that arose in her own mind was of her dear husband having to be in and out of the hospital because he had been gassed by the Germans in World War l.

She became pregnant with her third child unexpectedly. Her oldest boy was about to finish elementary school. Lucille was starting first grade.

When the baby boy was born, mama Liticia, knowing her oldest daughter would be overburdened, offered to let the baby come and stay with her in Cedar Grove until he reached school age.

Myra and Hilda continued to converse at the same time as they engaged with the I and me of their own selves-two trains a-runnin'.

For a moment Randolph studied mama and cousin Hilda. Then, seeing that they were no longer studyin' him, he looked across the road at the Campbell house as he did whenever he was here in front of the Baptist church. The place rotted and sagged more and more as its fond associations faded from his mental storehouse. He looked caddycorner from the churchyard to where aunt May's house stood. That old house was white and sturdy as if folks had been living there all along.

On school mornings when he walked down to the road in front of the church, he was mindful of aunt May's house being empty; it had been that way for a long time. On those mornings he closed out memories of when he was four years old and somebody stayed in that house.

Before cousin Hilda or Rob Roy and the other few folks who did not treat him like they were smarter than him cause they were grown, a youmg man, Reverend Winston, lived in that house. Even back then, everybody called it aunt May's house. Randolph had no memory of ever having met aunt May. She might as well be a haint for all he knew. Reverend Winston though, was the one who stayed there. And he was the first grown man or woman who treated Randolph in a way that he did not feel like he had to act like he was less than big people. The young preacher would allow Randolph to rummage through a musky old closet full of stuff that he hinself did not know was there. One day, little Randy found a bunch of cardboard pictures and a doohicky called a stereoscope you could look through to make the pictures big and clear. The colored drawings were of far away places. While trips into olden times in Sunday school books were his first journeys into exotic lands, the days Randolph came to visit with Reverend Winston and look at those pctures, were his first travels to places that you could look forward to actually going to when you grew up.

Randolph smiled. He was remembering what turned out to be a special day.

He found a straight razor in the closet-it was in its case. Reverend Winston who was at his desk writing a sermon, saw that the boy had taken the razor out of its case and had it in his hand.
Randolph's attention was divided between his fascination with his distorted reflection in the shiny-silver blade and the slow-quiet rising figure of the tall young preacher. Then, his full attention was captured by Reverend Winston because of the nearly motionless way his brown face and white shirt filled Randolph's peripheral vision. The sight of somebody moving so slow made Randolph wonder if he was imagining that the preacher was getting up from his chair.
"Hold still son." Reverend Winston extended his tapered fingers to remove the straight razor from the boy's little hand. When he had full possesion of it, Randolph heard him sigh. The feeling in the room told him that some kind of fear had been there. He had not known of its presence until reverend Winston's breath stirred it up.

"Randolph." He sat the boy on his knee. "This is a razor. It is sharp enough to cut your fingers almost in two." Before continuing, he took another breath. "I want you to promise me if you see another razor or a sharp knife, you will leave it alone." The sound of his voice scared Randolph. Noting the boys fear, the young Baptist preacher jiggled him, then injected a smile into his own tone. "I know you're a big boy, and you're not scared of anything. But there are times in life that even a big strong man has to be careful." He looked into Randolph's eyes and smiled. "Ah! Smart as you are Randy, you know exactly what I mean."

For as long as he could remember, Randolph had liked this preacher more than anybody except mama Letticia. Now though, it was clear to him that the tall man with strong hands and a deep 'Wings over Jordan' voice had something in him that was kinda like the slivers of sunlight that slid through the leaves in his and Arlene's mossy glade. He could tell, Reverend Winston would hurt just as much as he would if he harmed himself.

Fear leached out of Randolph completely. "Ok." He said this not only to let the preacher know that he understood. He was also saying, "You don't have to say another word. You have touched me inside where I go sometimes to wonder."

Since coming out of the dark world he lived in until he was about one and a half years old, four year old Randolph had wished many times that he knew enough words to express how he felt to a grown person. This time, he felt sure he did not need to. "Ok." was enough.

Randolph knew farmers who were buddies with one another. It seemed that all the older boys and girls around had good friends and running buddies. Now, he, Randolph had a friend. Although Reverend Charles Winston was a grown man, he was Randolph Wilford's running buddy. He would no longer have to fret that there were no boys his age 'round here. The pastor of Cedar Grove Baptist church was his friend.

Randolph did not know if he had stared at aunt May's house while he took the trip back to a period he had chosen to forget. It did not matter, he had reclaimed something worthwhile.

A short time after reverend Winston became his good buddy, it was time for the preacher to move on to his next assign-

218

ment. A new pastor came to Cedar Grove Baptist Church. Reverend Winston didn't say goodbye. Before Randolph knew anything, he was gone.

Since that first hurtful loss, Randolph had been sent to live with his real mother in D.C. Before he got to know him, daddy had died. He was anle to putthat behind him. He made friends and got used to the neighborhood. Then he, mama and Lucille moved to a new house, in a new neighborhood where he had to start all over again. Half the time, new friends there, suddenly moved. Down here, grandma, Jack, Rob Roy...he jerked his attention back to the sun, sounds and smells of the day.

Mama and cousin Hilda were still talking. Randolph looked at the thinning throng that had a short while ago been inside the church transported to another place just as he was, an even shorter while ago.

In that place-in that reverie across the road-he found a missing piece of himself. Whatever it meant he did not know. Yet, it meant something. Without intending to, he looked toward the tall yellow house that had been home for the past several years. At the peak of the tin roof the rooster-weathervane looked East as it had for all those years. More often than not, when he looked at the house from the churchyard, his eye caught that curiosity and expected it to tell him the direction of the wind. Then, one day, Mo had told him the vane had rusted in place a long time ago.

Randolph's gaze floated down from the roof to the base of the big oak tree-no buggy seat. All the slats were gone. For the life of him, he could not remember when he or someone else, threw the rotten pieces away. He brought his focus back to the church yard where he saw Mozzelle having a laugh with a few other women.

In the next moment, he took a peek inside himself. The notions he saw in his secret places were not in sharp focus. He looked back across the church yard, at Mo and her friends. The shapelessness of his inner notions and Mozzelle were connected because he remembered that when Reverend Esterbrook spoke of patience, during today's sermon, Mo jumped up from her pew and belted out a song he had recently learned.

FATHER ALONG WE'll
KNOW ALL ABOUT IT
FATHER ALONG WE'LL
UNDERSTAND WHY
CHEER UP MY BRO-THER
LIVE IN THE SUN-SHINE
WE'LL UNDER-STAND-IT
ALL-BY-AND-BY

Myra caught him off guard. She had come over to put her arm around him. It never failed to surprise... and please Randy when mama, who was usually distant, showed affection. "Well, young man, we're going home tomorrow."

'AND THE VOICE I HEAR
RINGING IN MY EAR
NONE OTHER
HAS EVER KNOWN'

Table of Contents